The Family Face

JUNE BARRACLOUGH

The Family Face

'I am the family face;
Flesh perishes, I live on.'

Thomas Hardy 'Heredity'

ROBERT HALE · LONDON

© June Barraclough 2000
First published in Great Britain 2000

ISBN 0 7090 6660 0

Robert Hale Limited
Clerkenwell House
Clerkenwell Green
London EC1R 0HT

2 4 6 8 10 9 7 5 3 1

Typeset by
Derek Doyle & Associates, Liverpool.
Printed in Great Britain by
St Edmundsbury Press Ltd, Bury St Edmunds, Suffolk.
Bound by WBC Book Manufacturers Limited, Bridgend.

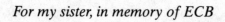

For my sister, in memory of ECB

INTRODUCTION

A Letter from the Past

Edward Bairstow had died in the late autumn of 1970, at the back end of the year, as they call it in the north of England. His wife was to outlive him twelve years.

All his family, and all the Bairstows before him, had lived from time immemorial in what used to be called the Yorkshire woollen district, the little textile towns that in Eddie's daughters' childhood were still separated by fields and woods, no motorway marching across them in a heedless hurry.

Each town had a fierce local pride. An outsider might have found their dialects indistinguishable, but the well-trained ear could pinpoint the town from which a speaker hailed. The district bred a tough, obstinate, forthright, down-to-earth race of men and women, stocky folk, most of whom were destined in Eddie Bairstow's lifetime, and even during the childhood of his daughters, Juliet and her sister Alison, to work in the mills.

Before they became manufacturers of worsted in the mills, weaver Bairstows stretched back centuries to the Middle Ages when they had been handloom weavers living on the Pennine slopes, and had combined their weaving with the cultivation of small intakes from moorland and valley. Their cottage looms lasted until beyond the end of the eighteenth century, when they were gradually taken over by steam power in the manufactories.

Nineteenth century Bairstows had done well for themselves in that urban world of gaslight and mill-buzzers, mill dams, scrubbed street-doorsteps, and clogs. Later, Eddie's parents showed no apparent nostalgia for it. When they spoke of the past it was to say how much better the present was. But when she was in a good mood, Eddie's own wife Kitty would enjoy recalling her childhood memories: breakfasts of bread and dripping eaten looking out of windows covered in the intricate Jack Frost patterns formed from the bitter cold outside and the fire-warmth within; dinners of tripe and onions; home-made clothes sewn on the old treadle machine.

Kitty's family, the Halls, had lived much closer to an older way of life. Her mother had worked from 1889, when she was twelve years old, as a 'half-timer' in a silk mill. Kitty, with her family, and all her numerous relations, had belonged to a busy little town, whereas it was felt by Eddie's daughters that their father had belonged only to himself. Yet the childhood of both their parents had belonged to a world of aspidistras, 'winter-edges' – clothes-horses parked round coal fires to dry wet clothes – toasting-forks, trams, and women in shawls, things that to Eddie's grandchildren were to seem like artefacts of the Dark Ages.

Eddie was not at all like the average Yorkshireman. Perhaps he had once belonged in some sense to his background, but his nature had never been hard or forthright or pugnacious.

At the time of her mother's death Juliet, Kitty's and Eddie's younger daughter, who lived with her husband Andrew Considine in a London suburb, was fifty, working part-time cataloguing books in a private library. Paul and Rose, her son and daughter, were both away at university. Paul had decided at eighteen that he didn't want a gap year; he preferred to start his studies straight away. Both offspring would be returning at the end of the autumn term to spend Christmas at home. The death of a second parent had made Juliet a rather elderly orphan, and since her mother's death she had been thinking a good deal about her childhood and youth.

The mysterious package arrived on a sunny morning in early October just three months after Kitty Bairstow's funeral. It was

Juliet's first week without either of her offspring at home or on their way home.

Earlier that morning she had been listening to a programme of piano music on Radio 3, enjoying several catchy gentle tunes – what they used to call 'swing': musical 'sketches', if such things existed. The last one had immediately transported her back in time. Back to a sunshine-filled room. Through the window of her mind's eye she had seen her father working in the garden, and heard her mother rattling saucepans in the kitchen. She herself was standing in the dining-room with the wireless on, laying the table for a meal. The house was not overstuffed with furniture; there was a lot of light-coloured wood around and pale wallpaper with a yellow frieze. . . .

The present-day Juliet, mop in hand, had paused in her washing-up, transfixed by memory as she listened. The music had taken her back on a magic carpet to the first time she had heard it as a child. The old scene was so clear and colourful behind her eyes that she had thought for a few moments that she was really back, or was hallucinating. But the glimpse flashed – and then was gone, like headlights disappearing round the bend of a long country road at night, and she was back in the present with the piano still playing on the radio. She could never go back – the past only existed now in her mind.

Half an hour later the post arrived.

She and her sister had recently been in touch with their mother's solicitor, settling her Will for probate. Kitty Bairstow had kept the same firm of solicitors who had always dealt with her husband's affairs up to his death and Juliet opened the firm's usual envelope, with the name on the back: 'Cudleigh, Holkham and Twist'. She was surprised however to find a letter not from David Jones, the man who was dealing with their late mother's affairs, but one from the senior partner, Robert Holkham.

She scanned it quickly. It seemed that it was not to do with her mother's affairs but with her deceased father's, which she assumed to have been settled long before.

She read the letter again more carefully:

9

Dear Mrs Considine

Just before his demise in 1970 I was instructed by your late father
to send you a certain package three months after the death of your
mother, his widow, whenever that death might be.

I am putting it in the post this morning by Recorded Delivery. If
you do not receive it within a day of receiving this, please telephone me. I am relying also on you to see that your sister is
eventually apprised of its contents. She was abroad when your
father sent me the enclosed and so he asked me to address it to you
both, but to your address.

Would you be so kind as to acknowledge receipt?

Yours faithfully
Robert Holkham.

What on earth was this all about? Juliet made another cup of
coffee, sat down, and read the letter again. There was nobody
available at present to tell about this peculiar communication
except Andrew who as usual would not be home from his work
until quite late. Her sister Alison had still been in the States when
their father died, had come home for the funeral and, not long
afterwards, for good. She was still living in England – but went
abroad a good deal with her new partner, Clive Sands. Juliet
thought they were not due back from Sweden until the end of the
week.

Today was one of Juliet's free days, so she could stay in to sign
whatever the postman brought. She might do some grocery shopping later: she still accomplished this on her bicycle, though ever
more worried at the volume of traffic.

The regular parcel-postman, a fresh-faced youth, rang the
doorbell about noon and she signed for a package wrapped in old-
fashioned brown paper. After pouring herself a drink, she took it
into the kitchen and put it on the kitchen table.

Had she any idea as she slashed through the sticky tape that
this posthumous package would reveal old secrets?

There was a box inside the stiff brown-paper packing, the sort

10

of box that has once contained typing paper. Upon investigation, she found a bundle of papers tied with green tape lying inside.

She took it out. Underneath, at the bottom of the box, there was a thick envelope addressed to her and her sister with:

Ally and July:
Please do not open this until you have read the enclosed typescript.
EB.

She drew up a chair, unfastened the tape, and placed the envelope back in the box under the papers.

The first page was pristine, but the second page had the handwritten words:

For Juliet and Alison, with their father's love: Pages from the Life of Edward Bairstow August 1970

All this mystery seemed unlike the father Juliet had known. But Eddie's death could still affect her, and often she felt as if it had happened quite recently, though twelve years had passed. She had known her father for much longer than she had lived without him, and her memories were predominantly those belonging to her childhood. He was no longer the afflicted man of seventy, as he had been when she had last seen him – and seen him die – but a father in his thirties when she and her sister were still children.

As time went by, these early memories had become paradoxically greener and fresher. When she was a child Juliet had loved her father more than her mother, and although she had become used to his absence – had got used to his 'not being there' – this new reminder was already making tears start in her eyes. She was sentimental, cried easily. It was their mother whom they were mourning at present. How long did it take to get used to the death of a parent?

Why wait to send this autobiography, or whatever it was, until his widow had died? Juliet's curiosity was aroused and she decided to begin to read it that very afternoon. She would not need to hurry over it. Her father had always wanted to be a writer. Perhaps this was his final attempt?

After eating a lunch of bread and cheese she washed her hands, and took the whole box into the sitting-room where there was a little table by the french window that looked out on to the garden at the back of the house.

Now that she was ready, she found her heart beating rather rapidly.

She turned over each typewritten page as she finished it, and made another neat pile on the table.

PART ONE

Pages from my Life

*Poetry is the flower of any kind of experience, rooted in truth
and issuing forth into beauty*
Leigh Hunt – the Story of Rimini: 1832

CHAPTER ONE

My childhood and boyhood

I was my mother's first child, and I was born at the end of the last century on the first day of January 1899. Mother – Lizzie Bairstow – was barely twenty. Years later I discovered that when I came into the world she had not been married for the statutory nine months. I think my sister Flossie realized this long before I did. I never took much interest in dates and if I had I would not have cared.

My parents were fairly conventional people but it had been no shotgun marriage. My father, John Bairstow, adored his wife and she basked in his love. I think he had been both happy and relieved to be forced to marry at twenty-one, for he did not get on too well with his autocratic father, my grandfather, Benjamin Bairstow. Benjamin had been forced to let him go, for John – his eldest son – was of age, so there was nothing he could do to stop him. There was plenty however that he could and did say, and he refused to attend the wedding in Woolsford. I heard all this much later of course, not from Father but from his great-aunt, my aunt Emily, who herself witnessed the marriage, along with Mother's own family.

Of my first two or three years I remember little. When they write of their early years, autobiographers always appear to recall a good deal, but I believe they are usually influenced by a photograph, or a relative telling them of something that happened to them when they were a baby or a toddler. But I do remember something that happened before I was three, for my first true memory is of the birth of my sister Flossie. At that time we lived in a house belonging to a terrace of identical houses near my grandfather's worsted mill in Thripley. We were to move in a year or so.

That first house was chiefly remarkable for the little garden where I played all day, and it was into the garden one afternoon, as I was squatting near a flower border listening to the tinny buzz of a bee buried in a rose, that my Grandma Sandall, my mother's mother, came out and shouted over to me: 'Eddie! Eddie! You've got a little sister!'

That summer afternoon of Flossie's coming into the world was very different from the night I was born. I have been told that it had been stormy and rainy, but that my mother had expressed a wish that her baby should wait to be born after midnight had struck, so that I could be the first baby born in the New Year in our city, the year that was the last of the century.

Poor Mother! Like many first-borns, I was not in too much of a hurry. The labour had probably gone on quite long enough when at one minute past twelve I arrived and the monthly nurse called down to my father who was waiting in the living-room holding his big hunter watch:

'It's a boy, Mr Bairstow!'

His reply had apparently been: 'One minute after midnight!' Then, 'Can I come up to her?'

I suppose he had to wait then until Mother was tidied up and I was presentable.

'A happy New Year and congratulations,' said Sadie Walshaw, the midwife, and they toasted me in the champagne my father had been keeping for the occasion.

Father worked hard – his own father, Benjamin, kept his nose to the grindstone. He started off as 'overlooker' for his father and then graduated to works manager. At that time all of them took very few holidays. Christmas Day was a bank-holiday, but on

Good Friday my grandfather insisted that the weavers had a day off. He was a Swedenborgian, an unorthodox sort of Christian, unlike Father, but he said:

'The death of Christ is not a day for working but one for mourning.'

Apart from these days, they had only the Whitsuntide and August bank-holidays – and a week's holiday in August – 'Wakes Week'. The owners of the mill had no more holiday than their workers!

When I was about five my grandfather leased a larger mill, and we moved house to a village called Wike, sandwiched between rural woods and fields and the ironworks a mile or two away on the way to Woolsford. Our house was similar to the first house in Thripley, but slightly larger and set back from the road. Outside the window, as I watched from my bedroom above the front parlour, which Mother called The Room, city corporation trams ploughed their straight way along shining rails, their overhead wires occasionally sparking at night and fascinating me.

As I have indicated, my maternal grandmother was staying with us when Flossie was born. Her husband had died that same year and Father had put forward no objection to his wife giving her mother a home. He would not have thought twice about it – he was a kind man. Grandma did not make work. On the contrary she was helpful with the cooking and cleaning, and Father probably thought it was up to his wife to express her preferences. As long as she wanted her there, that was that.

My grandmother, Emma Sandall, had facial features not unlike my mother's, but whereas Mother's aquiline nose, rosebud mouth and light-blue eyes added up to an impression of good looks, in Grandma's case the eyes were more clouded, the nose a trifle longer and the lips had thinned. My mother had golden hair when I was a boy and for the rest of her life it was fair, never grey. She was quite old when I realized that she must use henna, for it never looked artificial.

I suppose I did not think about age when I was a young child, though I knew that Grandma had married late. She must have been in her early fifties when I first knew her. Her husband, my Grandpa Sandall, had died of dropsy. I think it was Mother who told me this and I wanted to ask her what that meant. The name of his disease sounded sinister. Had he dropped dead?

When we moved to Wike, Grandma had a little room of her own at the back of the house. She never missed going to matins on Sundays, when she would put on her best black-silk dress and long coat, anchor her tall feathery hat with two long pins and then, her prayer book under her arm, cross the road opposite our house to the church half-way up the hill.

I often used to look at family photographs when I was a little boy. Mother put them all into a big album decorated with flowers and I liked to hear about the people, some of them already long since dead. Family photographs were added to the old cabinet portraits of the previous century when Father bought a Brownie camera. On one picture, which must have been taken by a friend who accompanied us, we are on a day trip to the Cow and Calf rock on Ilkley Moor. It is most likely a bank-holiday, probably Whitsuntide, Father having decided to make the most of his day off.

My father is dandling me upright, my bare feet just touching the ground, a dummy stuffed in my mouth. Mother, not yet pregnant with Flossie, is sitting on the grass next to him, and there are two other adults, probably neighbours who are also friends.

At the age of six I am standing with Mother in front of a hedge with the thick foliage of a beech tree taking up most of the background. Both of us are wearing hats, myself a large sailor's hat with the brim turned up and back, and mother a boat-shaped straw confection adorned with fruit. I am wearing my sailor's outfit: white blouse, kerchief and short trousers to the knee, beneath which are a pair of slim calves with dark stockings reaching up to a few inches past my ankles. There is a little lanyard round the collar. Mother once had an eighteen-inch waist, I do know that. How long she preserved it I do not remember but she was a fine figure of a young woman. Her dress is long, looks as if it might have been green, and she has a rose tucked into the fancy lace-covered bodice.

I am not wearing my sailor-suit on the next photograph which is taken a year or two later in front of our terrace house at 88 Woolsford Road. Instead, I wear a smock almost to the top of my knees, which are covered in long socks. A pair of trousers under the smock is just visible. The shoes are plain brown lace-ups. Mother is standing between me and Flossie. I have climbed on to the wall and am holding on to the railing. Flossie, on the other side of Mother, is in a pinafore and long boots and has a ribbon in her hair. Mother's dress has a big lace collar and she is wearing a belt with a large silver clasp. Her skirt is long, with two flounces. She is wearing her fair wavy hair in a bun at the top of her head, and a velvet choker at her neck.

The door is open behind us and you can see through the downstairs window – fancily curtained in net – a large Wedgwood-type pottery bowl bearing an aspidistra. There are two windows above, also lace-curtained, and a basement beneath where there is the coal-cellar and the washing-cellar where the washing takes place on Mondays.

My grandfather, Benjamin Bairstow, plainly terrified many members of his family. He was always kind to me as the eldest grandson but I think now that he did not sense there would ever be any rivalry between us. That sounds odd to say of a grandfather and a grandson, but Benjamin always wanted to be the best. He brooked no rival. He was always very aware of his talents, and his success in business was very important to him. He had put my father, his eldest son, to work in the mill at fourteen, since Father did not evince any inclination to continue his studies at the Higher-Grade school. Both Father and the next son, my Uncle William, suffered from their mother having died of TB when they were tiny children. But William stayed on longer at school, and at seventeen was articled to a solicitor. As I grew up it may be that my grandfather knew instinctively that I would never be a busi-

19

ness rival to himself or to my father or to those uncles who did not escape manufacturing. I believe that he thought I was a throwback to the family of his first wife, who had been country people, unambitious but kind and good looking. I don't know whether I was any of these things but maybe Grandpa thought so.

Of course as a child I realized none of this but I do remember being fascinated by Grandpa and wondering how he got everybody to run round doing his bidding. He would bark out commands in a gruff baritone. Especially it was my aunt Emily who did his bidding. She was just as kind and good as from all accounts Benjamin's first wife, her own dead mother, had been. In body Benjamin was short-legged and large-headed with a bald pate save for a snowy white ruffle of hair at the nape of his neck. He had an old-fashioned moustache, a luxuriant one like the Crimean veterans of his childhood. My father too kept his well-grown moustache almost into the nineteen thirties when only tiny 'eleven-a-side' moustaches like Charlie Chaplin's were fashionable.

But I must return to those dreamy days before the first war. I say dreamy because I think I passed much of my youth in a dream – a happy one. Father could not abide dreaminess and I must have often got on his nerves. I suppose he had not been allowed to waste any time when he was a boy in Grandpa Benjamin's house.

I was most content when I was on holiday on father's uncle Henry's farm at Thirksay in the North Riding, where I could go for long walks and dream unmolested. I joined in with my second cousins' games though, and I think they accepted me. Father sometimes said I was impractical, and I believe I may have often irritated him. He was however usually fair to me, even if a few conflicts were perhaps unavoidable given that we were so very different. He called me a dreamer, but he was not a man given to physical violence. A gentle rebuke or a sigh was usually all I got from him.

Flossie helped to defuse arguments, for she was Father's favourite. In fact my father was above all a woman's man – his wife's – and perhaps his daughter's. Father and Mother were happily married and so any difficulties we had, or whatever tragedies came along – and there was the tragedy of their third child my little sister Mary Jane dying of measles meningitis – they were all eventually come to terms with.

The relations between my father and his father were awkward on Father's side, and critical on Grandfather's. Father was a decent man, a good businessman according to his lights but limited in his vision. At least that is how I saw him as I entered adolescence, having on the other hand no desire whatever to apply any visionary powers I might possess to the god of Business. I suppose Grandpa thought I would eventually have to shape up in the mill later.

The Great War was to change many of our notions; the older generations like Grandpa – and even Father – were disorientated by it. Grandpa died three years after it ended, leaving his business to my Father and two of my uncles. Father steadfastly refused to believe there would be a war, either in 1914 or in 1939. He was a practical man, an optimist, happy and hard-working. He had done no wrong; it was inconceivable that his country should go to war. Lloyd George – or Baldwin – would sort it out. I think the worst day of his life was when I was called up in 1917. He left off wearing his daily rose in his buttonhole until the Great War ended.

As a child I was not much of a fighter and this did not help when I first went to school. It wasn't that I was afraid of the other boys, just that I refused to see how fighting could ever settle anything for good. There would always be another fight. Later, naturally I realized that might was right, and if you didn't defend yourself nobody else would. At least, that applied in the school playground, or at work. Not in the family. Flossie always stuck up for me even if I didn't always take much notice of her. Father once tried to teach me to fight but I could see his heart wasn't in it. I got on well with some of the girls, those who had not been brought up to think that boys should boss them around and get bigger pieces of cake than their sisters. The girls had names like Lily and Daisy and Gladys and Doris. They were much better behaved at school than their brothers.

I was six when Mother had her third child, Mary Jane. As I was older by then I can now remember more about Mary Jane as a baby than I can about Flossie's early days. Yet this was the little sister who was to die only two years later from complications attendant upon measles, and so all my memories of her in her cradle as a new baby are mixed up with later ones.

I had caught the measles first – I suppose from someone at school – and given it to Flossie, who had not suffered too badly with it. I remember feeling very miserable with a bright red rash, a sore throat and, later, earache.

Little Mary Jane had caught it from us. Later, I wondered if Mother blamed us for that. It was Grandma Sandall, who was still living with us, who looked after Flossie and me when Mary Jane was taken ill. Before they took her away to hospital, Mother sat up for three nights by her cot in the little bedroom we had at the back of the house, and I remember the terrible atmosphere of steaming kettles, and the doctor calling, and Mother weeping, and the sounds that I heard from Mary Jane herself when I crept one night to listen at the door. She was moaning: it did not sound like her at all. The next morning she was taken away to hospital so she might be saved and I was sent off to school.

Being practical, even at four years old Flossie was more help to Mother than I was. I always felt I was in the way. I suppose boys were of more use running errands; at least that is what they found for me to do. All the neighbours' children had already had measles and everywhere I went they did not ask how I was feeling but about Mary Jane. Had the doctor been? Was she delirious? It was nice not having to go to school but there was a terrible weight in my head and I did not know whether it was a real headache or a feeling of choked misery. The doctor eventually told us that our sister had developed meningitis after the measles. I tried to imagine how the word was spelled. Mary Jane was in hospital only for three days with Mother visiting every day, and then she died.

I remember the day Mother came back without her, and I

remember her face. I ran up to my bedroom and Flossie found me there. Flossie was not yet five but she seemed to understand. She told me that the baby had gone to the angels and Mother said I must come down for tea. Father did not seem to be there at all. A few days later he and Mother buried my little sister. I had heard them talking about her and whether they would bring her home first but the hospital said even a dead baby might be infectious and so she went straight from the hospital to the cemetery with Mother and Father and Grandma and some other relations.

The funeral was to be held in the big cemetery in the city where my great grandfather had been buried a dozen or so years earlier. Father had bought a brick grave – I heard them discussing that too. As my parents left in a carriage to ride to the city on the afternoon of the funeral, men workers from the mill stood bare-headed outside the mill gates at the end of their shift. Many of the beshawled women weavers were crying and clutching flowers which they gave to Mother and Father to take with them. I did not go to that funeral and neither did Flossie. The others all came back to the house for tea and nobody spoke to me. Mother looked so pale I thought she might die too.

It was my first brush with illness and death and it cast a shadow over all our lives. Father and Mother were to have no more children after Mary Jane. I felt guilty for years that I had given my little sister the measles. She had been the smallest and the weakest, the only one of us to develop measles meningitis.

When I was a bit older I reasoned that it had not been my fault – I had suffered the measles too and if there was anyone to blame it was the child who had given it to *me*. But then, who had given it to him? You could go back and back until everybody was to blame: It was God's fault – though I did not tell my parents my conclusion. I suppose my decision not to be confirmed when I was fifteen arose from that kind of attitude. My parents did not press me then, but I had the feeling that for Mother religion was part of belonging to a 'respectable' family. Later, I decided I needed a truth beyond social contingencies and I thought the Church was just part of those. I wanted a platonic truth that would be the same for all times and all places and all over the universe for ever and ever . . . and I could not believe that Christianity could provide it.

But I must return to myself at six years old. The mill was doing well, with markets still expanding, and Mother now had a woman to help with the housework. She no longer scrubbed her own doorstep or edged it with the donkey stone. Mrs Appleyard did that. I had begun at school when I was five and Flossie was to follow me less than two years later. It was only a short walk from Number 88 to this first school, an elementary school, as we called it then, and I attended it until I was ten, walking along the road every morning, returning home at twelve o'clock for my dinner, walking back at half past one and then returning finally, released at last, at four o'clock. I shall always remember some of the names on the school register of Standard Three, which class I went into when I was eight. There were over forty boys and girls in this class. The boys' register began with me and as well as Bairstow there were Bartle and Blamires, Crowther, Dewhirst and Firth, Gaukroger, Greenwood, Haigh, Hartley, Kellett, Ormondroyd, Pickles, Rushworth and Webster. They were the same names as the men called up along with me in 1917.

The school was a two-storeyed building with long windows and two asphalt playgrounds, one for the girls and one for the boys. As it was a Church school we got plenty of hymns and prayers. Father was not especially religious, though Grandma and Mother were C of E, and Grandma of course a regular worshipper. I think, before he left home to marry Mother, that Father had endured enough of his own father's religious turnings and windings. My grandfather 'went Swedenborgian' – the Church of the New Jerusalem – after his first wife, Father's mother, the country girl, died. I believe he thought he would meet her again in Heaven, and in the meantime by a mystical process would 'see' her again in his present life. He had remarried – had pretty well been forced to, left with three young children under the age of seven, but he had treated his second wife as a housekeeper – which she was. This had not prevented her from adding five more sons to my grandfather's tally. Grandpa was sure that in Heaven he would be reunited with his first wife . Whenever Father's cousin Annie came to stay from Thirksay my grandfather would make her perch on a stool at the mill, and there he would stare at her for hours on end because he said she reminded him of my grandmother. Annie did not seem to mind. She was one of fourteen children and for her it was a treat to sit down and be looked at even if she was not allowed to move.

Father was not as clever as his own father and had no time for the volumes of Swedenborg that his brother the future solicitor, William, devoured. My father was a good man, kind and gentle, as I have said, but he did not trouble his head about the Almighty and neither did he read very much. I could not discuss with him my later real religious doubts, when I found solace – and discovered that there were people like myself – from the books I saved up to buy from the covered market in Woolsford. But this was some time later, after I had left my first school. Strangely, I remember more about the elementary school than the 'Higher-Grade' boys' school I attended in Woolsford from the age of ten to fifteen. The little local school I had tolerated in a resigned kind of way. It seemed to have nothing to do with my real interests, though I did well in composition. Most of the boys hated this subject but the girls liked it, and so did I. I regularly got a star for my attempts and was allowed to take my exercise book home to show my mother. I was not especially good at arithmetic, or most of the other subjects we were offered, but I conceived my literary pieces with passionate aplomb. Above all, I enjoyed the verse our teacher Miss Robertshaw used to read to us at the end of the day and I vowed to write verse myself. I loved its rhyme and magic. It was not popular to admit to such things.

Once I heard Mother say to Father: 'Where does he get it from?'

I think this time I had written a description of autumn in the nearby woods. Father replied, as I hovered behind the door-curtain eavesdropping on them:

'Well not from me, Lizzie – but my father might have been a bit like that when he was a boy.'

Once, Grandpa was shown my book when he came on one of

his visits from the mill to take tea with Mother – by now they had patched up relations – and he said to me:

'Your real grandmother came from a very clever family you know! They wrote books.'

Both mother and father looked blank. It was years before my great aunt Emily told me that my grandmother's grandfather, who was spoken of in hushed tones, had not been married to my great-great-grandmother but was an aristocrat who had seduced a young woman servant at a great Yorkshire House. That servant had been my great-great-grandmother.

On the whole, the adults did not talk much about books in our house. They respected Grandpa's knowledge and bought me books if I asked for them, but were not themselves very interested. But Flossie liked reading, and also showed even more of an early talent for music. This time it was quite obvious where she got it from. Grandpa's brother and Grandpa's father had both sung in the Old Yorkshire Choir and attended the early concerts at the St George's Hall in Woolsford.

When Flossie was about six she asked to learn to play the piano, which she had been allowed to try out at school. My parents bought her a piano which was placed in the parlour that till then had contained only the best furniture and an aspidistra, and Flossie began to take music lessons from an old lady down the road. The following Christmas I was bought a violin. I loved listening to music but, alas, I realized that I had no real talent, however hard I worked at it. I would stick to books.

The first three books I owned were *Robinson Crusoe*, *The Fifth Form at St Dominic's*, and *Eric or Little by Little* by Dean Farrar. Some G.E. Henty adventures were then given to me at Christmas by one of my uncles. I had dreamed over Robinson Crusoe and decided I too would like to get myself shipwrecked if I ever got as far as the coast and found a boat on which to sail away, but I did not much like poor wicked Eric, and his school was not much like mine.

I was quite impressed when I visited the mill for the first time with Father. I was not taken that time into the weaving sheds, though I could hear the tremendous din from them. Instead, I followed father up some stairs to a large door of polished wood on which was inscribed in black and gold lettering MR JOHN. Later I discovered there was another door with the name MR BENJAMIN, and later still MR ALBERT, another of father's half-brothers, who was to join them. This particular afternoon I followed my father into the large comfortably furnished office where he did much of his work. There was a hat-stand in the corner and a big trestle table under the window piled with samples of 'tops' and 'noils' and pattern-books. On a shelf at the side leaned a whole row of tall ledgers, and in the middle of the room stood a large oak desk with quite a tidy surface, apart from a quantity of brown paper and string which Father set me to smoothing out and winding up into a ball.

'I have to speak to the burlers,' he said, and left me to my task.

I went to look out of the window from which I could just see the back of our house. What did Father do all the time he was here? I imagined he wrote letters and ordered wool and went down regularly to the looms, to check all was well. I did not know what a 'burler' was, but he explained when he returned and told me about the women burlers and menders who made good tiny imperfections in the 'stuff'.

There was a big upright telephone on the desk with a listening-piece that was suspended on a hook on the telephone when it was not in use. The telephone rang whilst I was there and I listened without being able to understand what my father and his unseen interlocutor were talking about.

That afternoon I was very impressed by the mill and my father's office.

Usually we spent our holidays in the North Riding on that farm owned by the brother and nephew of my dead grandmother – who were also descended from the aristocrat. I loved the rolling Plain of York and the busy happy life which that big family led up there. They were not very well-off but they were very kind people and I decided that Father was like them and might even have been happier working on the land than in the office and loom-shed of a mill.

The country relations all played cricket, the girls as well as the boys, and the family made up the greater part of the village team. Many were the long hours I spent on holiday in August, sitting in a field reading, waiting for the match to begin in the next field when all the work was done. I liked cricket; it was restful. My Clayton second cousins called me a quiet boy, but appeared to like me. It's true I was not a great talker. I usually had something to think about when I was by myself.

Whenever I returned home to start the new term at school and said goodbye to the holidays and the freedom of the farm and the fields I would feel depressed. The worst time was when I was fifteen and the war had just begun and I sensed this might be the last holiday in Thirksay for some time.

Long before then, during the summer when I was nearly eleven and had just left the elementary school, Father, who never stayed long with us on the farm – there was always work to do at the mill – greeted me with a second hand twenty-four inch bicycle he had bought from a friend whose boy had outgrown it. I was thrilled, and this was the beginning of my emancipation. Flossy could not ride a bike but I had practised on my cousin Edmund's at Thirksay.

Now I could cycle over into the woods near home and get further into them than ever before. They began only a mile away and stretched for many more miles. Some of them further west were on steep slopes and all had once belonged to one big forest. They were still almost joined to each other and stretched north-west, right over to the next parish, and north by a beautiful seventeenth-century mansion. A beck, brown and swift-running, ran in a narrowish clough at the bottom of the woods furthest west but my favourite wood was Horse Close, which was on more level ground and not so thickly planted. The stream there was broader and slower-running. I found, when I finally penetrated it one day, that the trees grew more thickly before joining on to – or becoming – another wood, the Great Royds Wood.

That summer I had left the little local school to go to the one in Woolsford. In future my free time would be even more precious. I remember that first term at the boys' high school, the same one my father had attended when it was called a higher grade establishment. Flossie was to follow me to the sister school to which we both travelled on the train. We were the third stop from Woolsford and the train came through the smelly iron-works area before arriving at the home station.

How I wished I need not do any homework and could escape on my bike and live in the great forest like Robin Hood, and be an outlaw. But I had things to look forward to, especially the prospect of Bonfire night with its toffee and 'moggy'. If you really tried, you found there was always something to look forward to; I wrote my first composition for Mr Pendlebury, my new English master, on the subject of Guy Fawkes.

By the time I was fourteen or fifteen I was beginning to find some of my school work more interesting. Not all of it, but particularly our English lessons with Mr Pendlebury and the French lessons with M Lépine. I was even presented with the prize for French in my fourth year, at what the gentleman called our *Collège Municipal*.

Most of the boys enjoyed maths and chemistry, which I deplored, and it was partly Mr Pendlebury's influence, I suppose, that set me off writing verse in earnest. I found I had great facility; words flew off my pen. At first I imitated the poetry he read us, or which the class stumblingly read aloud – Pope, Keats – those two opposite pillars of taste. Then I began to write privately of my days spent in the woods, of the birds and the trees, and the thoughts that arose in me as I walked alone or with Flossie.

Richard Pendlebury was a brown-haired rather handsome man of medium height. He had deep-set eyes and delicate hands. I believe his family came from Lancashire and lived not far from my grandfather's old house. I expect Mr Pendlebury was a graduate of some northern university. We were not supposed to have the best teachers, or the best scholars to instruct us at our school, for they went to be masters at the fee-paying Woolsford

Grammar. All grandfather's sons had gone to my school, father included, and the girls' section was attended for a year or two by my mother before she left to be a milliner. The education there was brisk, the teachers on the whole friendly. A man who was later to become a famous novelist was in the sixth form when I started there.

My favourite occupation on a Saturday afternoon was to go into Woolsford on the train and walk up the steep street to the market and there browse in Fred Power's book shop, or rather his collection of stalls crammed with second-hand books of every kind. Here I found books of local lore as well as poetry and books about books and realized that of making many books there was literally no end. I devoured Coleridge's *Christabel* – I'd received a complete Coleridge and a complete Tennyson for my fifteenth birthday from my mother and father, at my request. When I was a bit older, after the war, I reread *In Memoriam*, and later still introduced it to my future wife. It became her favourite poem.

At fifteen I learned *Gray's Elegy* off by heart, my favourite poem in adolescence, and I began to read essays of the kind they used to call belles lettres. I read Meredith and Pope – anything that came to hand, for once I left school I would have to make sense of the order of English literature for myself. One week I might be reading from Johnson's *Lives of the Poets*, and the next I could be trying to understand some peculiar book of mystical theology or a beautifully bound copy of the previous century's *Edinburgh Review*, both owned by Grandfather who bought books in job lots, being a great reader himself, especially in his retirement. But the year I left school I remember reading the short stories of Saki, the early plays of G.B, Shaw and the novels of Surtees, with equal relish.

I would have been happy to continue at school after the leaving certificate except that Father wanted me to attend the Woolsford Technical College in preparation for a post one day at the mill. Most boys did leave from the fifth form; many girls stayed on to take the Oxford Senior and then attend training colleges to become teachers. I ought, I suppose, to have asked one or two of the masters to intercede for me, represent my case to Father, that I was not interested in technical matters, specifically in the city business of textiles. I wanted to be a writer! But I did not want to disappoint Father, and how could I earn money at sixteen from an interest in books and the writing of poetry? I had begun to write pastiche in the styles of both Pope and Keats, and two of my efforts had already appeared in the school magazine. But I did not believe I was cut out to be a teacher and I would have to earn my living.

It was in the second year of what is now called the Great War that I was enrolled at the 'tech'. How soon all our lives were to be changed utterly! I had not realized how much when I went for the last of my boyhood holidays to Thirksay in 1915.

I noticed at about this time that Grandma was beginning to lose some of her memory. She would stare for a long time into space and often when you asked her something she would look puzzled. By this time she was in her seventies – she had been older than her husband. I suppose Mother noticed, though nothing was said.

I knew I would eventually be conscripted but I chose not to think about it. I did not want to be a soldier though I was patriotic. I wrote a poem about the war when I was sixteen and sent it to the *Woolsford Observer*, which printed it. Mother was very proud. Now I rather shudder when I read it but I suppose it was not a bad effort for someone so young.

Whenever I had a break from classes I walked alone to the park and sat reading or writing. Eventually I took my courage in both hands and decided to send some poems to my old English master. The subject of one of them was death. I was thinking of all the casualties and what spirit might live on after all the bloodshed. Had the grave truly been victorious? I think now of course that it had, but in those days, though far from being religious – which might have been some excuse – I tended to rely on the indestructibility of Man if not individual men.

Nobody took my writing really seriously at home except for Flossie who thought everything I did was wonderful. She was a sweet sister, but no critic. She wanted to be a teacher of small children but would be at school for another two years .

This is the sonnet I sent my old English master:

Victory over Death

Thou canst not kill, O Death, thou canst not kill!
Thy clammy hand may smite an earth-born thing;
Thy chilly breath may blast for good or ill;
Thou mayest strike the peasant or the king.
And yet, O Death, still shine the deeds of man!
The deeds of man are earth's eternal crown.
Tho' long his years on earth, tho' brief the span,
His deeds will live, and conquered Death may frown.
When dust to silent dust hath gone, and life
Lies mouldering in the tomb and hope is fled,
Then with a radiant grandeur o'er the strife
Men's deeds shout loud that man is never dead.
Vain Death! thy hopes are blasted hour by hour,
For in great deeds alone hath man his power.

I was very gratified when I eventually received an answer from Mr Pendlebury who replied after two or three weeks. I still have his letter.

Woolsford
20 Feb. 1916

Dear Bairstow
    Your must pardon my long delay in answering your letter; I have been overwhelmed with work connected with the School examinations, marking scores of essays and other papers. A few days of that kind of work makes a man disinclined for anything that will exercise his critical faculties: in fact they require a holiday. Nevertheless I was very pleased to have your letter and the accompanying poem which I enclose. I have read the poem with much interest as well as

pleasure partly because it is the effort of one of whom I shall always retain very agreeable memories, and partly because you have managed to show in your lines that far from having stood still intellectually and poetically since our last meeting you have made a very appreciable advance.

I trust that you will continue as you have begun and then some day I may shine with a little of the reflected glory from one who for a time was my pupil.

I imagine that you continue to read widely, and especially poetry. There is so much to read however that in these crowded days a wise discrimination must be used if any real benefit is to be obtained.

I like the way in which you have made a kind of exposition of your poem. It seems to show a grip of the thing, preparing the reader to find a poem which is an organic entity and not a mere cloud of nebular musings.

I have added one or two pencilled notes to those already inserted but wish it were possible to meet you face to face and talk over the lines as in the old time at school.

With apologies, thanks and very best wishes, believe me
ever yours sincerely
Richard Pendlebury.

CHAPTER TWO

War

I was just eighteen in January 1917 when I was enlisited into the King's Own Yorkshire Light Infantry, known as KOYLI. Its motto was *Cede nullis* which I remembered from my Latin was 'Give Way to None'. I had passed the medical A1.

A month or two later I had my new khaki uniform more or less thrown at me and was told to report again in the morning. I wrapped my civilian clothes in brown paper and was just in time getting home for I was caught in a sleet blizzard. I often think it was a suitable prelude to my time in the army. I remember so well how all my 'civvies' spilled out of the parcel just as I reached the doorstep. But my ardour was in no way dampened. It is difficult to recall how enthusiastic we were then, even I who was in no way a military type. When I got to my bedroom I examined my button-stick, the 'soldier's friend' which included toothbrush, knife, fork, spoon, razor and lather brush. Then I experimented with putting on those dreadful puttees.

I didn't sleep much that night. I was both excited and sad. Excited at the thought that I was going to serve my country but sad when I realized that I was going to leave behind me, perhaps for ever, those near to me, my mother and father, my sister and my grandmother. They were so much a part of my life that I did not realize how dear they were to me until I was on the point of leaving them.

The following morning I kissed them all goodbye and my father accompanied me to the station. Tears were starting in my eyes and I had a tight feeling in my throat. I thought, the dear old Dad! He must have felt sick at heart when he saw the train take me away but we said goodbye cheerfully enough.

I embarked upon months of training, to prepare us to serve in France. There were physical jerks, route marches, bayonet practice, drilling, firing and bombing. It all made me much harder in body – and also harder in soul. I realized what a sheltered upbringing I had received, for no one swore at home, but I learned to swear with the worst of them. I drew the line at certain other matters. They told me I would not be a full blown private until, like a 'real' soldier, I had caught some venereal disease and served my time at Lichfield Hospital. There and then I determined I would never run that risk.

But it did not take me long to realize that in future I would no longer be able to write a poem like *Victory Over Death*.

I was in the 9th Battalion of the 64th Infantry Brigade, 21st Division of the KOYLI. One of the first things I noticed after leaving Folkestone was an old 'swaddy' with his crown-and-anchor board: 'All weighed and all paid off and off we go to jolly war again.'

I was billeted in a stable belonging to the owner of a small *estaminet* in a village called Acquin. The battalion I was to join had just returned from the line and they were all ready for a guzzle and blow-out. They were survivors of Passchendaele.

A good tuck-in and free booze! What more could delight a soldier's heart? But I remember thinking that the beer was terrible – thin, French sour stuff.

There were six inches of snow on the ground and it was bitterly cold. Fortunately sleeping next to me was a huge Scotsman who kept out some of the draughts. The cobblestones in the stable were most tiresome and always found a way to my hip-bone.

Soon afterwards we left Acquin and marched I know not where. We passed through innumerable villages and most of the little boys could swear in English like the hardiest troopers. After some weeks of marching and resting, marching and resting, we arrived at a place called Hain. Here we experienced nightly air raids, and were quartered in some old French dugouts as lousy and dirty as you could possibly imagine. We were inspected by some brigadier or other who then left us for his champagne supper.

The marching had made my feet terribly sore and I was left behind with a septic foot when the remainder of the troop moved forward, so I was destined to miss the great German offensive of 21 March and only heard of it from the wounded who poured into the hospitals. I had left our battalion dressing-station, gone through the divisional rest-station, the CCS and a hospital in Rouen and was convalescent about four miles from Trouville, from where I was sent to our base in Étaples.

Whilst I was there hostile aircraft dropped two bombs in the square. (We thought the Germans respected neither civilians nor hospitals.) To add to the excitement, some colonial troops came into conflict with the military police. The Australians and New Zealanders did not believe in being penned up like cattle and were not accustomed to that exasperating discipline to which the Tommies generally assented. WAACS were prominent in Étaples, especially in the cook houses and dining rooms, and I must admit they had not a very good name. Or perhaps we were jealous of the colonial troops who had so much higher pay than ourselves. At any rate the WAACS could afford to despise mere Tommies and we in turn despised them a little.

I left Étaples along with a hundred or two other soldiers who were returning to join their various battalions. We were some miles from Rheims – I was never sure of exact distances, for at the time I rarely troubled my head about distances and places – when we saw something unusual was afoot. From the train, or rather from our cattle-trucks, we could see that the roads were full of refugees travelling in the direction opposite to ours. They extended for miles and miles, what seemed to me a never-ending column. Big farm wagons containing the remnants of their domestic possessions rumbled along, whilst the poor peasants trudged alongside. How many miles they had travelled I don't know but they looked worn out with fatigue and sorrow.

We arrived at a large French ammunition dump which appeared to be deserted. We had barely passed it when the train stopped suddenly. On our left we could see a village in flames. Shells were bursting in the neighbourhood. In the distance on the hillside we could make out the signs of advancing Germans. We had practically run into them unawares. French *poilus*, under cover of the low rail-embankment, were firing in the direction of a small wood not far from us on the left. It concealed a number of the enemy who began to fire on the train. This party was evidently in advance of the main body. Hastily we blocked up the door of our wagon half-way with boxes of bully and fired back at them. Two Germans advanced into the open and before we realized it one of our number had gone out to meet them. He brought them back – prisoners. It was a very cool piece of work. The two prisoners were young fellows of about seventeen or eighteen.

By this time our French engine-driver was beside himself with excitement and gesticulating wildly. After some delay he managed to reverse the train in order to avoid capture. You must bear in mind that we were men from a dozen different battalions on our way to rejoin them, and not a single fighting unit. I suppose it was the object of the officer in charge to deliver the goods and not to lose them. However, we retreated – a not unfamiliar procedure.

An hour or so later, we were transferred into open goods-wagons, and as we passed through various village stations we received plenty of black looks from the peasantry who still remained. Of course we had innumerable stops, and on one occasion somebody managed to scrounge a few bottles of champagne and some tins of Nestlé's Swiss milk, which made an excellent cocktail.

At last we arrived at a large French storing place. The wood huts were crammed full of long French loaves and they gave us pretty much what we wanted, our rations having already been eaten. I spent the night in a wood to the accompaniment of a prolonged air-raid – under the cover of a French transport wagon.

Early the next morning we marched off, hoping to find our respective units as soon as possible. The roads were still overwhelmed with refugees and wagons. It was a very touching sight and made me realize that the civilian population in England had not the remotest idea of the meaning of war. Certainly they gave their sons and daughters but their homes and personal possessions were intact, and were comparatively safe. These peasants lost their sons; their daughters were in many cases at the mercy of the Germans; their homes were destroyed and often their only possession was a bedding on which to sleep.

We arrived in a village named Romigny, which was near the French reserve lines and took up our position in a shallow trench. I was appointed batman to the officer in charge of our detachment. I had never held that dignified position before. I was elated at my promotion and shortly had a scrounge round the village. I came upon a deserted farmhouse, and entered what I took to be the kitchen or living-room. On a table, in the centre, were the remains of a half-eaten meal. The family had left in a hurry, not caring what they left behind in their confusion.

In the filth of the farm-house yard a couple of young calves were roaming about, enjoying their freedom. On the roadside, a few paces from the entrance to the farm was a barrel which had already been tapped, but I was lucky enough to be able to fill two bottles which I had with me, with *vin rouge*. A most welcome find! I had a good swig of the wine and then returned to our trench.

The night passed slowly; French field guns were firing most of the time. About dawn, I saw two aeroplanes which had been flying around for some time crash straight into each other. Both fell to the ground in bits. I don't know what became of the pilots – more dead, I suppose. A little later there was an unpleasant whiz of bullets, followed by the bursting of scores of shells just behind our position. We again retired, this time through shell fire, falling flat on our stomachs whenever a shell burst near us. We were in an awkward position since we did not really belong to anybody, and were more or less roaming about at will.

The day wore on steadily. In the afternoon, some of us attached ourselves to another body of Tommies, whom an officer was evidently collecting together as best he could. That night we had a few hard biscuits for supper, and slept in a large barn.

We left this lodging in the morning, and after marching for a while another fellow and myself decided to reach an object – the battalion – on our own account. We marched on dusty roads, and cut through fields and woods; the only troops we saw were French, chiefly French artillery.

We made a halt near a small stream, and came upon two stretcher bearers. They were more than fed-up. One of them borrowed a rifle; the other dipped his hands and wrists in the stream, and then held one wrist out for his companion to shoot at. The shot passed clean through his wrist. He was violently sick, but no doubt happier for the wound. A few minutes afterwards there was a tremendous explosion, and a large shell burst about twenty yards away. We must find the battalion, I thought.

A little later we begged some stale crusts of brownish-looking bread from a French camp, and towards evening we arrived in Épernay. Hungry and tired we begged a drink of water from a French civilian who looked at us closely. When night had set in, we came to a railhead, near which was a French hospital.

We had not been in the neighbourhood very long when a terrific air-raid commenced. A large hot fragment of a bomb just missed us. Later we were asked into the house of a Frenchman, and were glad of the shelter. It was pitch dark inside the house, except for the light of a candle held by someone underneath the bed. As a matter of fact we all crawled underneath like a lot of frightened rabbits. We had not been there long when I thought an earthquake had started. It was, however only a dud bomb which had dropped near our shelter. The next day, we were given a lift in one of our motor-transport lorries and eventually we reached the battalion which had recently come out of the front line. It consisted of about two hundred men.

Some weeks later, after relieving French troops and, by the way, assisting in the burial of three or four horses which had been dead for about a week – a very unpleasant job – I found myself at

Puchevilliers. From there we marched to Mailly-Mailly, and I was quartered in Hillside Villa, a corrugated-iron residence.

Often, in the evenings, I was on fatigue – carrying ammunition up to the front line, and I remember that it was here where I had to keep on my gas-mask all night and until early morning. I fell asleep with it on. They make one slaver like a winded horse. The trenches in this district consisted chiefly of liquid mud, although it was summer, and very hot, too. Gumboots were issued to us, but they are not good for the feet.

After this little spell at Hillside Villa I found myself in the front line. Our trench was a rough-and-ready affair, for real trench warfare was almost a thing of the past, and most of the fighting was done in shell-holes and the open country.

We were shelled heavily, a trying and nerve-racking experience. A few of my neighbours went down the line with shellshock. I received a parcel from home that day; the contents were hurriedly dispersed.

We advanced, captured an enemy dugout and some prisoners. Our sergeant was killed by the nose-cap of a shell, and our company officer died from a wound in the thigh. The poor chap bled to death.

By the time about half a dozen had claimed a shell-hole, it was already dark. During the night, I was startled by the loud crack of a rifle and the simultaneous yell of the young fellow next to me. He spun round.

'I'm hit in the heart – in the heart!' he kept shouting.

'Stop that bloody row,' said a sergeant, 'and let's have a look at you.'

Inspection proved that he had been 'sniped' in the right shoulder. It was dark – but they got him all right.

'Heart, hell!' mumbled the sergeant, who was an old hand at the game.

I often contrived to follow these old soldiers – old in service that is – since they often succeeded in missing the bullets. Later, we had to jump from the top of our shell-hole into a very shallow trench, and as each of us took the plunge, there was the sharp crack of a rifle, and a sigh of relief on our part as we landed breathless in the trench. When back in rest and listening to a concert party, it felt fine to be alive.

After the last big German offensive, in April 1918, the Allies had lost 400,000 men in three weeks. The Allies, who now included the Yanks, suddenly began to retaliate, and by the end of July fighting had resumed. Then we were to start our own offensive which was to lead eventually to the end of the war and our victory. Of course where we were we never got the whole picture, but we suspected that the Germans were better at attacking than defending.

The history books tell you that the Americans arrived in August, and that there was action near Amiens. The Germans were pushed back to the old Hindenburg line, and 30,000 German prisoners were taken on 30 September, the Allies sweeping all before them along the whole of the Western front. Then we won the Battle of Messine. This is what the history books will also tell you, but 1918 for me meant marching, being frightened, seeing men die and trying to believe that one day it would all be over.

We had marched all day in the hot sun and the revolting smell of mustard gas. Most of us had thrown our overcoats away. We reached a wide ravine dotted with captured German dugouts. Suddenly, there was a terrific roar and a loud explosion. It meant four men less. At night we crossed the river Ancre in single file. A shell burst about four men ahead of me. I held my breath, advanced through the stinking fumes, and found one of our chaps who had recently returned from leave, lying helpless on the ground. Where his legs ought to have been I could just discern a few shreds of puttees. Later I learned that he had died in hospital. During the night German prisoners kept arriving. '*Brot* ... *Zigaretten*,' they said.

I remember that shortly after this I had an attack of severe diarrhoea caused by the drinking of water from shell-holes, and I was forced to discard my braces and use a lanyard instead. This sounds very laughable, but I had not much time for laughter then.

About a week later, we were advancing in open country when

suddenly there was a regular rattle from machine guns. We had reached a road which was banked up on the further side. Below that bank one was fairly safe, but above it things were pretty hot. I was carrying a rifle with fixed bayonet, a large pick with only half a handle, and in addition the spare-parts bag for a Lewis gun. I waited and tried to judge the best opportunity for making a move, listening to the machine guns as they traversed the top of the bank.

I made the plunge. Bullets sizzled uncomfortably near. There were cries of 'stretcher-bearer'. Our sergeant-major was hit in the stomach and died from his wounds.

Out of breath, I reached a friendly shell-hole. Bullets hit the top and scattered the earth. I wished then that I could burrow like a mole or sink through the ground. Relieving myself of the pick, I made a dive for another shell-hole and eventually reached an old communication-trench.

The next day four others, myself and two officers, set out to do a little scouting. Shortly afterwards our colonel joined us. He looked worn-out and worried. I can still remember his pale face, made paler by three or four days' growth of black beard. Officer No. 1 climbed up the trench side to see how the land lay, and in doing so exposed the upper half of his body above the trench. In a couple of seconds there was the sharp report of a rifle, and he slithered down, with a bullet wound in his thigh.

Officer No. 2 shared a similar fate. The bullet entered just below the right shoulder and came out nearly in the middle of his back. The poor man gasped for breath and tried in vain to speak. His face became yellowish-white in colour. The colonel was kindness itself and tried to soothe him.

Four of us including myself then became temporary stretcher-bearers. In places the trench was very low, and when it was necessary to expose myself to the enemy, I had some strange sensations down my spine and in the pit of my stomach.

Lower down the trench a dead German was lying on the firing-step. He had red hair and his face was the colour of wax. He was covered with a blanket, but I could see his face as his left arm was thrusting the blanket away from him. His teeth were tightly clenched in great agony. A thin stream of blood had been running from his wound into the trench bottom. Not many yards away, one of our own men was lying in the trench almost face downwards. He had been shot through the head. Blood was congealed on his right cheek.

Perhaps if they had ever had any quarrel, the two men were now reconciled. Who knows?

Some years later when I read Wilfred Owen's famous poem, *Strange Meeting*, I vividly remembered those two soldiers.

I had not been wounded. I had suffered from a septic foot and dysentery, and a week or two after my sight of these two men I had a severe attack of Spanish flu and was sent once more to Trouville. I was convalescent when the armistice was signed.

Épernay ... Acquin ... Hain ... Trouville ... Étaples ... Rheims ... Romigny ... Épernay again ... Puchevilliers ... the river Ancre ... Trouville again. ...

Many years later I visited most of these places. I could not believe they were the same I had known in my youth.

Waste of war – *waste*. Inefficiency, muddle, boredom, discomfort, too, all affected me. I was very young, too young. The pain and blood and death of others was somehow mixed up at first with my more selfish memories. Only later did the real tragedy of it all detach itself: three-quarters of a million British troops dead – the 'lost generation': ordinary men like myself, officers, writers, poets – Saki, Owen, Edward Thomas. ...

Waste!

I had done my duty; I had not been especially brave; I had obeyed orders, occasionally accomplished a few things off my own bat.

Slowly it had hardened me, but the older I grew and the more I remembered, the more pointless I thought it had been. Yet I had been spared to live my life.

How could I make that life worth living?

*

After my experiences in France I could never again write a poem like *Victory Over Death*, the verses of a callow if sensitive youth, still almost a schoolboy. I had seen deeds of bravery, but they were not enough to erase death.

My writing had once been technically proficient, full of literary conceits: apostrophe, metaphor, repetition, archaisms, but I could not find words adequate to describe the horrors of The Great War.

My own paltry experiences left me with a sort of residual humanism. I had not been exactly religious before but now I thought religion all a big 'con'. By the time I was twenty-one, those eighteen months in France had changed all my feelings and opinions. I was not by nature cynical but I think I was forced to become so. I could not describe to Flossie what I had seen; it would only upset her and give her nightmares. Mother and Father were too pleased at my return to ask too many questions.

My grandfather, who was to die when I was twenty-two, wrote me a kind letter and enclosed a cheque for one hundred pounds.

I bought a motor bike.

CHAPTER THREE

Home Again

Grandma's mind had gone on failing before her body. Flossie had become very upset about this as she often told me in her letters. She said she felt guilty for burdening me with her anxieties, but I was glad to be a safety-valve. A letter I received just after the armistice told me that Grandma had died. She was old, so her death had been inevitable. Only when I arrived back in Woolsford in 1919 did I discover that dear Mr Pendlebury had died in the July of 1918 as a result of wounds suffered as a corporal in the Special Service Corps of the West Riding Regiment, where he had volunteered a few months earlier. He was brought back to die in a VAD hospital on the Yorkshire coast. Why had he sought to join our troops? Was it because so many of his old pupils had died that he felt he owed it to them? I felt it was a death that should never have happened and it made me feel paradoxically guilty that I had survived. My old English master had been forty-eight at his death and I saw this then as old. He was certainly too old to be called up. His death, which I continually imagined, became ever more shocking to me as the years rolled on. He should have stayed in the staff-room marking papers or walking home to Manningham to his parents and sister, for he was not married. It was all so pointless, and war was crazy.

Forty-eight. I think now, so young, so young.

I had myself been demobbed on 18 February 1919. In May the family intended to remove from Wike to a handsome new villa called Holmfield in a pretty village a mile or two away, one station down the line. After a few weeks at home readjusting myself to civilian life – or rather hoping my family would adjust to me – I was invited to spend April with my father's cousins in Thirksay. It was nearly four years since I had spent my holidays there but it felt more like forty of my own subjective time.

I took my new motor-bike on the train to Thirksay via Harrogate and stayed at Ox Close Farm with Father's widowed cousin Jane and her sons Ted and Gordon, the youngest two of her enormous brood. The boys had also been called up so I had something to talk about. It transpired that Ted had been in charge of horses on the Somme battlefields; if I'd been called up earlier I could easily have met him on my travels to and fro. He was a phlegmatic young man who cared more for animals, I think, than women. I told him about burying the dead horses and he listened sympathetically.

'Aye, they were the real heroes!' he said.

I was to enjoy speeding along the almost empty roads with Ted on the back of the bike. We went to Sutton Bank to see the White Horse carved into the hillside, and all over the Vale of York. I felt gloriously free after my two years of soldiering. Sometimes I just could not believe what I had seen and experienced over in France, but I would often imagine what it might have been like to have fought that war, dug those trenches, slept in those shell-holes, if they had been here in Yorkshire, in my beautiful land, which I thought was much lovelier than northern France. I was so glad to be home!

I had gone to Thirksay with the intention of seeing how life on the land might suit me. I dreaded returning to the tech where I still had at least one further year's studying to do. I had the half-formed notion that I might make the break and become a farmer.

I was awoken every morning by the crowing of the cock at dawn and I must admit I never wanted to get up from my comfortable feather bed. Ted and his brother were already up milking. I tried to put all my energies into helping them but it was tiring work. Perhaps the last two years had tired me out, or perhaps it was the flu that had left me feeling a bit weak. Whatever the reason, I think I soon knew that I would not make a farmer. I loved the country. I did not need the stimulus of the town, but I did need time to read, and here when work was done everyone went straight to bed, unless there was a cricket match going on.

In the army I had begun to smoke and now I would sit in the orchard smoking with a book of poems on my lap. I felt convalescent. Ted loved riding on my bike and in exchange took me for drives in the coal-cart to the station for coal, or to the market to sell eggs. As it was April it was different from my last visit when I had been there for the harvest and the fruit-picking and visited the agricultural show. I remembered the thistle-cutting and the clover-cutting and the rabbit-shooting. I was glad there would be none of that this time for I don't think I could have shot at a target, never mind an animal. War had left me completely against any sort of violence.

We visited all the other members of the large Clayton family. One had a little farm called The Laurels and one kept the village post office. Three girls had married away, two of them to farmers, one in the East Riding, one in the Dales.

But there was plenty to do and see, and I took walks as well, for I did not want them to think I only came to ride my bike, though I must admit it was at this time the pride and joy of my life. We walked by the little river and in the woods and my second cousin, Lizzie, showed me her magic tree. The tawny owls had begun to nest in the woods and sometimes at night when I woke from dreams of men dying in France I heard them hooting from that direction.

'You must come in the autumn or in August,' said Lizzie. 'We can go mushrooming then.'

Her father had a tandem bike and did not want Lizzie to sit behind me on the motor bike so I had one or two spins with her on the tandem. She was a healthy pretty girl of about sixteen but I did not fall in love with her although I liked her a lot.

There was an old lady who lived with Lizzie's family who must have been nearly eighty and I discovered that she was the older sister of my father's dead mother – my great-aunt in fact. Why had nobody pointed her out to me before? I knew Father called her Aunt Ann but I had not bothered my head about the relationship. Sometimes she came to visit my hostess and they would take tea in the kitchen and talk about the family. I listened in on these sessions and noticed they spent a good deal of time discussing my grandfather, whose husband Ann's sister had been.

'Forty-three years this April she was called away,' she said. 'She was my favourite sister. You look a bit like her.'

'Grandpa thinks Cousin Annie looks like her,' I ventured.

'Aye, I know – he was 'overseen' on Mary – still is! Not that she didn't deserve it, but still. . . .' She sounded as if men ought not to be so romantic. I knew then that like him I would be romantic about women.

Aunt Ann was very attached to a gosling on the farm. The attachment was mutual and it was very funny to see the bird follow her wherever she went. There were other geese on the orchard pond, quite fierce creatures.

After returning home from Thirksay I finally decided that I was not cut out to be a farmer. I had imagined I might be happy working on the land but that kind of labour left no time or energy for reflection, however beautiful the background to that reflection might be.

I was to take up my studies at the tech in September so I had four months to help Father at the mill, or at the office, number 120 in the Royal Arcade, a handsome covered street with two storeyed shops and offices, a beautiful piece of Victorian neo-Gothic. I suppose it resembled the Burlington Arcade in London, though the stone was darker and it was built later in the nineteenth century. A clock was suspended from the centre of the central avenue and there was a wrought-iron grille for entrance. The roof was cast-iron and glass, which let in the light and gave a sense of spaciousness to the place. Only a year or two ago was this beautiful piece of history pulled down – to build shoe shops!

One of Father's brothers also had an office there on the central avenue, and so I made myself useful to them both. I preferred work in the office to work in the mill, especially as there was always something interesting going on in Woolsford, and in my dinner hour I could visit the market and browse for books. Sometimes I felt that nothing had happened since I had last spent such hours in the market during those years before I was called up. It was still a world of eccentric mill-owners, often quite erudite men, readers, who retired to Morecambe – which they called Woolsford-by-the-Sea.

I really had no interest in working for my diploma in textiles though I knew I was perfectly capable of learning and reproducing my knowledge. But I had to qualify for some job or other and I could not think of anything I really wanted to do. Apart, that is, from reading, and writing poetry. I had written several poems at the front when we were becalmed not knowing what we should be called upon to do next, or where we were bound, and also during those long hours in hospital in Étaples. My poems at the front were all about homesickness. I kept dreaming of summer nights at home in England: I had thought if I could conjure them up clearly enough I could banish the dismal and terrible present. But who was I at nineteen to counsel wiser men than myself against despair?

Whilst recovering from influenza I had written a poem about war that was very different from the one I had had published in the *Woolsford Observer* when I was still an untried lad.

It began:

> *Ah, I have heard and smelt and seen*
> *I know the battle's bitter pain;*
> *The weary march and sharp attack,*
> *The marble faces of the slain;*
> *The mire and mud, the screeching shell,*
> *The choking cry from parchèd lips. . .*

It ended with an impassioned cry:

What of all our honoured dead?
Shall not all wars for ever cease?

I did not think when I wrote this poem that they had died in
vain. Later, I did wonder. Flossie had kept all my letters from
France and copied out the poems I had written there. I knew they
were not perfect but I had not stopped writing and that to me was
the important thing.

I wrote Flossie a poem for her eighteenth birthday which had
come around just after I returned home from the war:

Oh sister if! If thou didst but know
The warmth of feeling that I cannot show. . . .

I decided I would do enough work the following year at the
technical college to be able to make myself useful in the family
business, but that I would always reserve the better part of myself
for my leisure hours which I could spend reading and writing. I did
wish I could ask Mr Pendlebury for advice. I knew nobody else to
whom I could address myself, but formed a plan of sending some
of my better attempts to people whose work I admired, to ask
their opinion.

Meanwhile I learned about tops and noils and shoddy and
mungo and tried not to appear too dumb. Uncle Fred was a very
successful businessman in the worsted line and I did not wish to
appear stupid in his eyes. When I qualified I might even go on
working for him in Woolsford, if I did not go to the mill and help
Father. Our own business was not doing too well. The war was
over and the demand for officers' gaberdines and such like had
fallen off. Everybody was predicting a slump.

Uncle Fred took an intermittent interest in me and advised me
to learn Spanish in case markets could be opened up in Latin
America and I could be useful as a traveller. I duly enrolled
myself in the Woolsford Foreign Circle. I had enjoyed French at
school and I enjoyed my Spanish conversation lessons too, once I
had learned the essential grammar. There were one or two

natives of Spain or Argentina in Woolsford, and I decided that speaking Spanish was like speaking with a mouthful of crushed chestnuts.

I remained a member of the circle for years, although nothing was ever to come of my prowess with the language. Most of the pre-war foreigners had been Belgian or German, some of the latter having been in the city since the middle of the previous century, but the mood was still very anti-German. These families, mostly Jewish, had taken British nationality long ago and no longer spoke German at home, though Little Germany, the name for some of the district of warehouses in the city, still kept that name.

Very soon we had moved into our new house, Holmfield, and I was given a bedroom of my own looking out on to a daisy-starred lawn at the front of the house. We had a big hall covered in oak panelling and Father had hung the portrait of his own grandfather there in a large curly gilt frame.

He had also acquired a pianola, a magnificent mahogany piano with a perfectly good keyboard on which Flossie might do her practice, but with a secret panel in its handsome front which when opened revealed space for a thick rolled-up parchment, like a papyrus, of musical 'dots'. You hooked this roll into each side of the space and pedalled away. The keys moved magically under your fingers and the most heavenly sounds emerged. Beethoven's *Appassionata* sonata was my favourite. I soon perfected an appropriate posture, and finger 'business' which might convince an innocent that I was actually performing.

I also wrote the words for a few songs and hummed invented tunes to my sister which I hoped she would then set to music. Flossie had begun her two year course at the training college in Leeds. She was extremely musical but she was not creative, although she knew how to write music and had passed an examination in musical theory. I listened to more music than she did for there were now concerts in the city which I attended more often than Flossie.

'I'm sure *you* could write a better tune,' I would say to her, but she did not want to compose, would rather play what was given to her.

I wrote a patriotic Sailor's song, which I now find too bloodthirsty:

> *The salt sea-waves roll high*
> *and threatening is the sky*
> *O we are glad when danger's near*
> *For what, my boys have we to fear?*
> *When shells with thunderous roar burst o'er my boys,*
> *Burst over,*
> *We laugh and say, Roar on, roar on!*
> *We'll send you down, my German son!*

and several love songs. One of them I can still remember. I am amazed that it is so sad for when I wrote it I had no experience of romantic love, even if I was soaked in romantic poetry.

> *Far a down the vale of Love*
> *I heard a faint voice calling;*
> *Nearer, nearer come the voice,*
> *and Oh! for me 'twas calling.*
> *Ah those days of youth have fled*
> *And I am left a-sighing*
> *Longing for the light of love*
> *The love that's sadly dying.*
> *In the dell of pleasure sweet*
> *The birds for me were singing*
> *Oh to hear them once again*
> *Oh to hear them once again!*

I was longing for something. I did not quite know what, but I suspected it must be love – or rather 'falling in love'. Later, one of my new friends at the tech put these songs to music and Flossie played them for us. She was always busy practising the piano when she was not helping my mother with domestic duties.

Once I had started anew at the technical college I suppose my life was rather strange. By day I was listening to lectures on the subject of the woollen and worsted trade, had started my scrap-book of different types of wool, sticking samples on to special pages, some like the silky hair of a girl. But once my lessons were over I was back home, or reading and writing in the Mechanics' Institute library.

I found the new post-war poets quite a shock to the system when I finally got round to reading them. Before the war I had read some of the modern poets in magazines lent to me by Mr Pendlebury; now the war seemed to have loosened more of their tongues.

I still preferred Swinburne to the moderns and one of my own twenty-first birthday presents was to be a handsome white-and-gold edition of that poet which I put with the leather-bound Coleridge and Tennyson Mother and Father had given me – it seemed hundreds of years earlier – for my fifteenth birthday.

My years at the tech were chiefly remarkable for the friends I made among men of my own age or older. Those a year or two younger had been too young to be conscripted and there was a gulf between us, however much we liked each other. One or two of the older ones had gone through experiences similar to mine but after an initial conversation none of us appeared to want to talk further about our time in France. One friend, Jim Betts, was very musical. He had not fought in the war because he had bad asthma. He felt ashamed of that. I invited him round to Holmfield and found he was willing to put some more of my lyrics to music.

My other new friend, whom I got to know during my first year back, was a year older than myself, richer, and a bit of a mystery, I thought. Yet he seemed to like my company. He was called Alec Moore, and his family owned a large mansion set in a little park of its own in a wooded valley between Woolsford and Leeds called Knagg Wood. When he described it I thought it sounded like a mysterious domain. Later, when I read that story called *Le Grand*

Meaulnes by a Frenchman who was killed in the war, it reminded me of the place. Not so much the configuration of house and park, but the configuration of emotion I invested in it. By then of course I had been there myself.

Alec's father, Wilfred Moore, was a textile manufacturer, but a much more successful one than my own father. Mr Moore's firm had 'gone public'. Alec had a sister who had, he said, been away to school, but who, he said with a laugh, had never been 'properly finished'.

'If it hadn't been for the war, Father would have sent her to Switzerland – now she's at a secretarial college in Harrogate.'

'She wants to work then?'

'Oh, until she gets wed, I expect. She had a term or two at the Pudding School but she didn't like it.'

I had not yet asked Alec round to my home. He lived a good distance away; Knagg Wood was a mile or two north of Woolsford whereas Lightholme was six miles from the city in a westerly direction. Sometimes Alec and I would go together to the Sphinx café in the city for a cup of coffee. At first I did not reveal anything to him concerning my own real ambitions for I was shy of talking about myself. I knew that most businessmen despised poetry, and even more, poets, who were said to be namby-pamby creatures with a weak grasp of reality. Alec however had been to a good school and was a tolerant sort of chap. He had actually heard of some of my writer heroes.

'Why didn't you go to university?' I asked him, for it seemed to me that he was just as much a square peg in a round hole as myself.

'Father wanted me in the business, and I thought as I'd been over two years away in the navy he deserved a break. Our work here doesn't really interest me. All this "stuff"!'

Well, I expected he would inherit money and a thriving business.

'Tell you what,' he went on, 'you must come round one Saturday to our place. Do you play tennis?'

'Just about. I used to play with friends a bit, but I was never properly coached. We've just got a new tennis club in the village. I was thinking of joining. I need some exercise.'

As I said this I realized it was true. I needed a breath of fresh air. Mother's cooking would put weight on me if I let it. A golf club was starting in Lightholme that summer. Father was keen on the idea and decided he would take the game up seriously. Mother said nothing would induce *her* to play golf, and I thought I would prefer tennis myself.

'Right then. We'll make up a game. Perhaps Rhoda will bring along her friend from college.' Nothing more was said for a time.

It was now the April of my second year at the tech. I had not yet taken any girls out though I knew some of Flossie's friends. The town in whose suburbs our village now belonged intended to recommence dances in its assembly rooms, but so far I had not met anyone I liked enough to take there. At least I might soon practise my tennis, even if I drew the line at golf.

One day at the beginning of May, Alec, with whom I now sometimes went for a beer at the public house near the tech, said,

'Would you like to come over to our house to play tennis on Saturday?'

'You mean on your own grass court?'

'Of course. I'm sorry I couldn't fix it up earlier but Father has been unwell and Rhoda away. She's back now though, and a bit browned-off, so she suggested she asked a friend of hers over called Phyllis if I would bring a man along. We can play mixed doubles. . . .'

I said I'd like to. Fortunately I had just had my racquet restrung.

Alec explained how to get to Knagg Wood for this, my very first visit. As I have explained, it is in Woolsford but near the border with Leeds, where is found a mixture of suburb and wooded hills and valleys.

I very much looked forward to that Saturday. I realized that since leaving the army and abandoning my idea of becoming a Thirksay farmer I had been suffering from *ennui*, an emotion alleviated only by reading. What should I talk about with his sister, though? I racked my brains to prepare something suitably girlish.

Flossie's friends were all a little giggly, though she was not, so I had never had a proper conversation with any of them. At this time I was very interested in the Russian Ballet which I had read about and seen illustrations of but never yet seen perform. She might find that interesting? Or friend Phyllis might?

I imagined their house would resemble the one described by one of my favourite writers, Charles Lamb, in his *Last Essays of Elia*, when he says 'I do not know a pleasure more affecting than to range at will over the deserted apartments of some fine old family mansion.' Why in my mind's eye I imagined Alec's father's domain to be deserted I do not know. But I loved old houses and I knew theirs was a hundred and fifty years old. This was not very old, but when you considered how many really old houses had been demolished in the borough in the middle of the previous century, it was comparatively ancient. There was so little left around us that was really old, until you moved further away from the towns.

Before the war the house had apparently been extended, and new greenhouses and conservatories built. I knew it had delightfully large grounds, for Alec had told me about them and I had imagined a covey of gardeners, and a stable-block now filled with Rolls Royces. The latter were not very romantic but they were rather beautiful. I coveted a 1921 Bentley sports car but I'd have been quite content to have an Austin 7. Father was considering buying a car that would cost almost £250. More and more people were buying them. I read somewhere that at this time there were almost a quarter of a million car owners. Alas, I was not one of them, so I decided not to arrive on my motor bike but to go decorously by train.

Knagg Wood did not turn out a disappointment when on the following Saturday morning I made my way from the nearest station up a steep lane overhung with horse-chestnuts and beeches, fields falling away towards a valley over the high wall on each side. It was summer so the whole place was green. I caught sight of bluebells in a wood on my right, before the lane turned and there was a gate and then another path. I had come up to the house at the back or side. The carriage-drive curved round from the main road below me.

I pushed open the gate and heard voices faintly in the distance before I came out into a clearing and then passed through a wooden gate. There before me were the grounds proper of the mansion. The grey stone house had smoke coming from its chimney – even in May it was not often warm in Woolsford.

I shifted my racquet to the other arm and plodded on, hoping I was not going to make a fool of myself. But I remember I admonished myself: 'You have come through a dangerous war so there is no need to be frightened of a rich family and an old house.' Still, I hoped Alec's parents would not be too overbearing. I knew his great-grandfather had been a very successful if homespun wool baron, but two or three generations on, most of the *nouveau riche* were no longer rough and bluff.

I saw a girl standing on the mossy lawn in front of the house. She was wearing a shortish white skirt. Even I knew that fashions were changing now and girls no longer had to dash about a tennis court in long pre-war skirts.

The lawn rose in two terraces to the front of the house and there were urns filled with bright flowers. I saw that there was an orchard and a fruit garden on one side, and my favourite Lamb essay came into my mind again. I remembered that in the place he described there was a 'fiery wilderness' behind the house, with murmuring wood-pigeons. This however was a northern mansion, darker and more solid than the one I had imagined. I did hear wood pigeons, though, as I shook off my fancies and advanced towards the lawn.

'Rh-oda!' shouted the young lady. 'Come on out – he's arrived!'

So this young woman was not Rhoda. I was a little disappointed since I saw as I came up to her that she was blonde and curly-headed and quite pretty. Then Alec appeared in the porch followed by another young lady who must be his sister. This one was dark-haired and not so tall as the fair-haired girl. She too was wearing a skirt similar to the first young lady's.

Alec introduced me to them both. Rhoda's friend was called

Phyllis Crowther. The two girls shook hands with me politely, smiled, and were what I would have described as cautiously friendly.

There was a little breeze, not enough to spoil a game, and we decided straight away to do a bit of a warm-up for half an hour before lunch and then have a proper match after it, once we had recovered from the meal.

Although her long hair, coiled up in a 'Cadogan', was dark, Rhoda's eyes were blue and I thought she looked more Irish than Yorkshire. Alec decided she would partner me and he would join Phyllis on the other side of the net. The court was smooth and well mown.

Rhoda hit the ball quite well but with rather a lot of silent running around. Phyllis was a dab at long forehand drives and I had my work cut out to return them. But we were only practising, so if I missed a few it did not count.

After about twenty minutes of this, Rhoda said, 'I'm exhausted and terribly thirsty. Can we stop now and have a drink?'

We all agreed and decided on lemonade and trooped into the house. First through a large hall with portraits and a tiger rug and a few antique-looking swords hanging on the walls as if it was an old manor, and thence to a sort of breakfast-room. Here there was a trolley of drinks. Alec went into the kitchen and returned with a bucket of ice. I wondered where Mrs Moore was. Was she the sort of lady who would spend Saturday mornings drinking coffee with friends and then playing bridge with them in the afternoon?

I followed Alec into a sitting-room where Phyllis and Rhoda flung themselves on a sofa.

'I haven't played since last year – no wonder I'm exhausted,' said Rhoda.

'Oh, I had a game last week with that friend of your cousin Arthur's – you know, the one who came to Woolsford last year, the sheep farmer,' said Phyllis

'Do you play tennis every weekend, Mr Bairstow?'

'Please call me Eddie,' I said.

'Right – Eddie – question repeated.'

'Well no – not really,' I confessed. 'I quite enjoy a game now and then. I need more practice.'

'Are you a terribly keen sportsman?' asked Phyllis. What was she driving at?

'Edward is a writer,' said Rhoda solemnly. It must have been Alec who had been giving her my credentials.

'What do you write?' pounced Phyllis.

'Oh, well, I haven't much time at the moment,' I equivocated.

'He writes verse,' said Rhoda.

'How unusual,' said Phyllis. I felt a bit silly.

'Have you published any?' pursued Phyllis.

'A few times in the local rag,' I confessed. 'But not very much since I came out of the army.'

'You were an infant prodigy!' exclaimed Phyllis.

A gloom seemed to have fallen upon Rhoda's face at my mention of the army. I had better change the subject. But it was too late.

'Was the war just *ghastly*?' she asked. 'Alec won't tell me anything about the navy. Nobody wants to talk about the war any more.'

'Yes, it was indescribably horrible,' I replied shortly. 'Filthy and brutal. Though I served in France for twenty months.'

'Let's talk about something else,' said Alec.

'Well then, Eddie can tell us which poets to read,' said Phyllis. So I said, had they read Swinburne's *Forsaken Garden*, and they made me recite a bit of it. I was sure Phyllis was bored stiff but Rhoda said she loved Gray's *Elegy*, which they had read at school, and I could agree with that.

'It was my teacher's favourite poem,' she added. 'At school in York.'

At lunch, which was served to us in a small dining-room by a parlour-maid, I thought it was time to turn the conversation round but I wasn't very adept at doing that. I was damned if I was going to launch into Pope and Cowper and Coleridge, whose *Christabel* was at that time still my favourite poem, so I said politely to Phyllis:

59

'Do you play the piano? Or paint?'

'Both. Badly,' she replied shortly.

'Rhoda paints in water colours,' said her brother. 'And Phyllis here sings.'

'You must come to my house and we can have a concert,' I said boldly 'My sister is a good pianist and – she could accompany you.'

Whilst we were eating our pudding, which was a sort of 'shape' (I was surprised that the food was not very exciting) Phyllis asked me if I liked the business world. What should I reply?

'You mean the tech? It will lead to a job, I suppose,' I said.

'Are your family in textiles then?' asked Rhoda.

'Yes, but in a smaller way than yours,' I answered boldly. 'We have a family weaving-mill.'

'My father says things are not too good in business at present,' said Phyllis.

'But some people are doing very well,' Alec interrupted her.

It was true. I thought of my Uncle Fred with his world-wide contacts. I'd never be as successful as Uncle Fred. But I didn't want to talk about business. I had quite enough of that during the week. Rhoda too looked bored. She said, 'It's time for our match,' and smiled at me.

I used to enjoy tennis, unlike the rougher sports of rugger and football. I did not play brilliantly that afternoon, not as well as Alec, but my service was not disastrous and my volleys sometimes succeeded. Rhoda and I lost our first game but Phyllis flagged a bit after that whilst Rhoda still seemed to have plenty of energy, and we won the next game. After that, honours were about even until we decided to stop at about four o'clock. I heard the sound of a car on the gravelled path to the house and Rhoda said, 'That'll be Mother.'

It's hard to remember exactly what my feelings were that afternoon. I can remember finding Mrs Moore a bit daunting, Her Christian name was apparently Veronica and it was the first time I had met anyone called that. She was slim and stylishly dressed and had, I thought, a lot of self-confidence. One might have expected a pampered sort of rich man's wife, but she seemed perfectly intelligent and not overly concerned with her children's lives. I suppose that they had been under the care of nursemaids and then sent away to boarding-schools, so were not as close to their parents as I was to mine.

Alec introduced me to his mother as we filtered into a smaller sitting-room with comfortable chairs and small tables. An oak trolley was wheeled in by another parlour-maid. Mrs Moore shook hands with me and made some comment about being glad Alec had found a friend at 'that dreadful technical college'. She had a southern English accent. I believe she intended to be agreeable. She added, 'My husband is away on business this weekend.'

The tea consisted of cream buns and fragrant tea in china cups, and I enjoyed it all. Mrs Moore said no more as we drank our tea but I saw her looking at us in turn over the rim of her cup.

Phyllis was ribbing Alec about putting on weight. Perhaps she had designs on him. I listened to Rhoda who was telling me about her Pitman's course at the Harrogate secretarial college, and I wondered why she had chosen to learn something useful. Did her father want her to be his secretary? Really, I knew so little about them all, and I was chary of asking too many questions and being considered naïve. Would I ever meet Papa Moore?

Alec drove me down to the station to catch a train at about half past six. On the train it was Rhoda about whom I found I was thinking. I could not make up my mind what sort of young woman she was. She was not intellectual, yet she seemed intelligent and she had been friendly. I hoped she had been as interested in my conversation as I had been in hers. Phyllis Crowther had shown less interest than Rhoda in my remarks about the ballet. I wondered if she came from such a well-to-do family as the Moores. I must find another subject of conversation for both Rhoda and Phyllis, if there was to be a next time, which I hoped there would be. If they didn't want to make the journey to Lightholme we could meet in Woolsford perhaps, and go to the Alhambra.

As I sat in the train that Spring evening, absorbing my impressions of the day, I think I remember feeling myself physically attracted to both Rhoda and Phyllis, but more to Rhoda. I was twenty-one, and used to continually day-dreaming over impossible women. These two young women seemed approachable, but Rhoda appeared more mysterious than Phyllis, I suppose. That evening however there was nothing to indicate that I would soon be embarking on the most passionate adventure of my life, when my heart as much as my body would plunge me into quite novel feelings.

During term-time, Flossie lived in Leeds at the city training college. I wrote to her every week, for although she was only twelve miles away, in those days you did not make unnecessary journeys, and she was given an *exeat* only for family illness or emergencies.

The day after my visit to Knagg Wood, a Sunday, which day I usually employed writing letters or reading (I no longer went to church) I wrote Flossie a letter describing the Moore family and their house. I had found the place sympathetic, quite apart from the family. I was interested in the latter not because they were rich and their house well-appointed, but because they lived in a romantic place, steeped in the history of the last century. Apparently, so Mrs Moore had told me over tea, a century ago there had been secret passages in the shrubbery behind the house. She did not explain what they had been used for.

I hoped I'd be invited there again. In the meantime I asked Mother if I might entertain my friend Alec, and possibly his sister and her friend in Lightholme. Father looked at me a little quizzically.

'I could take them to play tennis on the village courts,' I said.

I saw Alec at the tech on the Tuesday after my visit to Knagg Wood.

'Would you like to come over to Lightholme for a game of tennis on our club courts?' I asked him.

'When?'

'Well, whenever it suits you. I have to book the court, you see.' I didn't tell him that I'd only just joined the village club and wasn't sure how long I'd have to wait for a court.

'Give me a few dates,' I said. 'If you'd like to come over ask the girls too, will you?'

CHAPTER FOUR

Rhoda

I can remember quite clearly the day I fell in love. It had been led up to by my poetry reading, I suppose. I never used to read novels very much; my favourite reading was still poetry and literary criticism. Anything exotic or lush or lyrical in the poetry I was reading seemed to predispose me to day-dream about women! One thing apparently led to another. I was well aware of the usual problems of the flesh; you could hardly be two years in the British army without experiencing lonely lust or seeing how others found ways of dealing with it. I was the same age Father had been when he married Mother, and they say the early twenties are the most difficult for a young man.

I however had been in the trenches so I should be harder than he had been, more disposed for action. I suppose I was tougher now, but I reacted against the pack mentality of young men, never went on binges of destruction and hated the idea of going to a prostitute. I was frightened of VD, but even more I found the whole idea of making use of a woman distasteful. You could say I was very romantic. I had enjoyed a gentle if not genteel upbringing that had yet enabled me to survive the war and had suited my temperament.

When I fell in love that summer I knew I had never felt like this before. I had felt desire, most inappropriately, before I was called up, for a young female dancer, dressed in 'Eastern' clothes at the

Alhambra in Woolsford where we went to see the pantomime *Ali
Baba*; I had a tender affection for my close family and my girl
cousins; and a sort of romantic yearning was aroused in me by the
poetry of Keats and Tennyson. This however was different, for it
had all these elements and more, perhaps most of all the romantic
yearning, at least at first.

I saw love as a bonus in my life, something secret and private
that I need not mention to anyone else. I was naturally a quiet
man and did not often talk about my innermost feelings, preferring to write about them. This is what I did immediately, writing
the first of over eighty poems over the next three years.

Even then it did not take me long to sense that my love would
naturally grow into a physical passion, and I guessed that an outlet
for it might prove impossible. I had been told that 'nice girls did
not' and that decent men respected them.

But all this was still some time away that Monday morning as I
raised a cup of tea to my lips in the college canteen, and there
flashed across my inward eye a sort of vision of happiness, and I
knew as I drained the hot sweet drink that I had begun to think
about my friend's sister in a special way.

From that realization to the next one: that I was in love with
her, was quite rapidly accomplished, though I said nothing to Alec
about any of it when he joined me before the lecture, nor during
the next week or two, except to ask him again whether we might
perhaps arrange some tennis with our original foursome, or
perhaps take the girls dancing one Saturday.

Alec said, 'We could meet you next Saturday in Lightholme – the
girls say they'd like an outing.'

'Do you mean – to play tennis?'

Suddenly I thought that I'd rather not waste my time with
Rhoda playing bad tennis.

'Well I thought that was the general idea, but we might just
come over and see your sights. We could all go for a drink in
Woolsford afterwards if you like.'

I said I wasn't sure whether I *could* book a club court in the village with only a few days' notice. It might be better to wait for time and be sure of it in a week or two. We could go for a walk instead, for there were pleasant walks around Lightholme, plenty of pretty spots, woods and streams within a mile or so, and most young folk went for country walks. I wasn't sure if I saw Rhoda or Phyllis as hikers. Flossie and I were quite used to walking.

'I can bring the girls over in my father's second car. He won't let me drive the Rolls!'

'It would be nice to go on to Woolsford afterwards. I can always return by train,' I said.

I decided I did not yet want to invite them for a meal home, though Mother was always saying my friends would be welcome.

'OK. You can show us some nice countryside instead of playing tennis. We can do that another day. I've never seen your neck of the woods.'

'Wouldn't the girls be bored?'

'Not they! My sister is a champion walker!' I was surprised.

When we had parted after this conversation I suddenly realized that Alec might want to get Rhoda's friend to himself for a bit. Why hadn't I thought of that before? Like myself, he probably didn't feel like dragging a young woman six miles for the sake of a game he might not truly care about. They could always play at Knagg Wood anyway.

So it was arranged and I planned a picnic either in Moon woods which lay about a mile and a half away north of Lightholme, or in the Horse Close woods of my childhood which were about the same distance away.

They arrived in a Morris which Alec stopped in the road in front of Holmfield. He tooted on the horn. Mother and Father were out, and as the women did not appear to need to 'wash their hands', we left the car up a leafy drive by the side of our house and walked up the lane by Titus Salt's spired chapel. Then I turned right and they followed me meekly as I led them down to the lane to where it goes over a little beck, where marsh marigolds and celandines grow in spring, and then further along past the big house with its park-like garden, set near to the Green, a collection of houses that was hardly even a hamlet.

We had walked about a mile from home when I struck across fields pink with sweet-smelling clover, over another field and down to a broader beck thaf sported an old water-wheel. There was once a mill here that used water power.

'It would be nice to picnic here,' suggested Phyllis.

'Oh, let's walk on a bit further – we haven't come very far,' said Rhoda.

If we followed the track right into the next hamlet beyond the stream it would lead to my old Horse Close woods which stretched right over to my previous home in Wike. Or we could turn in the other direction and walk to the steeper Moon woods valley. I decided I'd rather visit my old haunts that afternoon. It would be pleasant to take a lower path through woods to a spot further on where people often stopped to picnic.

Rhoda and Phyllis chatted away together until we all had to continue rather decorously in single file along a very muddy path. They did not however complain about their shoes getting dirty. There was not much further to go as we eventually climbed a stile and followed the path to the edge of the woods. I helped both women over it; fortunately they were again not wearing the ankle-length skirts that people like my mother still wore. Perhaps except for tennis the very short skirts that came in with the flappers were not yet there in 1921, except for schoolgirls, but you could still feast yourself on ankles and bits of calves!

I noticed the lights in Rhoda's hair as I walked behind her, she having let down her 'Cadogan' and tied her mane loosely back in a blue ribbon. Alec and I took turns to carry the small picnic basket which Mother had prepared for me – only a thermos of tea and some fruit. Then we were walking under beech and oak trees with the sound of the previous beck's tributary in our ears as the sun dropped its light through leafy branches in little gold coins. A few bluebells were still growing under the trees in a blue haze.

'It's lovely,' said Rhoda. 'How nice to live so near nature!'

'But you have a whole wood to yourself!' I wanted to say.

Maybe she was not used to walking on common paths? Still, I was glad we had decided not to play tennis.

Alec obviously wanted to rest for a while. I have noticed that women often have more endurance than men – or are more polite in not revealing boredom. I stopped under a tree where the ground looked dry. Indeed I had worried about taking a waterproof cover with us but I hated being encumbered.

'I think here will do,' I said, 'Are you thirsty? I haven't brought a meal, I'm afraid, except some bananas and apples. . . .' Fruit like bananas was still scarce and rather expensive but one of Father's business acquaintances had given him a crate of bananas in exchange for some machine order.

'We didn't expect you to feed us,' said Rhoda. 'Bananas are bliss, and a drink of tea would be heavenly!'

'It makes such a nice change to *walk*, rather than drive, or run about a tennis court,' said Phyllis.

I supposed they did not often spend their time enjoying such ordinary pleasures. Both girls had that slight lift of the eyebrow and amused tone that I have noticed in young women of well-off families who have been to boarding-school, but I thought these two were essentially simple and unaffected.

Alec lay on his back looking up at the sky through the leaves and I busied myself pouring out hot sweet drinks of tea into the metal picnic cups. Rhoda and Phyllis leaned against the tree trunk.

I felt quite content and I think they were too. What did we talk about? Not the war. Together, Alec and I had exhausted this subject long ago. His experience had been very different from mine. Straight from Uppingham to be a junior officer in Turkey and eventually invalided out with malaria just before the war ended. He said he wanted to forget about all that.

We did not discuss poetry either. I was wary of boring Rhoda, though perhaps I was waiting for her to ask me about my writing? We probably listened to the girls talking about their secretarial and cookery courses and how boring life in Woolsford could be. Both had been too young to enrol as nurses but they had done some voluntary work in the last six months of the war: bandage-rolling in convalescent homes. How different the life of an eighteen-year old girl had been from that of a boy.

How would I ever get Rhoda by herself? Would I ever be allowed to get to know her better? I felt sure there was a lot to know, as from time to time she bent the force of her sapphire gaze upon me. Perhaps we might soon go dancing? I was not a very experienced dancer but I had a decent sense of rhythm and could dance a waltz and manage the sort of dances Flossie had demonstrated to me, like the palais glide.

Alec began to talk about a trip to Switzerland he wanted to make next year or the following year.

'The Bernese Oberland,' he said, 'Just the thing – you ought to come with me, Eddie.'

I doubted I'd have enough cash by to go gadding abroad.

'Have *you* been abroad?' I asked Rhoda.

'Oh, before the war when we were little, our parents took us with them to spend a winter on the Italian Riviera. We were too young to enjoy it – we had a horrible nursemaid who kept us on a strict leash – we might as well have been in Scarborough, mightn't we Alec?'

'I'd love to go to Switzerland,' I said, thinking of walking by white peaks, glaciers sparkling in the distance, the sky blue and Rhoda in a woolly cap. There appeared to be quite a few things I dreamed of doing; the difficulty was how to go about implementing my plans.

Rhoda interrupted my train of thought. 'You're looking very serious!'

Was this my opportunity to tell her what was in my mind? No, certainly not. I could not say anything too personal with the others there. By the time I ever plucked up enough courage to tell her I'd like to get to know her better, or even that I was attracted to her, it would mean I already *did* know her well enough! I had never yet had a girl-friend. I consoled myself by thinking I was only in my twenty-second year after all. But I had no money and few immediate prospects. Why would she be interested in me? A young woman of nineteen would be looking for a husband, I thought gloomily.

But when we had all had our tea and eaten the fruit and were ready to walk back Alec decided to walk in front with Phyllis. It was now or never.

'Phyllis is a nice girl,' I began tentatively as Rhoda and I walked together. 'Have you been friends for long?'

'I've known her ever since school,' she replied, a little frown plucking at her forehead. 'But you know. Alec, he's rather impulsive – I believe he's become quite fond of her!'

I realized I did *not* know Alec all that well; we had never talked of girlfriends or anything more intimate than our personal ambitions. Would Rhoda think I was an impulsive sort of man? I'd never been thought to be so, but if I carried out my present desire and planted a kiss on her pretty cheek, she would be horrified. On the other hand, telling me this about her brother meant that Rhoda might be a little impulsively unguarded herself – or that she was upset and had to say something when Alec so obviously went off ahead with her friend. Did that little frown mean she might be jealous? Flossie had once said to me, 'Don't marry anybody but me, Eddie!' But she'd only been seven when she said it.

Women are strange creatures, I thought. They usually tell each other everything. I knew that the grown-up Flossie, who was not a particularly emotional person, still had a best friend, to whom she confided the kind of things brothers could not be expected to understand.

'I know how fond Alec is of *you*,' I replied. 'I have a sister too, you know – Flossie. I'm sure you'd like her. She's training to be a teacher.'

'Were you always close, then, as children?'

'Yes, I suppose so. We didn't go to boarding-school so we saw more of each other, at least till I was called up.'

'Alec used to have so many friends,' she said. 'Some of them were killed in the war and he's rather neglected some of the others, so I'm glad he's met you. He groans on about the tech. I think he'll be glad to leave and get on with a proper job, perhaps go in with Father. Father's thinking of building a factory near Glasgow.'

'It can certainly be a bit unsettling to have to go back to school, though I find it a relief after France,' I said.

She was silent, but as we caught the others up by the track across the fields to the water wheel, I felt I had been accepted as a friend. At last I had made contact, and I was jubilant. Rhoda had said something personal to me, even if it was not about myself. I knew women loved discussing people, and so we might one day proceed from generalities, or from the subject of her brother to the subject of myself.

Except that I'd really rather talk about her. I stole a glance at her as she walked along by my side. She had a very pure profile, a straight nose and a dimple on her cheek. I turned away hastily. I must not be seen to be staring. We were all quite tired when we arrived back at Holmfield. My parents had returned so I had perforce to introduce my three friends to them. Mother offered them a drink but they said they'd better get back as Alec and his sister were expected home for dinner. I decided not to accompany them back to Woolsford this time if I couldn't get Rhoda by herself.

When they had gone, Mother said, 'Those are two very well-brought-up girls, Eddie. I imagine your friend Alec's father is quite well off?'

There was nothing I wanted less than a discussion about money or prospects, so I just replied, 'I suppose so. Alec will inherit a good business. Not that I can quite see him as a businessman.'

'Why ever not?'

'Oh, I don't know. I expect the war has unsettled us all.'

Mother looked slightly worried. She knew that I had no real desire either to join my father in his business. The trouble was, what else was there for me to do?

Apart from thinking about Rhoda, which was most of the time, I was trying to make myself absorb technical things; we had to understand the power looms as well as the 'stuff' they produced. I was also busy sending some of my verse for honest criticism to the poets or writers I admired. Several took the trouble to reply to me and one, the man who had been at my own school a little before myself, and who was to become one day a famous and popular novelist and playwright, gave me good advice. He said I had 'distinct promise', which lifted my spirits – till he added that my poems were not yet good enough for publication. He told me to 'beat out my thought cleanly and nakedly' and not to make so much use of the obviously 'poetical'. I despaired: my style was hackneyed, my writing derivative! I must try to be less conventional. I was sincere, he said, but my manner was not. This was the opposite of what I actually believed, for I was not sure how sincere I was, yet I was truly sincere in my over-ornate manner! My mentor told me to read A.E. Housman and Edmund Blunden, which advice I did take to heart, and I believe my style improved.

I was aware that I had always written in an archaic mode, could not sincerely write in any other way, but I did enjoy imitating the styles of various modern poets just as I had previously consciously imitated older ones. I believe I had a real talent for parody. I read more, and realized that even before the war, and especially since the end of it, many writers had radically changed their whole approach, their style, especially in poetry. The trouble was that I could not bring myself to make that effort, for I thought it would mean becoming, as it were, another person. I had been influenced by the writers I still regarded as great: by Pope and Keats and Coleridge, and Tennyson and Swinburne – and by Mr Pendlebury, of course. Imitating them was the way I had learned to write since I began at the age of fifteen. I may be exaggerating when I say 'imitate'. It was more a question of the literary air I breathed. I now made an effort not to use archaic vocabulary, and schooled myself not to sound too rhapsodic, nor to make my rhymes too important for the sense of the stanza. I was good at rhyming but I knew it was often a prop rather than an inspiration.

Was there something the matter with me that I found that trying to be 'modern' went against the grain? I was still a young man, had emerged relatively, if not completely, unscathed from a terrible war, but my imagination was still seen to be cast in the mould of the last century. I had read and admired and was to read more, of Sassoon and other war poets, Rosenberg and Graves and Wilfred Owen, but I could not break up my literary style to write like them. If I did, I felt my words would emerge jagged and insincere. I should have belonged to the Romantic movement of the past century!

I was rather proud of my experiment, of writing a modern poem and then sending it to the editor of *Poetry*. I had written about a man at the ballet, because ballet was an art form that still interested me, now that I had seen it – only once – in Leeds, when a small offshoot of the *Ballets Russes* had come to the theatre for three nights. I was to be even more impressed later by the *Ballets Nègres*. I did not say to the editor that I had written my modern poem in a spirit of levity, nor I did I say it was meant to be taken seriously. I left it to him, not expecting him to publish it. When he mentioned it in the next issue, I was thrilled. He said he was not sure whether it was a parody. He had recently challenged the modern writers to write something characteristic of their art and he would then write deliberate drivel and the poems would be sorted out by a committee of critics selected by the modern writers themselves. Then they would see whether they knew the difference. Easy to see whose side *he* was on, and that was a bit disquieting.

These were my verses:

> *Kyasht! Pavlova!*
> *Goddesses divine!*
> *O hear my song; of your great Art I sing:*
> *Ah, now I see you glide*
> *On faery feet*
> *With music sweet.*
> *Your swan-like arms,*
> *You raise and lower,*
> *Fitful as an April shower,*

Pavlova! Kyasht!
Divine Goddesses!
My senses reel,
I feel,
Dazed.
O with what subtle charm,
My senses you infuse
With rhythmic trance
As you prance!

ii
I want the theatre attendant;
I feel drunk with delight
Where is the attendant?
You don't know ma'am?
You don't know,
Sir?
Ah, here he is:
Take me to the bar;
Whisky,
And a little soda,
And ice.
I shall recover,
Bientôt.

iii
Am I in my box?
Surely ...
But where are the dancers,
Pavlova, Kyasht
Divine Goddesses?
I cannot see them,
Tho' I strain my eyes:
They have gone?
I must have had,
One dozen whiskies!

Ah, a Voice, a Voice
In the darkness,
And I, alone –
Heavens! I shall go
Mad!
What says the Voice?
'Guv'nor,
Stay here.
There's your bench;
Take my advice,
And sleep on it.
Goddesses Divine!
Release you in the morning?
P'raps!'

iv
Do I hear swearing?
Is the air blue?
A trick o' the Fancy.

I read this to Alec who was a little puzzled – until I explained I was trying to be 'contemporary'.

'Oh, come on, Eddie,' he said, 'You know you were born a hundred years too late! That's your charm!'

Nobody rose to the editor's challenge though and the magazine went on criticizing the 'modern'. I did not think it would be worth while showing Rhoda the poem next time we met. Time with her was too precious, but I might show her one day a poem she had inspired.

We did not meet again however for another three weeks. She was away with her mother, visiting some cousins from Australia or New Zealand, and as it happened the tennis club was full up for Saturday matches until the middle of June. Alec asked me if I'd like to make up a party to go dancing, once she returned home. Phyllis would be there and we could have high tea before, or supper afterwards. Now the war was over dance-halls were opening in every town, modelled on the Hammersmith Palais. There was only one place anyone went to dance in Woolsford and that was the 'Horton Palais'. Wasn't it a bit low class for Rhoda and Phyllis, I asked.

He laughed. 'They like slumming,' he said. 'And actually it's quite well organized.'

The Charleston was just about to burst upon us after the popularity of a Negro musical in which it figured, and I believe some people already danced the shimmy and the black bottom after they arrived in the provinces, but I still preferred tangos and waltzes. I loved the rhythms of both: the slow waltz was Romance and the tango was Sensuality. I could imagine nothing more delicious than holding Rhoda in my arms dancing either of them, though I favoured the waltz. I knew the steps of the tango would be fiendishly difficult to master properly, for me at least. I'd never be a very good dancer.

I don't think Alec had any idea of my feelings for his sister. After all, so far I'd only met her twice. I was very happy to encourage him in his not yet official courtship of Phyllis without his realizing why. I suspected he was seeing Phyllis anyway, when Rhoda was not there. Since the war, people had given up chaperones. Not that the women of my family had ever had them but I thought the Moores would probably make a fuss about whom their daughter went out with, even if they were no longer able to vet them in advance.

Rhoda looked lovely that afternoon, or rather early evening, when we all gathered in Woolsford for a quick meal at the Sphinx eatery before going on to the Palais de Danse. Alec was a bit quiet and Phyllis seemed rather morose, so it was up to me and Rhoda to keep the ball of conversation rolling. I enjoyed that, and managed to catch her attention when I described the ballet I'd seen, and then the magazine article I'd read on the subject of the tango.

'Oh I *love* tangos!' she replied. 'They're supposed to be very naughty though, aren't they?'

We were eating fish and chips and Rhoda said they were her

favourite meal. I tried not to stare at her and I don't think she noticed that I did often look at her and that I addressed my remarks principally to her. I wouldn't have minded if she had, though I was still shy of saying anything too personal.

From something she said, I believe Phyllis noticed. By then we were in the big dance hall though not many couples were yet on the floor. We had taken a table – they still had them in those days if you paid a little extra, and although they didn't run to champagne, there was beer. Alec and I were not great big beer-drinkers and the girls drank fruit-juice. People didn't come to such places to get drunk; there were plenty of pubs in Woolsford for that. My first dance with Rhoda was a military two-step which was hardly my favourite dance. But she moved with gusto and I could just about manage to get my feet in the right place. Roll on the tangos and waltzes! Alec and I had decided to swap our partners now and then, so I was dancing a waltz with Phyllis when she said:

'Rhoda is a good dancer – I expect you've noticed?'

'Yes, I wish *I* were. . . .'

'Practice makes perfect – but I expect you have other talents.'

If it had not been Phyllis I'd have thought she was flirting with me. As it was, I think she had long ago set her cap at Alec even if he thought he was making all the running.

'I'd like to try a tango and a slow waltz,' I said. 'I shall have to learn how to dance them properly.'

'I expect Rhoda could teach you – you'd like that!' she said.

'Have you both been to lots of dances?'

'You mean private ones? We hardly ever go to hops like this – but it's fun, isn't it? I've been to lots of dances with Rhoda – in big houses and at house parties. Sometimes her father organizes staff dances at work where he likes his wife and daughter to show up. He finds them decent partners – some of his minions, usually.'

I was silent, feeling gloomy. I was not likely to be asked to such a dance, nor did I frequent house parties. Rhoda must find all this small beer and think I was a dreadful dancer. I saw her sitting out talking to her brother and they were both laughing.

When my turn came round to dance with her again it *was* a slow waltz. I'd like to have held her more closely but I didn't want to presume. I knew I didn't suffer from sweaty palms and I'd gargled before leaving home so as to have sweet breath, but when it came to the point I just wanted to hold her tight and shut my eyes. She felt lithe and light. She was silent as we negotiated the steps where we turned, and then she said,

'Do you like dancing, Eddie?'

This was my chance.

'I like dancing with *you*,' I said. 'I wish I were a better dancer – you deserve one – but I haven't had much practice.'

I thought, I've never really wanted to dance like this with a woman before – I suppose it's only an excuse to hold her, but I can't tell her that!

'I like dancing with you too,' she said simply.

She was such a nice young woman. I looked down at her fondly. Could she have any idea how attractive I found her? Lots of men must have felt the same.

'Will you come to the theatre with me next week?' I asked boldly. 'They're doing a musical at the Alhambra.'

'Oh – do you mean on Saturday? I think we're going up to the Dales next weekend but I'd love to go another time.'

Fortunately, I hadn't yet bought the tickets.

'I'd like to see some ballet,' she went on.

'Then I shall enquire – that little Russian company might perhaps come again to Yorkshire.' We finished the dance in amicable silence. I felt I now had a future.

This first dance on a Saturday evening ended with my saying goodbye to the three of them outside the station. The last train to Eastcliff and Lightholme would leave at eleven o'clock.

Rhoda said, 'It's been so nice,' and Phyllis said, 'We must do it again!' Alec added, 'See you Monday, old boy.'

And that was that. But I had made a start, and now it was up to me to invite Rhoda out without the others. Would her family want her going out regularly with a young man? I had no idea of the *mores* of Knagg Wood. Flossie had never been out alone with a young man and she was about the same age as Rhoda, but she had often been out with a group of friends who played tennis together. Flossie was a shy girl anyway. A sophisticated young woman like Rhoda would often, I imagined, pop over to shop in Leeds, and would not dream of asking her father's permission to go out on a Saturday night.

Anyway, I knew her brother, and I could always invite her through him. I was sure Alec was succeeding in getting Phyllis by herself. What did most people do? There was a code for courting in Woolsford and surrounding towns but I was hardly cognizant of it. I had been away too long. Did I see myself as 'courting' Rhoda? Surely you could go out with a girl many times without tongues wagging? I knew my mother would be interested if I took Rhoda out more than twice so it was important to let the family think we were all going out together. This might even go on being the case, alas! I couldn't help wishing she lived nearer; I was constantly thinking of her.

I seem to have gaps in my memory for that summer. I suppose my feelings were engaged early on, but I was often solitary and spent more time thinking about her than seeing her. I wished I had a car. Would she consent to accompany me on the motorbike? But if she did, I would worry about her safety.

In the meantime I would write to her. Girls liked letters. Then I'd ask her to the theatre as soon as the ballet returned to Leeds – or even better came to Woolsford and I had saved up enough for the tickets. I wished I had a proper job but I'd have to wait till autumn for that. Even then I'd be lucky to find anything and it would most likely be Uncle Fred I'd be working for and that wouldn't mean much cash!

I spent hours over my first letter to Rhoda. I did not want to appear to dazzle her with my wisdom or to put her off by hinting too much, but I did want to let her know I thought highly of her. I would try for a light touch, so I told her how much I had enjoyed dancing with her – I dared not say how beautiful I thought her, nor that I had begun to miss her when there was no 'next time' to look forward to, but I enclosed a short poem about the woods and our walk there.

I suppose any young lady receiving even my toned-down missive would have scented a rat or at least imagined there was something behind my need to write to her.

I waited impatiently for a reply. Alec was away from college with a cold. I hoped Rhoda had not caught it. She ought to have received my letter on the Tuesday but when on Friday there was as yet no reply on my leaving home for college, I decided I'd ask Alec when he returned if she had received it.

When on Friday lunch time I went by myself to the Great Northern for half a pint of bitter, what was my surprise to see him sitting with Phyllis in the lounge.

'Hello, old thing – I thought you were ill?'

He looked a bit shifty. 'Oh, I'm feeling better, and Phyllis here was shopping in the city so I decided I'd come in.'

'Are you coming for the practical this afternoon?'

The 'practical' was a sort of test we had every Friday afternoon when we were presented with various hanks of sheep's clothing and asked to describe how we would deal with them.

'Oh Lord, I suppose I ought to – but I don't think I will!'

Now was my chance to ask about his sister.

'Did Rhoda get my letter?' I asked casually when I returned to their table with my drink.

Alec looked puzzled but Phyllis said quickly, 'Yes, she did and I'm sure she'll write you an answer from Harrogate.'

'Oh, is she staying for long?'

'She's with Aunt Madge,' Alec explained. 'Rhoda gets bored at home and she says Harrogate has better shops.'

I thought, she most likely goes on lots of family visits. Our family went only to Thirksay but Father's sister Emily had not long ago extended an invitation to us all to stay in the house she and her stepmother had retired to in Bare, near Morecambe, Woolsford-by-the-Sea.

Grandfather had died a few months before this at the age of seventy-three, and Aunt Emily had waited a long time to retire to the seaside.

'I wanted to tell her that the little Russian ballet company is to visit Woolsford in three weeks.' I said. 'Would you like to come along too? Rhoda told me she enjoyed the ballet.'

'Not for me,' said Alec, 'but I'm sure Rhoda would love to accompany you.'

Phyllis smiled. I wondered what the two girls had been saying about me. It was upsetting being there with the two of them with Rhoda absent so I soon said my goodbyes and asked Alec to send his sister my regards.

'You can always telephone,' said Phyllis. I had not thought of that. Father had just acquired a telephone at home – we had used the one at the mill for years in case of emergencies, but Mother had recently agitated for a personal machine. So far, I had not used it. A black contraption, about a foot tall with a listening tube hooked on to the side of the stand, at the top of which was the large round speaker rather like the overgrown trumpet of a black daffodil, it sat in the hall under the big portrait of my great-grand-father.

'I must take your number then,' I said. Alec wrote it down for me. I wondered why he had never offered it to me before. I took it gratefully and departed to the boredom of Friday afternoon. A light drizzle had begun to fall; spring seemed to have gone away for a time.

When I got home after a hour in the Mechanics' Institute reading the newspapers, Mother said,

'There's a picture-postcard come for you, Eddie, by the last post. On the table in the kitchen.'

It was from Rhoda and was of the Stray in Harrogate.

'Thanks for your letter. See you soon. I'm having a nice time here. Back next week. Love from Rhoda.'

She had sent me her love! Did it mean anything?

'That from your new friend?' Mother asked.

'Alec's sister,' I said shortly, and did not elaborate.

We had a supper of ham and eggs with Father, who had been staying late at the mill doing the accounts. I went up to my bedroom to read.

I think it was at this period of my life that I formed the habit of reading in bed. I kept the current books I was reading and reread-ing on my bedside table and often read past midnight. It was here too that I would write my poems and my letters, both of which were usually addressed to Rhoda Moore.

It was my favourite month of the year – June – when at last I saw Rhoda again. Alec told me she had been staying with another relative in the south of England and I had eventually received another postcard, but with no address. I was shy of asking Alec for it; I was not quite ready to declare to him the growing feelings for his sister which were burgeoning within me.

The day came, however, when he told me she was back home. I telephoned Knagg Wood the same evening.

I still had bit of cash in the bank left over from the hundred pounds Grandfather gave me when I was demobbed – what had not already been spent on the motor bike – and so I was ready to buy two tickets for the promised visit to the ballet, if she would agree to accompany me. A new company was doing *The Sleeping Beauty*.

Alec and Phyllis were not interested in making up a party. I don't know what they got up to when they went out together; I think they often took his father's second-best car to the Dales and toured around in the long evenings. How lucky Alec was to have money and a car! I still didn't trust myself enough on the bike to risk Rhoda on it. It had no side-car, but perhaps she would consent to sit in it if I saved up to buy one?

I had not seen her for over a month when we met outside the theatre in Woolsford, the first time such a ballet company had visited the city's principal theatre, and I felt nervously exalted. As it was a warm evening, she was wearing a straw hat and a longish flowery dress with a little bolero. I tried not to stare at her but she looked so lovely and fresh and young. She seemed perfectly calm, smiled, thanked me again for my letter and said it had been 'a bit boring' staying with her relations whilst she was waiting for the opportunity to start work in the office of one of her father's friends in Woolsford. All her own friends were either abroad or still at college, or just living at home helping their mothers, which was even more of a bore.

'I expect some are already married?' I offered boldly when we were finally ushered into our seats in the stalls, the most expensive ones I could manage.

'One or two,' she agreed, 'but I think it a mistake to marry too young.'

'So many girls a little older than you had sweethearts who were killed in the war,' I said and felt a lump of sympathy in my own throat.

She looked at me swiftly and replied, 'Well, it's all over now, isn't it? I'd like to travel more and enjoy myself before I settle down.'

Her words made me feel a bit depressed. But what was more innocent than wanting a bit of independent experience when you were twenty? I must admit though that in those days I was a romantic and connected the idea of being in love with marriage. I had better be careful! In my heightened state of infatuation – I suppose I must call it that – I might put her off.

We both enjoyed the ballet. The costumes were not sumptuous and there was no full orchestra, but the music, played by a pianist, a few string players, a wind instrument and a timpanist was, I thought, lovely.

I bought us ice-cream in the interval when the red plush curtain was down.

'What gift would you want to give a child at its christening?' she asked me suddenly. 'Or what *wouldn't* you want to burden a person with?'

I thought hard. 'Well, apart from the dangers of pricking fingers, I suppose I'd not want a person to be unkind – and the best quality I'd want someone to have would be intelligence – no! – imagination.'

'Would you rather a person was beautiful or clever or good?'

Had she been thinking up topics of conversation?

'It would depend whether it was a man or a girl, I think.'

She laughed. 'So you'd want a girl to be good and a man to be clever – or imaginative – whatever that means?'

'No, I'd want both males and females to be imaginative, I think.

83

More important than beauty or brains, though I'd like a girl to be beautiful too,' (like you, I wanted to add).

'I suppose you mean that they'd compose music like Tchaikovsky, or write poetry, or paint pictures? I'm hopeless at all that!' I knew that like Phyllis she had occasionally tried her hand at water-colours.

'Appreciating things needs imagination,' I said. 'You don't have to be creative.'

'*You* are,' she said. 'Have you been writing more of your poems?'

I'd like to have told her that I had written several about *her* but it wasn't yet the time, and certainly not the place.

'A few,' I answered vaguely. 'Actually, Russian dancers make me want to write. Dance is different from the other arts, isn't it? I don't think I quite understand it. I mean, could it be done without music?'

'You *are* funny!' she said. 'The choreography is written to music, I think. And with ordinary dancing – even fox-trots – how could you dance them "cold", without music?'

The curtain's going up cut into this discussion. Rhoda laughed and looked at her programme. I hadn't been able to convey to her exactly what I meant. Some dancing came before music surely? It was hard work maintaining a balancing act between trying not to look too keen and yet conveying I cared about her. The very gap between us made me feel I could love her even more.

I decided to be bold, and as the dancers executed a *pas de deux* I took her hand and squeezed it. She let her hand lie in mine though she did not return the squeeze. I looked at her profile. She was caught up in what was happening on the stage and looked solemn. The audience began to clap the two dancers so I had to take my hand away.

'How are you getting back?' I asked her as we came out into what was still a light evening – it was almost the longest day in the year.

'Oh, Bert Robinson – that's Father's chauffeur – is meeting me at the Midland Hotel,' she said. 'I told him half past ten – I hope that's all right? I knew you'd have to get a train back to Lightholme or Eastcliff, but I thought there'd be time for a drink first.'

The way she took it for granted that I'd take her for a drink to the Midland, which at that time was rather chic, pleased me and worried me at one and the same time. I just hoped I had enough cash with me. The programmes and the ice-cream had been quite dear. Fortunately, she opted for a lemonade and I bought myself half a pint of beer. I didn't want her to leave. Why could we not stay talking all night, go for a walk in the park, see the sun rise?

'I wish you didn't have to go,' I said.

She turned to look at me.

'Most girls are not allowed to go out to the theatre with a man their parents don't know,' she said, 'never mind drink in hotels with them. But Mother has always been good about things like that. It's my father who's stricter. Anyway, you've met Mother. You must meet Father as well. Alec says he intends to have a party for his twenty-fifth birthday and I can invite whom I want. Would you like to come?'

'When's his birthday?'

Birthdays were not the sort of information men swapped with each other.

'It's at the end of July. Your exams will be over by then, won't they?'

'Yes – then I've got to look for work.'

'Don't look so anxious,' she said, 'I'm sure you'll find something. I believe Father knows your uncle Fred – you can work in his office for a bit, can't you? In the Arcade.'

'I suppose I shall have to.'

'Then we'll be able to meet for a sandwich now and then, because Father's friend Reginald Parker – the one who needs a secretary, has an office there too!'

'You take this job seriously then?' I asked her.

'Mr Parker's got one secretary – I mean a proper one – but I've always wanted to earn some money of my own. I passed the

Pitman course quite well, and his firm needs an extra girl to see to odds and ends and do a bit of typing.'

'Oh, I see.'

Just then she waved to someone standing at the revolving doors who touched his cap then disappeared back on to the pavement. 'It's Bert – he's come for me. I shall have to go.'

We had finished our drinks so we stood up and I took her out to the waiting car. I didn't think I wanted to kiss her goodnight in front of the chauffeur, however discreet he might be, so I just took her hand and said, 'May I see you again soon?'

'Thank you – it's been lovely,' she said, without giving me an answer. 'I hope you don't have to wait too long for your train.' Then she was in the car, and off it went.

I walked to the Exchange station where my train would leave in a few minutes. I had a compartment to myself so I shut my eyes and thought over the whole evening, oblivious to the sooty smell and the sepia posters of Llandudno. Why could meetings not go on for ever?

It was just about this time that Father bought Mother a birthday present which we all enjoyed. It was an HMV gramophone that came complete with wax records and a big horn to amplify the sound. It had a clockwork motor and I spent many hours turning its handle for the family. There were several pieces of music I wanted to save up for or ask for on my next birthday, and at Christmas. My musical tastes were not quite those of my parents. Mother's favourite song was 'I'll walk beside you', and Father liked 'Keep right on to the end of the road'. Flossie, however, loved some of the composers I loved when she heard them on the gramophone: Delius, Gounod and Grieg. I had not heard them very often 'live', for there were concerts in Woolsford only on Friday evenings once a month at this time. But Flossie was not as fond of Debussy as I was myself. She said he wandered all over the place!

I accepted Alec's invitation to his birthday party, though I was not quite sure what kind of party it was to be. He said. 'Oh, dinner for a few friends and we might dance a bit – if it's fine we can have the garden lights on. . . .'

Knowing the inhabitants of Knagg Wood, I wondered if I should wear a dinner-jacket. This I did not yet possess. Father however did, though he was heavier than I was, even if about the same height, or just a little shorter.

Having made myself wait for Rhoda's letter thanking me for the visit to the ballet, I replied with as much passion as I dared to reveal.

This was, I suppose, the first of the many love letters I wrote to Rhoda during the next two years. I enclosed a poem with it, and this too was to be the way it would be in future. I think I wrote as many poems as I wrote love-letters. In the future I was to write to her every day after parting from her at lunch-time when we both went back to work, or if we had seen each other in the evening. But I must not get ahead of my story.

At first I did not send her all the verse I wrote, afraid she would think me mad or importunate. Some poems I kept in a special drawer where I would later add any replies I had from her.

I remember trying to find a metaphor for my love and failing to do so satisfactorily. I saw it as a 'white flame' that licked round her heart. The flames were white, I think, because I thought they were innocent. She fanned the flames in my heart too and made me feel that the centre of my being was in her. I wanted the two fires, from me and from her, to fuse and allow us to arise like spirits from a mutual conflagration. I wonder what she made of that poem.

More often I wrote of moonlight and clouds, of evening, of the sea, of colours. The first poems were written before I knew whether Rhoda might share my feelings; later, when I thought she did, my lyrics became more passionate though my dreams were still sweetly romantic. If not quite all my verse was written to Rhoda or about her, it all arose from that peculiar heightening of feeling that love brings about especially when you are young.

Everything I saw or did seemed to have a heightened meaning that arose out of my love for her. My writing and my love were one and the same. She had cast a spell over me and the first time I truly realized this was at Alec's party.

Although in my opinion Knagg Wood was an ideal place for romance, being 'romantic' in itself, the dinner and the guests might have conspired to make me feel uneasy or out of place. Yet because Rhoda was present and possibly because it was a warm moonlit night. I felt easy and happy. Old houses always effected a transformation in me, and this one, with its winding paths under trees, and its terraces, and the way it looked as if it held a secret, the way it curved round from the front elevation, the statues on the terrace – even if they were not from Italy – the fountain on the front lawn, the sense of dark gardens stretching all around, was an ideal place for my dreams.

Yes, I kissed Rhoda that night for the first time. Along with a dozen or so of Alec's friends, we had drunk a birthday toast in champagne, and eaten a delicious meal. His parents had been there for the dinner but had left the young people to dance on the terrace to music from a more splendid gramophone than ours at home. We had drunk some wine but I was not drunk – not with wine anyway – and I had stared at Rhoda in the candle-light. Then she and I had drifted out to the further terrace under the moon. Other couples were either dancing, or sitting laughing and talking on the top terrace where coloured lights had been put in the bushes, or strolling together. I believe Alec was with Phyllis.

Rhoda had been quite happy to walk with me. She looked so beautiful that night, her eyes very deep and dark blue and a little flush on her cheeks. When I kissed her I felt I was performing some sort of sacrament. She did not pull away but stayed quietly in my arms for a few moments. I don't think anyone saw us but my heart was beating so loudly I imagined it could be heard on the upper terrace.

Eventually she said, 'We ought to go back, Eddie.'

I loved the way she spoke my name. I took her hand, and I said, 'I do love you Rhoda – did you know that?'

She was silent.

I did not dare ask her what she felt about me. This was only a beginning.

I returned home very late that night but I could not sleep. I sat up in bed and began a poem. First of all I wanted to use a line that had been echoing in my head all the evening: *The eyes of night are bright with love*, but I could not think of a new word to rhyme with love, so I kept the line in my journal and started again. I began:

> *I saw the sailing clouds,*
> *Sweep by the harvest moon;*
> *The yellow moon's high light*
> *Made night as sweet as noon.*

This conveyed some of the atmosphere of the terrace and the dancing but then I wanted to bring in Rhoda. I decided to concentrate on the stars and the moon, and being together. I continued:

> *Above the fragrant trees,*
> *We watched the peeping stars,*
> *And rims of rolling clouds*
> *Like lustrous silver bars:*
> *The night was ours, my sweet,*
> *The wind was in your hair*
> *And when I saw your eyes*
> *Saw my love brimming there.*
> *High moon, O didst thou see*
> *My hand upon her heart?*
> *A cloud obscured the moon,*
> *We knew that we must part*
> *A little while, my dear.*
> *How could I let you go?*
> *And still I knew I must*
> *O sweet, is life for ever so?*

When you are young you can summon enormous energy but also

react so quickly to whatever life throws in front of you that your feelings go up and down like a yo-yo. When I woke next morning I was still thinking of Rhoda, but now I was worried that she may have only tolerated my embraces. I would never know because she would be too kind to tell me.

I resolved to spend a solitary afternoon after helping Mother with a few domestic tasks. As it was Saturday, Father was at work, for the mill always worked on Saturday mornings.

I managed to get up to my room even before lunch and decided to look through my books. In pride of place I still had my beautiful leather editions of the collected Coleridge and collected Tennyson, and I had Keats too now, along with Wordsworth, both of which had been at my bedside ever since I left the army, along with Johnson's *Lives of the Poets* and Boswell's *Johnson*, Laurence Sterne, who had once gone to school in Lightholme, Leigh Hunt, and De Quincey.

I had just finished the *Autobiography* of J.S. Mill and Meade's *Twelve Years in a Monastery*, and they were on my bedside table. I had Burton's *Anatomy of Melancholy* too and Lamb's *Essays*, my favourite poems of Gray, an old copy of Surtees's hunting stories that had belonged to an uncle, and some of Swedenborg's strange books that my grandfather had left me, and several collections of essays. I spent all the pocket-money Father gave me on books.

I loved them. I believed in what it said at the front of all the Everyman editions: *Books are the precious life-blood of a master spirit.*

In a strange way I don't think I could have fallen in love with Rhoda the way I had if I had not been weaned on literature. I was reading more of the moderns now. Everyone's darling, Rupert Brooke, had given way to D.H. Lawrence, whose novels I was collecting. I still read and reread Saki though, who had perished at the front. Flossie had advised me to read Galsworthy's *The Man of Property* and *In Chancery*, which had just come out as part of *The Forsyte Saga*, and I thought I might lend Rhoda that. I was not sure how much of a reader she was. I did hope she was, for I wanted to share everything with her. But somehow I thought she would like Galsworthy more than Lawrence.

Recently I had been rethinking my thoughts about religious belief. I decided I might be an atheist – I was not sure. Was I a free thinker, what was called a 'rationalist'? I found much in the world that was incomprehensible to reason. I believed in life and its possibilities, life that was such a mystery, and I imagined I might, through love, be able to begin to understand its mysterious meaning. Love, poetry and music were in my opinion its deepest manifestations. I could not live without *them*. What was this atom of the universe, made up of millions of cells, this atom called Myself? We all looked at ourselves and wondered why we wondered! That all of the universe was a sort of stage-set, invented by God so He might observe man's struggle between good and evil seemed to me an inadequate explanation. Flossie believed it and I suppose Mother did, and even Rhoda, though I had not yet had time to investigate her thoughts on the matter. Maybe she just did not bother her head about such things.

I sat in my old chair and looked out of the window thinking these thoughts. We all lived in two worlds, the physical which we could see, and the intellectual which we could perceive and feel. If we could combine both in their just proportions, then we should be gods indeed! But to which world did Rhoda belong? I knew my love for her belonged to both, but principally to the latter, for she was most alive in my thoughts. I had the feeling that I should love her for years and years and that my inner life would run along underneath all the time. But that inner life must be fed by the outer, and I imagined taking Rhoda to Thirksay, to the Lakes, to the coast, perhaps to Aunt Emily's in Bare; I imagined walking on the moors with her. If Father bought the car that Mother was always on about I'd learn to drive and then my dreams could become reality.

In the meantime, I finished my new poem and sent it to Rhoda with a letter that said how much I had enjoyed last night and how dear she had become to me. This time *I* would write the first letter. I wanted to tell her about my reading and all my thoughts but I did not want to bore her, and knew I did not yet know her well enough. But when I was with her, or missing her, she seemed more important than all the books in the world.

I also wrote to Mr and Mrs Moore to thank them for inviting me.

CHAPTER FIVE

Work and Love

For the rest of that lovely summer I saw Rhoda whenever and wherever I could. Sometimes at the weekends Alec and the two women came over to Lightholme and we played tennis on the village courts; another time Alec took us all to Grasmere in the car his father had now given him for his birthday. Both Rhoda and I sketched the little lake on that occasion and I found it entrancing to sit with her and be occupied drawing and at the same time watching her draw. I wanted to paint what I had sketched but was always dissatisfied with my efforts. When I was with Rhoda I took every opportunity to hold her hand but was still shy of the others seeing me do it, though they must both have been well aware of my feelings.

Both Alec and I heard in September that we had passed our final diploma exam, and I began to work full-time for Uncle Fred in the autumn. As I have already explained, he had advised me to learn Spanish for the overseas markets and I was still enjoying the meetings of the Woolsford Foreign Circle.

Rhoda was soon installed in an office in the Arcade and apparently enjoying being of use. We could not at first meet for long over a midday snack as her hours were rather different from mine and Uncle Fred was a stickler for my presence. She told me her parents could not understand why she would want to work for her 'pin-money'.

That autumn I was sometimes over at Knagg Wood at week-ends, and wished I had the skill to paint the place. I remember the marvellous colours of the trees as they slowly changed from summer green to vermilion and yellow, scarlet and pale brown. Knagg Wood was a. deciduous paradise in September and early October: it smelled of falling leaves and the soft piles of last year's leaves in hidden dells and overgrown pathways. There was always the sense of some hidden treasure at the heart of it all, and for me of course that treasure was Rhoda. *She* took her home quite matter-of-factly and grumbled about the damp. One afternoon we walked together under tall beeches, right to the boundary of the estate.

'I shall carve our names here, together!' I said and took out the penknife I had brought with me for the purpose.

'Oh Eddie – you are a baby!' she said, but she did not stop me and I managed an entwined E and R whilst she went looking for beech-mast to take, she said, to the village Sunday school nearby for a sale of work.

'You don't sell beech-mast?' I enquired, baffled.

'No, silly – the children make brooches from them.' I remembered Flossie doing something similar.

Rhoda looked so pretty when she returned with her skirts full of beech-mast and early conkers.

'You don't teach at Sunday school?' I enquired.

'Oh no they just like to feel we take an interest. It's a Baptist church and we're C of E.'

Once I began to work in earnest for my uncle I was often tired. This was partly because I stayed up late at night writing to Rhoda or reading. Whenever else could I have time for myself? I had to burn the candle at both ends, had to get up when Father did and take the same train to Woolsford. By nature I was a nightingale, no lark.

Later that winter I often felt a bit under par. I think it was partly still a lingering of the long-ago influenza and the whole of the war trauma, and partly the foggy winter, when I was liable to get sore throats and quinsy.

Slowly I got used to seeing Rhoda and the others at weekends until the day came when I told her I wanted to see her by herself and not with the others. I had still not been introduced by her to her father separately – I had only shaken hands with him at Alec's party – and was rather dreading it. I guessed he would not consider me a suitable friend for his daughter if my designs were other than those of mere friendship. And they were. I loved her and I thought I was just the right man for her. I had decided pretty quickly that I wanted to marry her and that I would propose to her when I was twenty-five. In those days people did not marry in haste and Rhoda was two years younger than I. Had she any idea how serious I was? She did not always let me kiss her goodnight, but she was always most friendly and charming to me when we ate our lunch-time sandwich, and often said, 'See you tomorrow.'

Alec said nothing to me about our relationship but she must have talked to him about it, for one day in 1923 she said: 'Alec thinks you ought to meet both my parents since I have met both yours.'

It was true she had been to tea with my mother and father, who thought she was a lovely girl but were very much against my being serious about any young woman until I was established.

'Can you come for tea on Saturday? My father will be there, and Alec has promised to be there too,' she said on the telephone.

I accepted of course. I did not quite know what to expect. But I decided to speak to her first.

I had written her a love-letter that very week, enclosing a poem, and I was worried lest either had come into her father's hands. But why should I care? I was not acting dishonourably, and I was used to being teased about my romantic thoughts. We were not living in the Middle Ages or even the era of chaperones. The letter however had been private, meant only for Rhoda's eyes. She had told me once, that she kept all her private letters – and my poems – in her handkerchief drawer, and I had been rather touched.

The poem, which was a description of a sunset had started with the line:

The sun dipped down behind bright bars of gold.

I had been exalted as I wrote it and very pleased with it when I had polished it as much as possible. I always took many hours over my verse, enjoying juggling with words.

The second line was a little exaggerated and I had nursed some misgivings, but let it stand:

Evening's fires festooned the fervid sky.

I described the colours of evening: palest green, pale lemon, rose, dying grey, mingled with purple and hazy crimson. They were the actual colours of many sunsets we saw on the Pennine heights and I never ceased to marvel at them, and at the great galleons of clouds moving always in our skies. This poem however had the line:

She curled her lip and I was left in scorn

as night fell and

far above the churlish stars were born.

This was the line I had wanted to use. It had seemed a pity I could only bring it in if I made the writer scorned by 'she'. I hoped Rhoda had not taken it seriously. I should not have sent it to her, for I told her repeatedly that all I wrote, especially about her, was felt from the heart. Rhoda had never curled her lip at me but I suppose I was allowing myself to imagine the exquisite torture of her actually doing so, wanting my poem to end in 'dark night' after the splendours of the brilliant sunset. I knew this was called the pathetic fallacy, but Rhoda probably did not.

I wanted to add, *The love within your eyes, my sweet, has*

banishèd the night, but I dared not. I realized I had known Rhoda now for almost two years, but did not yet know yet if *she* could love *me*. She knew *I* loved *her*. I was patient, but perhaps it was about time I declared myself formally, or at least made it plain I was serious. I did not know what to expect from her father. I could not imagine my father receiving a suitor for Flossie with anything but pleasure, though I was not sure. Our manners at home were not formal, and making declarations not part of our way of life. There could not have been much formality when Father proposed to Mother, or even when he told his father he was going to marry her: he was twenty-one, he was working, and his girl was 'expecting'.

I would gauge the atmosphere when I met Mr Moore, and act accordingly. But I had to ask Rhoda first. I was a bit older now but although I wanted to marry her, I had little money from my ill-paid work with my uncle. Father would surely have to take me on at the mill if I got married? But business was not good and I did not expect anything as of right.

I longed to improve my prospects – but only on her account. I did not care for myself; I was sure we could be just as happy on a small wage. I had always hoped to earn money through my writing but that seemed hopeless, even if I had not yet given up hope. I would not want Rhoda's father's charity, nor an offer of work from him. Nor was I truly interested in becoming a manager. I'd work only for her. Not that I imagined any such offer would be forthcoming for I guessed the sort of son-in-law Mr Moore would prefer.

And then I thought, I am mad! I have only kissed her a few times and visited Knagg Wood a few times, though I have known her now for ages and written her long letters and sent poems to her, and here I am thinking of spending my life with this one woman. Yet if I had been rich I'm sure we'd be able to get married there and then. If she would have me.

I needed three more years, I thought, before I could decently propose with any expectation of being accepted. In those days that was how things were.

In the end, I telephoned the Knagg Wood number. Luckily it was Rhoda who answered.

'Oh, Eddie! You are coming over on Saturday, aren't you?' she said, I imagined a little anxiously.

'Of course – but I just wanted to ask you. . . .'

Now I was struck dumb but managed to add: 'ask you what you have told your father about us. . . . Can we meet on Thursday at twelve-thirty? I know you'll be busy but if we could just have a coffee together at the Sphinx. . . and then you can brief me.'

'He knows I go out with you sometimes,' she said after a pause, 'He said he'd like to meet you – he knows your Uncle Fred.'

'Yes, I know he does,' I answered rather impatiently. If he thought I was anything like my Uncle Fred he would be in for a disappointment. 'But I want to ask *you* something first – I can't do it over the telephone!'

'All right. I'll be there on Thursday at the Sphinx.'

She sounded nervous. Surely she must know that when a man like me was in love with a girl the way I was with her, his thoughts might turn to marriage, however far in the future that might be?

My intentions were honourable, however much I had to admit to myself that I wished I could go further than just a few kisses, however impassioned. That was why many men did marry, but in my case it was only one of the reasons I wanted to live with Rhoda. I thought it was girls who thought about weddings all the time but Rhoda had never said she wanted to get married, whether to me or anyone else.

I felt I still did not know her well enough in ordinary ways, and the feeling depressed me. She had accepted my adoration, or at least I thought she had, but maybe she had not said anything much about me to her parents. I often wondered if Alec wanted to marry Phyllis; he had never said anything to me about that either.

She was waiting at the Sphinx with a coffee in front of her when I entered the café that Thursday. It was the only place in Woolsford that made coffee, and was the result, I suppose, of all the previous century's émigrés from Germany with their Continental habits.

A few of the regular visitors were already there, and downstairs lunch had begun for those who had the time and money to indulge themselves.

I went straight over to her and she looked up and smiled.

'I got here early – you sounded so solemn on the phone!'

I ordered a cup of coffee for myself. When I was with her I found it hard not to sit staring at her, drinking in her presence, but I felt shy this morning.

'It was because your father wants to meet me. What have you told him about me – about us?'

'Just that you often take me out. He said he'd like to meet you. I told him you wrote poems.'

'Did he ask you if you were serious about me?'

'No – nor whether you were about me,' she said mischievously.

'Rhoda – listen – I want to get things straight. . . .'

Now it had come to the point I felt awkward. She looked at me earnestly. 'I wish I could tell him – tell your father – that,' I lowered my voice, 'that I *love* you.'

She blushed. 'Oh, Father would be embarrassed. He's a businessman, they don't talk about such things, you know.'

'Well, your mother might.'

'Mother never asks me about such things. I think they see me as a little girl. I don't believe they talk about me very much.'

'But surely they would not be too amazed if – if someone – one day – wanted to – to marry you? You are now of full age, as they say, and that's not too young to marry.'

Rhoda was not experienced or blasé enough to riposte with something on the lines of, *Is this a proposal, sir?* which the heroines of smart plays would have done. Instead, she looked at me with a little frown on her forehead.

'I'm sorry, I know I should not have blurted it out like that,' I said, 'but how else? Surely you know I'd like. . . one day. . . if you wanted me. . . I'd like to marry you?'

Now it was all out. She continued to stare at me.

I thought, she is going to say the thought never entered her head.

But instead, she said, 'But Eddie – your poetry – your ambitions – you wouldn't want to be burdened with a wife. Not yet!'

Did she mean I hadn't achieved anything much, or that men without fortunes did not marry rich girls, or that she really thought my writing was more important to me than love? I took the last meaning and replied, 'You help me write – you are my subject matter at present!'

'Look, Eddie,' she said after a pause, 'you know I'm very fond of you. I like going round with you, but we've got all our lives in front of us. I don't think I'm ready to marry just yet.'

'But one day, Rhoda – say in two or three years? I should have saved something by then, and you'll be twenty-four. Lots of girls are married by then! Would that be too soon?'

I was pleading for myself and did not like the sound of my own voice. I tried to recover ground but I was not used to this sort of talk. All I wanted was to hold her in my arms – for ever.

I went on, 'It was just that I thought your father might ask me my – intentions, you see. I know he is a very successful man and men like him want their daughters to marry successful men like themselves. . . .'

'He's never mentioned anything like that to me,' she said firmly. 'I think he's just interested in my friends, and I've never had a friend before quite like you. He's met all my girl-friends too . . .'

'Does he ever talk about you to your brother, do you think?'

'Oh, Father never discusses things with Alec – Alec is too prickly.'

'Well, I sometimes fear that your father has probably lined up some young man for you,' I said.

'Don't be so gloomy, Eddie dear, I can't remember any man he's ever particularly praised to me, unless it might be Cousin Arnold or his brother . . .'

'Who are they?' I asked suspiciously.

'Oh, relations,' she said vaguely. 'They're to do with wool or something in the Empire. I believe Father had a business arrangement with them over wool prices.'

'I won't say anything to your father about you then. But I can't help it if he guesses I'm in love with you!'

'I'm not in purdah, Eddie. I know lots of girls who go out with young men – you know, for fun, for theatres and things – and I'm sure they are not all thinking about weddings!'

'Your brother might be – with Phyllis,' I answered.

'Oh, surely not?'

She looked quite shocked. I did not say that I did not doubt what Alec and Phyllis got up to. I was puzzled. Educated girls with well-off fathers might be expected to behave more formally with young men, but on the other hand their manners were often much franker and freer than the girls of my own class. Not that Rhoda was an aristocrat or anything like that, she just happened to have been born with a silver spoon in her mouth.

'I wish you were poor!' I blurted out. It was her turn to look puzzled. It was one o'clock – time to be going. I felt miserable. Had I put my foot in it? Had I ruined things between us? 'I promise I won't ask you anything, except to accept my adoration,' I said in a quiet voice and she looked searchingly at me.

'I've never met anyone like you, Eddie,' she said finally. 'And I think you're sweet. I'm sure Father will like you as much as I do! Now I have to go back to the office.'

I took her hand as we went out and she leaned over and kissed my cheek as we parted in the arcade, she to the Parker office on one avenue and I to Uncle Fred's on another.

The first thing Rhoda's father said to me, as we sat in his drawing-room sipping tea from china cups, was, 'Rhoda tells me you are a poet.' I admitted this, trying not to choke into my tea.

Mrs Moore tried to rescue me, saying, 'How unusual!' Then she spoilt it by adding, 'Have you published anything yet?'

'Yes, as a matter of fact, I have,' I replied. I had already mentioned to the others about the war poems I had had published in the in the *Woolsford Observer*, but the editor of *Poetry* had seen fit to print me, parody or no.

'Fred Bairstow is your uncle isn't he?' asked Mr Moore. 'Not much poetry about him! Where'd d'ye get it from?'

I agreed about Uncle Fred. 'My grandfather Bairstow was a great collector of books,' I ventured, 'and another uncle is a good linguist. Most of the family are in textiles though.'

'Not much brass in writing verse, I don't suppose?' he went on. I agreed.

'My husband's grandfather was Mayor of Woolsford,' said Mrs Moore. 'You may have heard of him?' I agreed I had.

'Tell us where you were in the war, then. Alec was in the Royal Navy.'

Alec was not present at this interrogation. He had probably taken the car to the Dales. I did my best to summarize my not particularly distinguished career in the King's Own Yorkshire Light Infantry.

All Rhoda's father said was, 'You don't look old enough to have been in it all!'

There was nothing I could say to this. Eventually Rhoda and I escaped and she took me to look in the old stables which now housed her father's cars. I hoped I had passed muster. There was a little constraint between us after all we had said on the Thursday and it was too wet to play tennis or go for a walk. I saw her mother looking out of the window as we passed in front of the drawing-room on our way back to the house.

Rhoda and I were to go the cinema together in Woolsford that evening but I do not remember much about the film, silent of course. It was to be another six or seven years before the talkies arrived in Woolsford.

That summer Father bought a car, a Morris, and the family went on several jaunts. I was longing to drive it myself and to invite Rhoda to join me but Father was a bit reluctant at first to let me try. He had only just learned himself, but he was a good driver, being a man capable with his hands, and practical. During the next few months we visited Aunt Emily on the Lancashire coast, and stayed, overnight, going over to Wordsworth's Grasmere, my choice, the next morning. Then we went further to Mother's grandparents' old village near Lincoln, and of course to Thirksay.

That was where I wanted to take Rhoda, so that she might see how much the place meant to me, but she could not go on the day I asked her.

Perhaps I ought to have another go at being a farmer. But there wasn't much money in that, unless you were a gentleman farmer, who had money anyway. We had not alluded again to my proposal but I had written several poems to Rhoda that tried to express what I could not say to her face, or not so easily.

Father eventually relented and let me practise my driving with him sitting next to me. I rather enjoyed it, once I had got the hang of it. Reversing was the most difficult procedure; once I had to go all round Ilkley because I could not put the car into reverse. That would be a good place to take Rhoda, I thought, before I dared venture further afield without Father by my side. We could leave the car there to walk on the moors.

This did come to pass. Some weekends Rhoda and I went for walks on the moors together. For longer journeys, though, Father and Mother wanted to go too; after all it was their car. Rhoda, or Flossie with a girl-friend, would occasionally accompany us. We were not yet engaged, either officially or unofficially, and I constantly felt I wanted to sort out the future. Rhoda seemed to accept me; she could have no doubts that I loved her. But I still felt there was something she might not be saying and I even tortured myself imagining she was secretly in love with someone else. But who could it have been?

By the end of 1923, after a whole year of more friendship, more walks, occasional tennis-parties and lunch-time chats, I began to hope we might get engaged. Mr Moore had apparently said no more and Rhoda had never broached the subject. She did however begin to acknowledge, if not answer at much length, some of the letters I wrote to her when we had not seen each other during the week – and sometimes even if we had!

Holmfield
Wednesday

Sweetheart Rhoda,

I am on my lonesome this evening, everybody's out except the cat and her last kitten so why shouldn't I write to you? It's the next best pleasure to being with you and I hope you won't mind a second letter this week since we have not seen each other at work since Monday. I always look forward to your replies. How I wish you were here. Somehow I feel particularly alone – the evening is so cool and the sunshine so brilliant and you are not here to share in the delight.

I am not unhappy, but there is something – a great deal in fact – missing, which leaves an ache in the heart and makes me feel terribly lonely. And you, Rhoda, are the only person who knows the true reason. It seems an age since I last saw you. You were rather quiet then – a bit distant – at least I thought so, but perhaps I am imagining all these things?

Forgive, dearest, the imaginings of a man very much in love with you. You have such a sweet uncomplaining way whilst I keep asking so much of you in various ways. I wish it were possible – I wish I were in the position to ask you to be my wife *now*. You know that. That is my grandest ambition. We should bring each other happiness, which is I think the only success in life. You are always in my thoughts and I love you more dearly than anything else in the world. Will you wait?

I have thought very much on the problem and I don't want to be unfair to you. People have tongues – very long ones some of them! – with which they give advice to young people but it is only a matter to be settled one day by you, by looking deep down into your heart. Love is a thing of beauty and beauty is a joy for ever. I'm sure you do understand. Our life is in our hands as far as living is concerned and it is our business to mould it for happiness.

If you stand with me I need have no fears and it is a wonderful thing to step rose-crowned into the darkness. My sweet Rhoda, don't upbraid me for being sad. I love you dearly, and sadness is a necessary part of life. I know you will not misunderstand me.

104

Rhoda, I worship you and love you very deeply. I pray we may one day 'keep the faith'. I am longing for Saturday when I shall take you for a walk on the moors and when I hope your cold will be better – and then we have the dance in Woolsford to look forward to. I'd like you to put my name on the whole of your programme! Until then, sweetheart with all my love

Eddie

Holmfield
18 May

Dearest,

As I shall not see you to-night I'm writing instead. I feel very tired after a busy day, so please excuse my non-appearance at Knagg Wood. I did not forget last night when I put my head on the pillow (not at set of sun but about 11.30 p.m.). You didn't forget, did you? I had a most delightful evening on Friday for which I cannot sufficiently thank you. I think that walk we had in the park was the pleasantest evening I've ever had and I hope we can go there again before long, and sit by the lake and feed the ducks.

Do you remember my describing my 'Fourth Step' on Friday? I'm sure I could write a lovely story called The Fourth Step. Would that I were able to take the final one. Don't you wish it too? Money's a blessed nuisance, isn't it? It's a nuisance when you haven't much of it and I believe still a curse when you've got plenty:

O, damned gold!
O cursed gold!
Thou art the miser's pleasure:
Confounded gold!
O filthy gold!
For me thou'rt hidden treasure

Where does that verse come from? I ought to know. Has anybody in your house perused the book of modern poetry I lent you yet? I think the other verse I quoted last week ought to appear with the title <u>England</u> in order to give a true picture. England's countryside certainly is an English characteristic but after all we are an industrial people, taken as a whole.

We English think not very much of the fields in 'England's green and pleasant land' – we pay the agricultural labourer the least of any class of worker. But who's written a sonnet on a steel magnate or an ode to a soap-maker, or a triolet on a rotund brewer? And yet we are governed by industrialists. We are in the power of Mammon; workers are slaves. Their wages are given to them after they have done the work; and they fawn at the feet of the powerful to obtain favours. Had an Eastern monarch more power? They certainly don't cut off heads here but they cut off stomachs – they say 'Do as I bid or starve!'

I suppose I ought not to think these thoughts as all my family is in business. Don't think I'm a Bolshevist or a socialist – socialism is only the name for a theory – I'm none of these. I don't covet other people's goods; you know I don't desire to be rich. I only want suffi-cient to pay my way. Most people don't want mansions. But most people have got to be wage slaves just to live.

I hope you're not yawning by now! I thought these little reflections might interest you, which brings me back to the woods the fields and the sky. These are free subjects and eter-nally wonderful. I'm surprised that some millionaire hasn't made a contract for cloth to cover us so that we cannot see the sky! And then charged us so much for a peep. Sixpence to view a foot and one and six for a yard. There's only one reason why it's never been done; it isn't practicable. I'm certain it would come to pass if it was possible. You've even to pay a few coppers to see Bettwys-y-Coed.

But the thrush sings for rich and poor alike; the cuckoo doesn't wait for his fee; the fiery sun in the evening gives his gold to him who will take the trouble to glance at him; the rainbow is lavish with its delicate colour and the scent of flowers, if unpreserved, can be had for nothing. And, greatest of all, Rhoda, love is free. It is the greatest of gifts. It makes life worth the living. It does not pander to the rustle of bank notes. If it does, well it isn't love. If you would one day tell me you loved me I would count myself as one of earth's happiest men.

We are busy straightening up at the office and I don't think I shall be home as early as usual on Friday. I hope I shall have a letter from you as soon as ever possible.

With deepest love my own little Rhoda. Four kisses till we meet again.

Eddie

I wrote Rhoda many such letters. I poured out everything to her that came into my head, but I do remember being occasionally worried that she might believe my diatribes against the state of society were directed against people like her father. I had no designs on Mr Moore's money. The trouble was that I rather despised money and also hated it because I hadn't any. I suppose that is the situation of many young men.

When we met on Saturdays we often sat in a park in Woolsford or further afield and talked, and I always ended up kissing her. She accepted my kisses, and sometimes returned them, but by the summer of 1923 I still had the uncomfortable feeling that I was not getting anywhere. Had her father actually expressed his disapproval and she was not telling me? I dared not ask her. I had still not formally asked her to be my wife and had decided not to do this until I could be sure of her answer, before asking her father's permission, which was, I believed, the way to proceed.

I truly thought that this was not for my sake but for hers. I had a horror of embarrassing her. I could write all that was in my heart but I found it much harder to say it. I could imagine what it would be like with a woman I loved who loved me in the same way and knew I would have asked that woman over and over again to be my wife even though I had no money saved. But I wanted Rhoda to come to love me in the way I loved her and perhaps the fact that she did have money also made me hesitate, and depressed me.

One day Alec called in at my uncle's office and we went out for a drink after work. I had not seen him to speak to for weeks; he was always busy on his father's business, often now away from Woolsford. I decided I'd ask his advice.

I began by asking how Phyllis was. I thought he looked a little shifty.

'Oh – well, er, we don't see as much of each other as we used to.'

I was surprised. I said, 'I thought you two would get married!'

'Phyllis has other ideas,' he replied and twiddled his glass between his fingers.

'You mean – another fellow?'

'Not exactly – more than one, I suppose! I never asked Phyllis to marry me, so I can't complain.'

'Do you wish you had?'

'Phyllis and I had good times together,' he said. 'But I don't think she's the woman I'd want to wed.'

I thought, perhaps he means they've had what the family call a flutter and more sophisticated milieux call an affair. Did he mean she was the wrong kind of woman, the sort *he* had possibly made her? He couldn't have been in love with her, surely. Was he a man who divided women into those who did and those who didn't? He'd been away in the Navy and must have had more experience – 'women in every port' – than I had acquired in the trenches of Flanders, or refused to acquire elsewhere. I wanted to ask his advice about his sister but he wouldn't see Rhoda as another woman, or one like Phyllis.

I began, 'You know that Rhoda and I still see each other?'

'Well, of course. She's very fond of you.'

'But, Alec, I want her to be more than that! I'm serious about her. What does she really think about me?'

'You mean you'd like to *marry* Rhoda?' He sounded amazed.

'It's not all that unusual a wish – we've had ample time to get to know each other!'

'Yes, but – well. . . .'

'Do you think your parents would consent to Rhoda's marrying me?' I asked him boldly.

I saw he was embarrassed and realized he was thinking about the fact that I hadn't much – or any – money. He did not know how to put it. But surely some people had married for love, even in his family?

I tried again. 'I thought your parents might have said something.'

'No'

'Well, Alec, I know I can't offer much in the material sense but if she loved me as much as I do her, that wouldn't matter!'

And that was the trouble. I still did not know how much Rhoda loved me. I thought she did, a little. She would receive kisses and hold hands and listen to me but she never evinced the sort of passion that very often took me over. Did women not feel as we did? And anyway, was it necessary for a woman to return a man's love, feel as he did? Or was that just my own romanticism that wanted it, needed it? I was certain that my having more or less money would not be the deciding factor to predispose her to love with me. Rhoda was just not that sort of girl. It didn't alter the case that she might not be – probably was not – in love with me. My being as rich as Croesus wouldn't alter that.

'I don't know what to say, old chap! Father's never mentioned you in that way and I don't know whether Rhoda has ever told him how you feel about her, or how she feels about you. We just don't talk about such things much in our family.'

'Has Rhoda never said anything to you about me?'

'Well, I just assumed you were good friends. I suppose one doesn't see one's sister as a grown woman! I expect Mother has her eye on someone for her – don't let that get you down.'

Did he not take his sister at all seriously? I chose to take *his* words seriously.

'But, Alec, we don't live in the Middle Ages! Parents don't arrange marriages any more in England!'

'You'd be surprised,' he said. 'Not that Rhoda would marry anyone just to please Mother – or Father.'

Be grateful for small mercies, I thought. I did not wish to ask her brother to plead for me, so I just said, 'Well, now you know – at the end of ten years I'll probably still be saving up.'

'In 1933 we shall all be millionaires,' he said unseriously. 'Cheer up!'

I'd like to have asked him if he had ever been serious about Phyllis but thought better of it. I felt he was about to say something like, there are plenty other fish in the sea, so I hastily changed the subject and we talked for a bit about work.

Then he said, 'I wanted to sound you out about something else. I thought of going this summer for a week or two to Switzerland and wondered if you'd like to make up the party. There'll be a fellow I used to know at school. No women. We might do a bit of walking. . . .'

I was flattered he'd asked me, but had I enough money? If I hadn't enough to be able to get on my knees and ask Rhoda Moore to marry me I ought to be saving up what I did have, not squandering it on trips abroad. But I was sorely tempted.

I needed a change. Life since being demobbed nearly four years ago had been one long slog. Rhoda was all that had kept me going.

'I'll think about it,' I said.

My sister Flossie had now finished her training but she did not want to teach in any of the local schools. They were rough and Flossie was a gentle sort of young woman. Help came in the form of Father who stated that there was no need for his daughter to teach. Her mother needed her at home now that they had a much bigger house and garden, and if Flossie cared to help with the housekeeping he could give her pin-money which she could supplement by giving some private music lessons.

I was doubtful that she was doing the right thing but I imagined she would eventually marry, so there was no point in her following a profession for which she was not really suited. She loved children in ones and twos and threes but the classes of over forty after the war were a different and difficult proposition. Much needed to be done to improve social conditions in the city of

Woolsford, and in the towns nearer to us. Flossie was trained, and had a year's experience, so she could always find a job once the schools settled down and had smaller classes, or she could work in a private school.

One day she said to me that she thought she might never marry.

'So many of the young men we used to know as children have died, you see. There won't be any husbands for many of us.'

Flossie still usually accompanied us when Father took us on outings in the motor. Even when I took Rhoda without my parents, which was not often, Flossie would sometimes come along as well. I would have preferred to be alone with Rhoda but Mother always said, 'Oh, do take Flossie – she doesn't get out much,' and so I would. My mother was clearly being prudent, thinking we should not be alone together. She liked Rhoda and wanted us to get engaged. I knew this without her saying anything. One day, however, I heard her say to Father, 'Rhoda is keeping him dangling and should put him out of his misery!'

My father grunted something in reply. He always preferred to keep out of emotional tangles.

'I expect it's her parents,' Mother went on. 'Eddie's not good enough for them, I suppose. They'll want her marrying a rich man.'

I was angry. Alec had hinted much the same. But if Rhoda loved me. . . .

That autumn, Rhoda and I were still seeing each other regularly and I was still trying to gather up my courage to propose formally to her. The protocol was that a young man should ask the permission of the lady's parents but I wasn't sure at what stage he did this. I decided to try to discuss it sensibly with Rhoda.

We were sitting in an alcove at the Picture House tea rooms one Saturday. She was nibbling toast and I was drinking cup after cup of tea since my mouth felt so dry.

'I have something to ask you, dear,' I began.

She paused in her nibbling and looked at me.

'If I asked you to marry me, Rhoda – no, don't say anything yet.

I don't want you to decide anything – but do you think your parents would ever agree to your marrying me?'

She was silent at first. Then, 'If they thought I'd be happy they wouldn't object, I'm sure, Eddie!'

I caught my breath. I so much wanted to force her to a decision but knew I must not.

'Will you think about it, then?' I said.

'Yes, Eddie,' she said in a small voice. 'I'm very fond of you, you know.'

Meaning she was not in love with me yet? Or would never be? Or that she was already fond enough of me to marry me?

'I do love you Rhoda,' I said.

She took my hand and squeezed it. 'I wish people could live together before they got married!' she said.

I was surprised. I had not thought of her as an unconventional girl.

'I mean, how can you know whether you are suited to someone? We see each other a lot, and I know you are sure of your own feelings – but I just don't know. Forgive me Eddie. Ask me again in a year and I promise I'll tell you then. Let's just enjoy each other's company for the present.'

'I won't mention it again before next summer,' I said solemnly. 'But just tell me, darling, is there anyone else you might want to marry?'

I did not see how there could be for I saw such a lot of her there was hardly time when she was not at work that she could be seeing someone else.

She looked quite startled but after a fraction of a pause, 'Oh, no, Eddie, I don't think so,' she said. I breathed a sigh of relief.

I took my week's Continental holiday later that autumn along with Alec and Anthony Sheard and Ben Dyson, and the others stayed on for another week when I went back. I had been in two minds about going; I had hoped – and had therefore taken the chance – that in the end Rhoda would come along with her brother. She did not. The four of us stayed in Lucerne and then Interlaken.

I had resolved not to think about Rhoda and to concentrate on the Bernese Oberland and writing my travel notebook, and I did manage during the day to give myself up to new sights and new sounds. I believe it did me good; I certainly felt healthier and rested in spite of our long walks. We often went drinking in the Bierkeller or the cafés in the evenings, though I did not much like the beer. I had not liked French beer in the war either – thin stuff, I thought, after the good old warm English ale. After these holiday evening convivialities I would usually feel depressed, and it was in the middle of the night that thoughts of Rhoda would refuse to go away. I should not have come, I thought, I should be saving every penny with the object of marrying Rhoda. How many days and weeks and months would go by before I might ask her for her hand in full expectation of a positive reply?

The new year, 1924, came in hard and frosty, and with it my parents' idea of visiting the British Empire Exhibition in Wembley in July when they could stay with some of Mother's cousins. There would be no holiday abroad this year for me, nor a break at the seaside, so I reckoned that if I could go on a little ahead of them and wangle things so that Rhoda might be there too, we might have a few days together away from both our families. I didn't say anything about this to Mother and Father or Flossie but intimated that I'd prefer to go to the exhibition alone or with a man friend, rather than acccompanying my parents. Father said he would give me five pounds to spend on myself. He knew his brother didn't pay me very much. I felt a little guilty that any spare money I had ought to go to the Rhoda fund but five pounds would hardly set us up in married life. And anyway I wanted to spend it on her.

Then the bombshell fell. Rhoda was to go to Europe in the middle of July with an aunt and uncle whom she was to meet in Paris before going on to Venice and returning home via the French Riviera, and I don't know where else.

113

I had waited long enough. Two or three days together did not seem much to ask, when we could settle things one way or the other. It was now or never! We could, indeed must, meet in London when she was on her way abroad. I was determined about that and so laid my plans, which I revealed to Rhoda at the end of May.

It seemed there was no way of her getting out of the long Continental holiday. I suppose she could have refused but it turned out that the man she worked for in the arcade was moving his office to Manchester and she would lose her job in September in any case. I would regard her holiday abroad as a preliminary to an engagement, for I had decided to propose to her formally in London. If she accepted me I would approach her parents on her return. My idea was that Rhoda would have tactfully prepared the ground with her father by a letter from Europe!

To cut a long story short, Rhoda agreed to meet me in London. It would be quite easy for her to snatch a day or two with me. Her relatives were to meet her in Paris, her luggage having been regis-tered and sent along ahead, before she herself took the *Golden Arrow* to Paris. All she had to do was to fix a date to meet them after 'a few days with a school friend' in London. This in case they mentioned to her own parents that she was not travelling with them.

Why did a grown woman need such a subterfuge? Rhoda was twenty-three after all.

I arrived in London the day before Rhoda and made my way from the 'diggings' Uncle Albert had found me in Wembley Park to the north entrance of the vast concourse. Rhoda was to meet me the following day at ten o'clock. She was to alight at the north end station and had promised to be in front of the Colonnade café by the east side of the garden next to the main entrance.

I pored over the map and the guide. There was too much to see, and yet perhaps I wouldn't care if I never saw any of it. I might visit the Palace of Arts though; I had better make the most of this solitary day so at least I should have something to recount at home.

I walked down Raglan Gardens to the Palace of Arts and prepared to be impressed. I was not so interested in the engineering wonders or the various pavilions of our far-flung empire. It cost sixpence to enter the Arts Palace for it covered an area of 40,000 square feet in eight main sections. And this was only one little building among two score mostly much bigger ones, not to mention the lakes, the gardens, the amusement parks, and the bandstands. I thought Rhoda might be interested in the Palace of Horticulture but I wanted above all to see the paintings and so I went first into the gallery which was exhibiting portraits from Hogarth onwards – Reynolds, Gainsborough, Romney, Raeburn, Millais, Watts, Burne-Jones.

I was entranced. Never had I seen so many great paintings together, some of which had never been exhibited to the general public before. There were modern paintings in another gallery, and sculptures as well as the period rooms and a display of theatre art. There was too, a special gallery housing the Queen's doll's house, the most popular exhibit in the whole exhibition and I was sure Rhoda would like to see that. You had to pay extra to see it.

I was not so interested in the artists of the Empire but I wanted to see the six furnished apartments from 1750 onwards through Regency, mid-Victorian and William Morris styles, to that of the present day, and I'd like to see the bookbindings, and perhaps the theatre models.

Rhoda *must* see the doll's house. If she wanted to see the Horticultural Pavilion as well, we'd have our work cut out. We should have to miss most of the exhibition unless we returned the next day. You needed weeks, not a day or two, to make the most of it all.

She was to meet me at two o'clock and I was there in good time. I was in a fever of impatience lest we miss each other, or that her friends would insist upon accompanying her. I waited in front of the Colonnade café, but it all seemed much bigger when you were

115

there than it had done on the map. I had just begun to worry, thinking she might go to the wrong restaurant or café – my programme told me there were, believe it or not, thirty-three different ones, when, there she was! I saw her turn the corner by the garden and make her way in my direction. I ran towards her and when she saw me she walked more quickly and then we were together.

I hugged her with joy. 'Oh, Rhoda – you're here! I can't believe it.'

She took my arm, saying, 'I'm dying for a cup of tea. Can we go in?'

We joined a not very long straggle of people waiting outside the door of this handsome café – it was too late for a meal – and were soon sitting at a table.

'Tell me all about it,' she said.

I spread the map out, reluctant though I was to waste my precious time alone with her. 'It would take weeks to see it all,' I said, 'and for that you'd need a plan, but they give you a list of the star turns. You'd love the Queen's doll house. I've read all about it and I'm sure you would.'

'Oh yes. I'd like to see that!'

'And there's a theatre and a fountain they light up at night,' I went on. I passed over the biggest knife in the world and the oldest cricket bat and the kitchen-range from the 1851 Exhibition.

'Look! There's a mannequin parade every day in the Palace of Industry,' she exclaimed.

'I'm not sure when that takes place – I did try to discover—'

'And there's a gramophone room,' Rhoda pointed out, looking over my shoulder again, 'and lots and lots of machines of all sorts—'

'I see enough of them at home. I'd prefer diamond washing and sculpturing in butter!'

'And a pearl necklace it took thirty years to make – with every pearl a different colour,' said Rhoda, still reading.

We both began to laugh.

'And a twenty-foot-high pineapple and Nebuchadnezzar's

amulet and a Burmese Buddha and Indian jugglers – and a cheese that weighs one and a half tons. . . .

'It's all about making things, really, isn't it?' she said. 'Let's just go and see that doll's house. We'd need six months, not weeks, to see all this!'

'Don't you want to see the gardens?'

'There won't be time, will there?'

I took her hand. 'I don't care what we go to see so long as you are with me,' I said.

There in the middle of that crowded café, instead of during some romantic moonlit tryst, I wanted to blurt out, *Please let's get married straight away, Rhoda, please.* I could scarcely hold myself back from uttering the words. Instead, I just said, 'I do love you, Rhoda.'

'I know, Eddie,' she replied. I thought she looked rather sad. We got up and she followed me out of the café. Then she came up to me and took my arm and said, in a different tone of voice, 'We could be together, you know – really together. Nobody expects me back tonight.'

I was amazed – unbelieving. I stopped, and she stopped, and I stared at her. I was sufficiently master of myself to say, 'There's nothing I could want more,' all the time thinking, I don't want it to look as if I am proposing to her after she has stayed the night with me like a married woman – if that *is* what she means. I must propose to her before – before whatever she intends to happen. I felt my heart beating rather loudly in my ribs.

As if hearing my unspoken thoughts, she said, 'No Eddie – darling Eddie. I know you love me – but don't ask me yet.'

I was immediately suspicious: 'Has your father said something?'

'I don't want to talk about it. Let's just enjoy ourselves.' We were now walking along the path back to the Palace of Arts. 'Aren't I grown up?' she said in a low voice. 'Can't I do what I want? I'm going abroad because I want to.'

'Do you really want to go? I shall miss you so?' I asked, all at sea.

'I just want to feel free for a bit,' she replied after a pause. Then she smiled. 'Show me the Queen's doll's house.'

We waited patiently with a large crowd of others and when we finally got into the gallery Rhoda was thrilled. The doll's house had a scale of one inch to one foot and everything was made to the same scale. There is something about the miniature that fascinates; there were even fountain pens and chessmen and toothbrushes, soap, scent, tobacco, hot-water bottles, playing-cards. There was water in the taps, and electricity moved the lifts. Rhoda might be grown up but she took a childlike delight in this miniature mansion and it really was wonderful. It was nearly as tall as Rhoda, and nearly nine feet long. Everything in it had been made by artists and craftsmen. The front of the building was lifted up on pulleys so you could see everything, every room furnished in detail: dining-room, library with tiny books, drawing-room, bedrooms, bathrooms, nurseries, sitting-rooms, kitchens, cellars stocked with fine wines, a garage with a fleet of cars and a garden planted with flowers that would all eventually bloom.

Rhoda exclaimed about the golf-clubs and the taps with running water, the electric lifts.

'It took two and a half years to make,' she said looking up from her programme. She looked entranced, really happy, so I felt happy too.

'Would you like to live in a house like this? It's a palace really, isn't it.' I asked her.

'No, but I'd love *this* house! Isn't she lucky, the Queen, having all this to herself!' She took my hand. 'I'd love to plan a house. I'd like to have been an architect, you know, but they didn't want me to train for that – they said there weren't any women architects.'

'I've never heard of any. It's not too late to find out if you could.'

'Oh, Eddie, you are sweet. I think it's too late now. Anyway, they let me be a secretary.'

I decided to plunge in as we walked away. 'Would they let you marry me?' I asked.

'Father doesn't want me to get married yet. I don't know why. Most people want their daughters to wed, don't they?'

'Depends to whom, I suppose,' I replied. 'Anyway, you can get married without your parents' permission – once you decide.'

I wondered if she would want the sort of smart wedding the rich go in for. I felt I was pushing things too much, and yet I wanted her to know that I was an honourable man and was not going to embark upon an affair with no marriage in sight.

But Rhoda said, 'I'll let you know when I have!'

I am approaching the most difficult part of my story to write. For so many years I have cherished certain memories, never spoken about them to anyone else, and now that I come to write about them I feel curiously shy.

What happened was that we went to a little hotel in Bloomsbury where we spent two nights together. There, I proposed to her again. She said neither yes or no, but she promised she would write to her parents to test the water, and then write to me whilst she was away with her relatives.

'I shan't tell Mother or Father, or anyone, that we spent these nights together!' she said.

Of course I didn't want her to tell her parents, but I wondered how she was going to broach the subject of our marriage. I dared not ask her whether she truly accepted my proposal on her own account, never mind what her mother or father might think. They surely had some idea of the way the land lay, if not from her then from Alec. I had the impression that she was still holding back from committing herself but that it was mainly on account of her father. But had not those two nights altered her feelings for me? I knew they had altered mine for her – made them even more profound, made my love stronger.

Who can describe love-making? I was inexperienced but I think I made up for it by tenderness. My love for Rhoda had naturally been mixed with desire for a very long time, but I can truly say that lust was not my overriding feeling. Rhoda was quite passive and lay looking up at me with big eyes, yet she was not coy. Had she done this before? I did not care whether she had or not. I ought to have cared, and was amazed, thinking it over later, that I did not: I just wanted her *now*, for mine. The present was what mattered, not her past or my past. I had resisted camp-followers when I was in the army, though there had not been many of them around except when we were on leave in Trouville, but I did not see why I should resist my true emotions. What surprised me more than anything was that Rhoda was not filled with the usual embarrassment and fear and timidity that I imagined afflicted all nicely brought up women.

'I am a bad girl,' she whispered, and smiled.

'No, you are a very good girl,' I replied stroking her hair. She sighed.

'Why can't we just elope?' I groaned later when we awoke together with the pale dawn light coming in though the Bloomsbury Square window.

'You are rash, Eddie darling.' Rhoda distrusted some of the intensity of my feelings although I believe she was flattered by it. 'You are so gentle,' she said.

Had she expected me to be a ravening beast? I told her how I still longed to take her to Thirksay to see the Vale of York and my father's cousins, how I wanted to take her everywhere, never be parted from her.

Yet after one more day together we should be parted.

We spent it sitting on the tops of London omnibuses, getting off to walk when we saw something we wanted to explore. In this way, we went into some of the city churches and, right on the other side of London, sailed down Park Lane, alighting to walk in Hyde Park. It was a warm day and we stood hand in hand by The Serpentine and walked over to Kensington, which Rhoda seemed to know quite well.

The second night I made her promise again she would write to me from Paris.

'I just can't bear to be parted from you,' I said. 'I shall miss you so much.'

I believe I knew then that she would not miss me in quite the same way and this made me feel so sad that I actually said to her, 'Will you miss me, Rhoda?'

'I'll be back by Christmas,' she said. And then, 'I thought you might not mope so much if I stayed with you, Eddie.'

'I shall wait for you,' I said, meaning not only her return from abroad but until she felt ready to marry me.

At first I tried to look cheerful on Victoria station the next morning when she boarded the *Golden Arrow* for Paris, and I kissed her goodbye. Then I felt that the train was gathering together all my life and that it was taking it away along with Rhoda. I ran along beside it as she waved to me gaily, and it puffed slowly away. How I missed her already, feeling both happy about my time with her, and terribly sad, and I went on missing her when I finally returned to Yorkshire.

Rhoda was as good as her word and I received a card straight away from Paris. Paris was very hot but soon they were all going on to Switzerland and then Innsbrück and Salzburg before a week or two in Vienna where others would join them. She would write to me from the Tyrol and from Vienna. After this their plans were vaguer but they intended to be in Nice by September.

I thought of her in the mountains, placed her where I had been with her brother, and wished I had a magic carpet to join her there – along with some money, of course. But she appeared to be enjoying herself, whilst I was back slaving away for Uncle Fred.

When no letter arrived from Rhoda for two weeks, I telephoned Alec. His parents were in Scotland for the rest of the summer, he said, and he expected Rhoda was too busy enjoying herself to write. He had received only one postcard, from Innsbrück. Of course he knew nothing of my meeting his sister in Wembley, nor how I felt how that must have changed our relations for good.

But was it for good? For me, Rhoda's trip abroad was a hiatus, a treat I could not grudge her, but a weary time of waiting before I could see her again. She had promised she would tell her parents about us, hadn't she? I had heard nothing from them, but that was understandable if they were away from home.

Her next letter arrived two weeks later, in mid August, from Salzburg.

121

Dear Eddie, I hope you are well and that you are not finding work too bad. I am having a wonderful time. Some of Mother's cousins joined us from Paris and we decided, before we went back to France, that after Vienna we would stop over in Venice. Just imagine, in an old palazzo owned by an American friend of a cousin! I'll write to you from Italy. I just want to say now, thank you for being such a nice man. With love from Rhoda.

I was puzzled, but I wrote back immediately to the address in Venice she gave me at the end of her letter. It would doubtless await her arrival there in a week or two.

She did get my letter, for her next one to me was written from the Palazzo Esti in Venice in September. She was just off to Nice. Venice was wonderful but 'we want some autumn sun on the Riviera and we shall probably stay for the whole of next month.' She made no reference to her parents nor to our time together in London. Reading between the lines I found her letter a little incoherent. I feared the worst – that she had regretted her two nights in London, that she despised me for being poor, that her father had forbidden her to have anything further to do with me. . . .

Her next letter was from Nice in October. It was much worse than anything I could have imagined. She need not have written to me, I suppose. It said,

I am sorry, Eddie. I know this will be a shock. I tried to tell you before but I could not. You see, I am with my cousin Arthur Marriott, and we have got married at the British Consulate. Please forgive me. I have been in love with him for a long long time and never thought he would want to marry me. I shall not see you in England, for he is taking me straight away to his home in Wellington, New Zealand. I shall never forget you – please believe me, and forgive me,

Rhoda.

122

I telephoned Alec frantically that evening and probably did not make much sense.

He was quietly sympathetic, said, 'I don't know what to say, Eddie. It was a surprise to all of us too. She's known him for years – apparently he proposed as soon as he saw her this summer. I'm sorry, Eddie, but Rhoda's always gone her own way.'

'Did you know she was fond of him?'

'Well, I suspected there was always something up between them. Whenever Arthur came over to England, from years back, they used to spend a lot of time together and I believe whenever she stayed with her aunt she may have seen him. Shall I – would you like to meet in Woolsford?'

'I don't think I could bear to see anyone at the moment,' I replied. 'But for God's sake let me know any news you have of her. I don't know where to write.'

'We could go and get drunk together if you like,' he said.

'One day, perhaps.'

I put the phone down. I could not tell my parents what had happened. Not yet.

Of course they eventually discovered and I became the object of sympathy. But I would not let Mother say a word against Rhoda.

I did agree to talk to Alec eventually. He was back in Woolsford and invited me to lunch at the Sphinx. Of course, I tried to discover why Rhoda had left me in the lurch. I had received no more letters from her, though I had sent several to be forwarded. Alec was terribly embarrassed.

'She was sweet on that cousin of ours years ago when she was only a kid – she used to write to him, and I suppose it all came to a head when they were cast together abroad. I shall miss her myself, you know – I was never very fond of Arthur – a bit too much the glamour boy.'

I shuddered inside, but managed to get out, 'What does your mother think about it?'

'As I told you, my parents knew that Rhoda had once had a G P for Arthur, and they didn't object.'

'I suppose Arthur is rich?'

'Wildly so, old boy. I'm sorry, Eddie.' He added as we parted, 'I'd much rather she'd married you.'

The next two or three years were dreary. Now and again I had news of her in New Zealand from Alec, but then he moved away to work permanently in Scotland so even that link was thin, since he was not a very good correspondent. Eventually we lost touch completely. Before this he told me that his parents had gone over to Wellington a year or two after Rhoda's marriage. By then they were grandparents. I often used to wonder if Rhoda had wanted to see the New Zealand pavilion when we were at the Wembley Exhibition. If she had told me then that she was in love with her second cousin Arthur Marriott, had been in love with him for years, what would I have done? Would I have wanted to spend those two nights with her? Why had she suggested them if she loved someone else?

I could not help believing that in some strange way the affair between Rhoda and me was not over. But she never communicated with me or gave me any grounds for this, and I was not of the race of adulterers.

Occasionally I saw Phyllis in Woolsford. She had not yet married and we met once or twice over a drink. I think she knew I only wanted to go over the past and talk about Rhoda, though I tried hard to concentrate on other things.

Once she said, 'We both lost out, you and I, didn't we?' Another time I asked her if she had known about Arthur Marriott, but she said, 'Rhoda never talked about him. I knew there was someone, of course. I'm sorry, Eddie.'

She however knew nothing of my snatched two days of happiness with her friend. I did not want to see too much of Phyllis, because the fact that she was not Rhoda, but was connected with the happiest time of my life made me miserable. Also, I knew – and Flossie also intimated – that Phyllis might have her eye on me as a possible future husband.

I thought I would never get over my love for Rhoda. In some

ways I never did, if by that one means holding a remembrance of extreme happiness and extreme sadness. I knew that most people would have seen her treatment of me as shabby, yet I wanted to forget what had finally happened. I understood that she must have dreaded telling me the truth, and her lack of candour was because she did not want to hurt me. I had loved her, and did love her, if you can go on loving a person you will never see again. Sometimes, later – not at the beginning – I would dream of her and I think there was always a depth-charge waiting to shatter my submarine defences.

At that time, right up to 1928, my thoughts were far from marriage. In 1926, and during the three years that followed I sent out half a dozen stories to twenty different magazines but had no luck. I remember the titles of some of them: *The Dreamer and the Magician, The Working of Chance, Slade, Mrs Redway Entertains*. I tried to put some of my feelings about the loss of love into these stories but I expect they were too gloomy for the mass market.

During the same period I also wrote four plays. *Finding the Man* was one, and there were three others whose titles I forget; brittle comedies that were of the type fashionable at the time and totally the wrong thing for me to be writing. I should have tried to write something about my war on the lines of Robert Graves' *Good-bye to All That* which came out in 1929.

During these years we often visited Aunt Emily on the coast and often motored to Windermere or Coniston, and once to Cambridge, as well as to the moors nearer us, and to Thirksay and the Vale of York. I liked one or two of my female second cousins there and sometimes imagined I might marry one of them and set up as a small farmer, but it was a pipe dream. Chicken farmers were two a penny, and failing right left and centre, and there was much unemployment, with ex-servicemen selling matches on city streets. The war to end all wars had brought nothing pleasant in its train. I had better stick for the time being with Uncle Fred.

It was hard for Father and Uncle Albert to keep afloat at the mill, and would soon be even harder, with a slump and the depression, though somehow they managed. No good my going in with them just yet; Uncle Fred had more export contacts than Father, and I continued to practise my Spanish at the foreign circle.

Four years after the last time I'd seen Rhoda, in 1928, at an extramural class on Greek civilization, in our nearest small town, I first met Kitty Hall.

Within the year we were married.

CHAPTER SIX

Marriage

Time's glory is to calm contending kings.
To unmask falsehood and bring truth to light
Shakespeare: The Rape of Lucrece

Her romantic young father!

Juliet had put her father's typescript down just before he married her mother. She would finish the whole story after she had refreshed herself with a cup of tea.

It was still the same October afternoon, warm and sunny, everything the same as usual out in the garden that she could see through the window. Only a few hours had passed, yet it seemed like days since she began to read. It had all brought back her father so poignantly.

Nobody but herself and her father would have read his story, unless Mr Holkham the solicitor had bothered to investigate. He would most likely have been too busy, or incurious about the private affairs of his clients.

She would finish it before her husband returned from work at about seven o'clock.

Lying in the box was the large sealed envelope addressed to 'Ally' and 'July', their father's pet names for herself and her sister.

Juliet was puzzled about Rhoda, for Rhoda seemed to have liked her father, if not been in love with him. In Juliet's experience, *I love you but I am not* in love *with you*, was usually a

127

cop-out clause for young men rather than young women, who were far more likely to imagine they were 'in' love'.

Had Rhoda ever lied to Eddie?

She wondered too if her father had felt less himself after his marriage. After the end of the love affair that he appeared to regard as so important in his life, had he ever done what *he* wanted?

Later, after her cup of tea and a cigarette – Juliet was always about to stop smoking – she read the rest of the typescript.

How he had hurried over the last half of his life, in the chapter he called *After Rhoda*. He began by quoting the poet Cowper: a poem called *The Winter Evening* from *The Task*. She well remembered his quoting it in her childhood. Perhaps he had considered it summed up his married life?

> *Now stir the fire, and close the shutters fast,*
> *Let fall the curtains, wheel the sofa round,*
> *And while the bubbling and loud-hissing urn*
> *Throws up a steamy column, and the cups*
> *That cheer but not inebriate, wait on each,*
> *So let us welcome peaceful evening in.*
>
> The Winter Evening

She went on reading, hoping to find something about herself and her sister.

I do not propose to write about my marriage to Kitty in detail. Rhoda had abandoned me, but Kitty was a faithful wife and there are some things which nobody has the right to discuss when two people are involved. I know she will not read this, but that doesn't make any difference. I was a different man in my thirties from the one who had been so in love in his twenties.

I will say however that as I did not expect as much from Kitty as I had once expected from Rhoda, I was quite content. Also, Kitty was what in those days they were not quite calling 'career girls'. She was more intelligent than I was, I think. She didn't nurse an ambition to write but she read a reasonable amount and was a good 'all-rounder'. She was better at physical things than I was: a better dancer, a better swimmer, a better singer, and she had been an amateur actress as well as a very good teacher before we married. She could not go on with her profession; in those days women had to stop if they got married. It was only during the next war that they were begged to return to the classroom. Anyway, when the children, Alison and Juliet, arrived – we were married in 1929 and Alison was born fifteen months after our wedding, Juliet eighteen months after that – Kitty had her hands full. I was still not earning very much and trade was very bad. Eventually, I think it was in 1933, Father suggested I went in with him and his youngest brother at the mill. I left Uncle Fred's office where I'd been for more than ten years, and tried to feel enthusiastic about weaving-sheds. Father made me works manager as I was supposed to be friendly and good with people.

I know Kitty thought I was not ambitious enough, and it is true that I was quite content, once my working day was over, to return home, eat my supper, say goodnight to the girls if they were awake and spend my evenings with a book, unless it was the evening for my visit to a class or the meeting of a society. I had left the foreign circle and joined a literary society in Woolsford; and a little later I was to occupy myself in the winter researching and writing biographical and critical accounts of some of my favourite authors to be delivered at future sessions of the society. I introduced the members to the atheist and eccentric Samuel Butler and to other writers I'd read years before and still enjoyed.

In 1937 things looked up a bit at work and we were able to move from the terrace house we were buying on a mortgage to a modern house, both of them only a mile or two away from Holmfield. These two years before the war were happy years for me, and I hope for Kitty. I helped in the house – laid the fires and polished the shoes and dug the garden, and I took the children for walks. They were very different. Alison, the elder, whom I always called Ally, was a rebel, later to become a 'Bohemian' in her youth, though for a Bohemian she married young. She was less literary than Juliet and more extrovert, a popular girl with many friends, and very attractive. I always considered her Kitty's favourite, and that may have been because she was more like her mother in character. I know it doesn't always mean that you like the people who are more like yourself but I think in this case it was true. Kitty of course never showed it; indeed she got angrier with Alison than with her sister. On the other hand our younger daughter, Juliet, whom I called July, was more aware of adult approval and disapproval. When she was a little girl, she was more of a clinger and a bit over-sensitive. She hated change, wanted everything to stay the same for ever. I could sympathize. I marked Juliet out to be a librarian. She was a great reader, whilst Ally was more active and had more friends who wanted her to 'play out' with them. Juliet was, like me, a little unobservant, lost in her own world, and rather impractical. I think she was a bit jealous of her big sister but tried not to let it show. As I have said, 1937 and 1938 were, in spite of the threat of war, very happy years for me and my little family.

When I married Kitty I made a conscious effort to forget Rhoda, and life carried me on so that, in time, my youth – that now seems so near – moved further and further away from my conscious thoughts. I may have made mistakes in my marriage. I certainly felt that Kitty was its driving force. Perhaps she was the kind of woman I ought to have fallen in love with earlier, instead of Rhoda. After I married Kitty I still kept in an old trunk over eighty love poems written for or about Rhoda between 1921 and 1924. Kitty knew I had been in love before but she never read these poems. She had heard of my old friends Rhoda and Alec but I don't think she would have treated any infatuation of mine very seriously.

I have just recently reread the poems I have quoted in my story – and many more written in the throes of my romantic passion. I used to keep them hidden among wads of paper and exercise books in an old tin trunk. Kitty would ask me every spring to have a good tidy round and I would tidy up the little box-room where I kept my things but I never cleared out the trunk. It stood there for years. Sometimes I felt it was a silent reproach, not to my memory of Rhoda but to my early literary ambitions. I shall not leave the poems to be found by Kitty after I die. They will go for safety to the bank for the girls.

I did not love Kitty in the way I had adored Rhoda, but I'm sure she never knew that, and was satisfied. I was grateful to her, and absolutely faithful to her, but our love began as a married love, just as, like all romantic loves that endure, it would have become eventually in any case. I often wondered; if Rhoda had married me, what sort of life we would have had. My love was never put to the test, and I do still regret that.

Odd that it was Kitty, before we were married, not Rhoda, who visited Thirksay with me. Kitty liked the place, I think. I was still half hoping I could one day live there and learn to farm but Kitty said it was a pipe-dream and that she would not be very success-ful as a farmer's wife. To her the countryside was for walks and holidays, not for day-to-day living.

I continued working for my father. Our new house was bright and breezy. We had a bathroom with greeny-blue tiles and a prim-rose bath and a kitchen with green chairs and a range fed by a deep coal fire gas copper. In the two rooms downstairs where my bookcases stood we had some solid furniture. The coal fires were a lot of work, but I loved them. The garden was on three sides and gave me plenty of toil. Two crab-apple trees grew there, as the land had once been a market garden.

When I think of those years I always hear a piano piece called *Green Tulips* played by a man called Billy Mayerl who was often heard on our wireless at the time. Even now that tune can bring it all back: the girls sitting by the fire reading, or at the table with their paint-boxes; Kitty darning stockings, and myself in my big armchair reading.

For a time I went on attending the extramural classes where I had met Kitty. She was a clever woman and perhaps she would have liked to accompany me to them but she said I needed an evening out away from the children and I could tell her what I had learned. Later, when the children grew up and could be left, we attended classes and joined societies together. Even then, though, she would never accompany me to the village inn, The Black Horse, for a drink, where I used to see friends on Sunday mornings before returning for Sunday lunch with the family. It was often on Sunday afternoons in winter that I would sit before the fire, and if there was nothing I ought to do in the garden, I'd write verse. I never stopped writing, though it was no longer love-poetry, more often parodies and satires.

When the children were small before the war and just after it for a year or two we all had family holidays on the coast. For the next year or two after that, the girls were old enough to take walking holidays with their friends and to go abroad for weeks in summer staying with French friends or on trips planned by their school.

The years after the first war and before my marriage appear to have lasted for centuries, the time when I was not yet a father, the time when I was in love with Rhoda. The Great War had been the first watershed for me, the second had been my love for Rhoda. Fortunately our daughters were just too young to have to serve in the next war. When I look back at the years between my marriage and the beginning of the Second World War, they seem to have passed in a swift dream: the births of Alison and Juliet, our new house. . . .

People talk about depression a lot nowadays; I stopped writing love-poems after Rhoda left me, so I suppose I may have been 'depressed'. But I kept my nose to the grindstone. Work, and a glass of beer now and then, kept me going for a bit till I met Kitty Hall. I don't think she had any idea why I was so obviously unhappy – she thought it was either that I didn't enjoy my work or that I was still reeling from the blow about human nature I'd received during the war. No good telling her the blow I'd had from Rhoda was far worse.

Soon there was another war on the horizon. I joined the LDVs, the local defence volunteers, who were soon to become the Home Guard. Things had looked up at the mill at the end of the 1930s, and we were never so busy as we were in the second war. For once there was no slump. Our stuff was in demand, for officers' great-coats, for gaberdines, even for parachutes. Kitty went back to teaching part time in the war, and then full time when the girls eventually left home.

By the time Kitty and I could go abroad together in the early 1950s, both daughters lived away. When she was only twenty-three Ally had married an American she met at university and had gone to live in Chicago for several years. Juliet was away at university, afterwards working in London before she too married. They were luckier than my generation. I suppose I could have left home to work in London but there had been few jobs when I was in my early twenties. Nobody expected Juliet or Alison to follow me into textiles. Women did not then aspire to management positions and they were hardly like to have become weavers. Neither would I have advised any son, if I had had one, to follow in my footsteps.

Uncle Fred had been officially retired for years; he lived twenty-seven years longer than my father who died a few days before the war broke out. Fred never really let go his grip and still kept up with a skeleton staff, occasionally making money from mysterious deals.

Later, when I was in my mid-fifties, work once again became a problem; there was too much Far Eastern competition, and finally Uncle Albert, my father's old partner, sold up the mill. I worked for nine years in the office of another company.

As long as I had my books, I was content. I had never stopped reading, and for many years was busy writing my literary papers, taking part in debates in the town, visiting old houses with Kitty, and going to concerts and art exhibitions. Kitty and I have enjoyed holidays abroad for fifteen summers. Whenever we were in Italy, I used to wish that we could have stayed there and never returned home. We went to Spain too, where I tried out my long-ago-learned Spanish – I found I remembered quite a lot!

I am writing now in the March of 1970. Alison has told us her marriage is on the rocks. Our grandsons Thom and Mick, are in their early teens. Juliet married Andrew Considine ten years ago, and their daughter, my little granddaughter Rose, is nearly eight years old, her brother Paul six. We see them whenever we can, though they live in London and we are still here in the North.

Kitty possibly guesses I am writing something, but now she is retired she is busy looking for antiques with her friends, and as I do all my writing when she is out of the house she has never seen it. Sometimes I paint little pictures of the village and the church and the skies which I do show to her.

I believe another quotation may speak for me now. This is by Edward Gibbon:

> I must reluctantly observe that two causes, the abbreviation of time, and the failure of hope, will always tinge with a browner shade the evening of Life.

I know that I am mortally ill, and I know that Kitty knows it too, but I do not know if she knows I know. Neither do I know how long I shall have. She will probably have been told that I am going to die before the end of the year; that is my guess. I have thought it wiser so far to say nothing to the doctor about how long I might still have. This is not to spare myself but to spare Kitty. So long as she thinks something can be done to keep me alive she will be able to carry on.

I have told her many times how grateful I am for my married life. I hope I have made her happy. I am leaving her a private letter separately from this account.

She has been a good and loyal wife to me. I wish I had been a better husband.

I have just reread this short account of my life. My story stands as I have written it, but it will need a final coda which I shall not be able to write myself. I have had a happy life, all things considered, and I don't want to go. Apart from the cancer, everything in me works perfectly well. But it is never 'apart from', is it?

I trust I shall be seeing my daughters and my grandchildren

many times before I die. If it were not too dramatic to bid them farewell now as I write, whilst I am still feeling myself, I should say it here, but when they read this it will in any case be a second farewell – for who knows how many years after the first? I expect they are both thinking, How unlike Father all this is!

What there remains for me to say will chime so ill with the rest that I am adding a little codicil in a special envelope to be read by my daughters – by, you, Juliet and you Alison – when you have read the previous little exercise in nostalgia.

Sometimes I lament that I have done so little with my life. I believe any virtues I have had have been negative ones, but several times in the last quarter of a century – just after the war and twice later – my life has been turned upside down, and my inner life become turbulent. I did not breathe a word to anyone at either time, so nobody knew. Kitty was away nursing her sick mother on the second occasion, so did not accompany me on a hurried visit to London.

I must break my silence now. It will be up to you, Alison and Juliet, to decide what to do about it.

You will find in this box the envelope on which I have written <u>Please do not open this until you have read the enclosed type-script</u>. Open it now. I believe you will find the contents are self-explanatory.

Bless you both and all my grandchildren.   Eddie Bairstow.

PART TWO

PART TWO

CHAPTER ONE

Juliet

Juliet sat for a long time in the dusk thinking about her father's story. His childhood and his time in The Great War especially interested her, but she couldn't help wishing he had devoted more space in his story to his marriage and children. She supposed that for most people it was usually the first half of their lives that was the most exciting: when they were young, and full of hope, and everything was being experienced for the first time. She wished she had known her father when he was in his twenties.

How on earth had he remembered what he had written in the letters to Rhoda? Had he reinvented them, or had she sent the letters back to him? Perhaps he had taken copies, and kept them out of nostalgia? She recalled reading somewhere that in the last century people often used to make copies of the letters they sent. These letters were only sixty years old, and the 'last-century' would soon be the twentieth. . . .

She cast herself back in thought again to her own early years, and searched in the evening for some old family photographs, which she found eventually in an album. There were cabinet portraits of Eddie's babyhood and a few snaps of the family on Ilkley Moor all mixed up with some of her and her sister, their babyhood and childhood. Her mother must have stuck them in later. Even when you looked at them carefully, it was easy to confuse babies of different generations if it were not for the fashions in women's clothes. That was the comforting thing about babies – in a changing world they stayed the same. Her father, the baby of 1899, had worn longer clothes and always been wrapped in a shawl; there were no romper suits then, or 'Baby-Grows', but the years of his babyhood and childhood were not in the Dark Ages. In the very year of his birth, aspirin for headaches had arrived in England. During that first year of his life everyone must have been talking about 'the end of the century'.

Juliet looked more closely at the photographs in the album. The first was a cabinet one taken in Woolsford when he was about six months old. Propped up against a cushion, he was wearing a long white dress, ribbons at his wrists, and little leather shoes with pompoms peeped out from underneath the white skirt.

His eyes were wide open with an expression of amazement; the eyebrows were already marked and lent a certain quizzical quality to his gaze. His mouth was slightly open; his ears were large and shapely; his fair hair was swept into a tiny quiff. The fingers on the hand that was visible were long. It could have been any late Victorian or Edwardian baby, but it was her father.

On another photograph, he was about eight and her Aunt Flossie six, already wearing glasses for her short sight. They were both staring straight into the camera. Eddie was wearing a sailor suit with a wide-brimmed collar over a dark jacket, and Flossie was in a dark dress with a very fancy collar of lace, and a little locket on a pendant. Her hair was long and straggly, light brown, and she wore a flat bow at the back. The children were leaning towards each other. Eddie looked just as he did when he was a baby – big eyes, half-open mouth, large ears.

As a child Juliet had always been interested in Aunt Flossie's tales of her grandparents' lives. Some people are born nostalgic. Her sister Alison had never been like her in this. Alison did not believe in wasting words or living in the past. As a child, Alison had looked very like Eddie's mother, and Juliet had envied her curly golden hair and deft fingers. Going away to live in the States had been partly a symbol for Alison of cutting away the roots of the past with no regret.

When Andrew returned home he was tired and busy so Juliet told him only the bare bones of the story. He did not seem particularly surprised that his father-in-law had left them the story of what had mattered to him in his life.

That night, Juliet went to bed but was for hours unable to sleep. When she did fall asleep, thoughts of her father's past and her own life were still going through her mind. She kept surfacing from sleep, thinking about herself as much as her father. To think that most of what she had read that afternoon had happened before she herself was even thought of, before her father had ever met her mother!

Was Rhoda Moore still alive and, if she was, where was she now? Did she still live in New Zealand? She had never heard her father mention her, though she remembered a vague reference he'd once made to the British Empire Exhibition. Her father had clearly not kept up with Alec Moore, who appeared to have moved away from the district. Was he still alive?

Thoughts about her father, his childhood and youth, and about her own, were still tangling around in her head in the morning after that restless night.

The whole affair with Rhoda did not appear to her to make much sense. Had he been totally deluded by the young woman? She did not understand why Rhoda had dumped him in such an unpleasant way. Surely it couldn't have been because she'd gone to bed with him? They'd known each other for four years, after all, and she had the distinct impression from her father's story that Rhoda was not exactly inexperienced. He said that he did not know whether she had allowed other men to make love to her, but Juliet imagined that he did not consider this at the time, only later.

In the morning she tried to telephone her sister in Cambridge, where Alison was now living with Clive. As Juliet had thought, they had still not yet returned from the conference in Sweden. Her nephew Thom told her they were expected home in two days.

What moral had their father wanted them to draw from this story of his lost love? Or was there no moral and he had just felt like unburdening himself?

She had put aside the big envelope, had as yet said nothing to Andrew about it. It might contain some of her father's poems. She would wait to open it in Alison's presence.

She was wrong about the poems, for whatever the truth of Eddie Bairstow's life had been, it was what was in the as yet unopened envelope lying innocently on the table beside her that was to surprise them all most.

Having now read the story of her father's trials and tribulations, Juliet thought she might one day commit her own memories to paper. She could begin by writing down a few impressions of her family, especially of her father, whilst she waited to tell Alison about it all. Edward Bairstow's words had brought back forgotten events in her own past, had reminded her of her own unrequited loves, and all the ups and downs of her own youth. After more than twenty years of marriage, that all appeared distant, belonging to another world, as far away from her now as her father's youth. Perhaps though she had been luckier than her father.

She thought about her own early memories of him, as he had been in the latter part of his story after his marriage. She'd like to reflect systematically on what he had written, compare it with her own recollections, but the more she thought about him, the more he appeared to slip and slide away. She tried to remember what he had told her as a child about The Great War – not much – and also spared a thought for her mother, intrigued by their relationship. What she had just read certainly obliged her to reassess her father, and to reconsider her own character, as well as those of her parents.

Had the father she had known been a quite different person from the one she had always imagined she knew well? His revelations were not, she supposed, extraordinary, unless you had known the man himself. It was the manner of their arrival, so long after his death, that was untypical, and there was still the question of the unopened envelope still at the bottom of the box.

At the end of the week, Juliet finally got through to Alison who said she would come to London in a few days. On the phone, she summarized the news about their father's early love. Alison listened, a little dismissively, she thought.

'This Rhoda probably distrusted his romantic nature – though she'd be flattered by his devotion,' she said.

During the afternoon while Juliet sat waiting for her sister to arrive, she was still caught up in thoughts of her own youth. She had been rereading some of her father's story, and the envelope was waiting on the table for them to open together.

Alison arrived about two o'clock, looking preoccupied, but smart and healthy. Juliet offered her a cup of coffee, since Alison said she'd had a snack on the train. Over the coffee, Alison expatiated upon her husband's work problems and about her younger son Mick's new job in a lab; then she said,

'Well – where is it?'

Juliet brought the box up to her. 'You'd better take it with you and have a good read – unless you want to stay the night and read it here.'

'No, I've to get back tonight. What does Andrew think about Father's story?'

'Oh, he had a quick look, but he's busy. I thought he might be quite interested in the war bits. Father seems to have spent an awful amount of time just getting lost. I can't find on the map of France all the places he mentions.'

'They were probably just little villages and tiny rivers. Were you thinking of making a pilgrimage there?'

Juliet sensed a certain amount of dry irony in her sister's voice. She was aware that Alison thought her sentimental.

'I told you I'd wait for you to open this,' she said. 'Father wanted us both to have read his story before opening it.'

'Well, you conveyed the gist to me,' replied her sister. 'I trust your powers of précis. I think we had better open it now together, don't you?' But she looked as if the envelope might bite her when Juliet handed it over.

She took it, then put it down, again, saying, 'Has the autobiography made you believe that nobody in the family really understood him?'

'Are you reluctant to take the plunge Ally?' Her sister was silent, so Juliet went on, 'I suppose it's hard for children to see their parents as young and fallible? Father didn't seem too complicated, did he? I always supposed that long before I was born he'd come to terms with his lack of success.'

'I hate those phrases "come to terms with", "settle for". Why should people settle for what they don't really want in order to pretend to be happy? Some people just aren't happy. Why should we be happy anyway?' stated Alison fiercely.

'But, Alison, Father was not one of those people. He had quite a happy nature, I think.'

'But what you are saying is that if he hadn't nursed further ambitions, if he'd been more like his parents, he'd have been even happier.' Her sister was a great arguer.

'Who knows?' Juliet answered, adding, 'How rich some people's inner lives must be! – people who glimpse things that others don't bother their heads about, or just miss. I mean, I know music meant a lot to Father, and country walks – just as they did to Auntie Flossie, but he got something special from words. What do you think of when you think of him? I think of books. How would *you* have described him?'

Alison thought for a bit, and then said: 'He was good at making slip-knots. I used to envy his neat parcel making. And he was very obstinate. Also, he enjoyed playing billiards at the village Conservative Club, and he loved Italy. Will that do?' She cocked her head on one side.

Her elegant sister was very decided in her views, Juliet thought. 'What about his writing?' asked Juliet.

'Yes, his writing. Perhaps he was meant to be a consumer of literature rather than a writer.'

'But he was so creative!'

'All right then, have it your own way. Now, that envelope. We'd better open it,' said Alison brusquely.

'Your turn,' said Juliet, 'since I had the pleasure of seeing the rest before you.'

It felt quite bulky. Alison was handed a paper knife and opened the envelope neatly.

Inside the big one, there were other envelopes all neatly numbered. Alison took them out one by one. 'When did Father sort all this out? Surely Mother would have noticed?' she remarked.

'She'd be out with her friend, Miss Hoyle. You won't remember – you weren't in England. When there was a remission, Father always told her he preferred to stay at home and read and she must get out to enjoy herself.'

'And the last remission lasted about six weeks, didn't it? He probably imagined she'd have some nursing of him to do before the end.'

'Yes, but he died very quickly once he got to hospital for a blood transfusion that last time.'

They were quiet for a few moments. Alison put down the paper knife, but then with a sigh she took it up again. 'This is what he wanted us to do,' said Juliet.

On the outside of the envelope on the top was printed:

FOR MY DAUGHTERS

Letter Number 1
(Read this first.
E.B. August 10th 1970)

The date was less than three months before he died. The other letters were numbered in turn 2, 3, 4, and 5.

Some of them looked as if they were in the envelopes in which they had been posted to their father at his business address, some with old New Zealand stamps.

Alison handed Juliet the paper-knife, saying, with a pretence of boredom, 'Your turn now.' Was her big sister even a little nervous?

Juliet slit open the first envelope, one that had no stamps on it.

The letter inside was dated July 10th 1970 and was in their father's flowing hand that made long loops of the 'g's and 'y's.

145

My dear Ally and July

You will by now have read my unremarkable story. I wanted to write it before I died and I also needed you to read it before you read the contents of the other envelopes here.

At the end of 1946 I received a letter from a young man called Archie Marriott who had been in the army during the last two years of the war and ended up waiting to serve in the Pacific – which fortunately never happened because of the detonation of the atom bomb and the end of WW2 in August 1945.

I was not sure whether to believe what he said in his letter. I'm afraid I tore it up at the time and now wish I had not. What he told me both amazed me and also horrified me. I replied to him though, and he wrote to me again the following year (see letter no. 2, 1947) to tell me that his father had died. To make a long story short, he came over to London to see me eight years later, in 1955.

Juliet may remember the April week when her mother and myself were staying with Kitty's cousin George in West London. You were already married, Alison, and in the States, but you, Juliet, were living in Pimlico at the time of our visit. I remember your mother was very critical about your domestic arrangements.

One afternoon I took the opportunity to visit the Charing Cross Road looking for book bargains, but I also met Archie Marriott at a Lyons Corner House. He was thirty years old at our first meeting and was just about to be married. Read the letter (no. 3) which he wrote to me on his return home. He did marry shortly afterwards and became the father of a son, Alexander.

Ten years later – five years ago now – in 1965, he wrote again. His mother had just died (see letter no. 4.) I met him again when he was in Europe with his wife Thelma, and their son Alexander, who was now almost ten years old.

The fifth envelope is the one to read last and tells you all you need to know, but I expect you will have guessed by now that Archie is Rhoda's son.

If you think all this is nothing to do with you, I do earnestly beg you to believe what you read. Read the letters and then act upon them. Do not turn over the page till you have read them all.

There was another fresh page to follow but they did as they were told.

They held their breath as Alison opened the second envelope, and all the following letters, which they then passed between them. Letter no.2 was dated 2.9.1946, and read:

Dear Mr Bairstow,

Mother wants me to let you know that her husband Arthur has just died.

I too wanted to tell you this. As I explained in my first letter to you last year, I have wanted to meet you ever since Mother told me the truth. Don't worry – she will not come over to England! – and I have no wish to interfere in your life. I just want to keep in touch with you now and again, if you will. What Mother did was unforgivable – she says so herself but she wants you to forgive her.

There was an addition in Eddie's hand:

I wrote to Rhoda in '47 and she replied saying it was as if a burden had been lifted that she had been carrying all her married life.

Letter no. 3, 1955 had a pencilled note:

This was written after meeting me in London. E.B.

Dear Eddie,

It was wonderful meeting you. I had to tell Mother all we said and did. As I told you in London, ever since her husband died she has been a different person. . . .

The letter went on to describe Archie's feelings at meeting Eddie for the first time. 'It was all so natural,' he wrote.

Alison and Juliet were passing these letters backwards and forwards to each other, reading and then rereading them.

The fourth letter was dated 1956 and it said:

Thelma gave birth to a son this morning. Mother is delighted and is already looking for resemblances. Thelma knows Mother's story. . . .

The fifth letter said:

I am the bearer of very sad news. Mother died yesterday – very suddenly – of a totally unexpected heart-attack. Alex is inconsolable – he was very fond of his Grandma. I wish we could all meet without subterfuges – ourselves and your wife and daughters and your English and American grandchildren but we will go by your advice not to upset your wife. . . .

They returned to the page they had been told not to read before all the other letters had been read.
'Read it aloud,' commanded Alison.
Juliet read out what their father had written to them:

Now you have read all the enclosed letters, you will have guessed that Archie is my son, and that you have a half-brother. Make no mistake about it, Archie is who his mother told him he was! Rhoda had no children with Arthur Marriott.

It is my earnest hope that you will arrange to meet him on his next visit to England. He is an intelligent man and travels round quite a lot in Europe and the States. He's a businessman, as you might expect, involved in import and export, but he is a cultivated person.

I am enclosing a snapshot of Archie and his wife and son taken recently. . . .

Juliet looked up. 'There are still a few more paragraphs. He doesn't seem to want to finish, to stop writing, to leave us.'
'Let me see the snap!' exclaimed Alison.
Archie was of medium height and dark. Maybe he had some of his mother's looks. His wife was small and pretty. The fair-haired boy was the image of one of the cabinet photographs of their

father that Juliet had been looking at just recently. On the back of this photograph Archie had written: *We think Alexander Edward looks just like his grandfather*.

'No pictures of her husband,' said Alison. 'Was Rhoda dark?'

'Yes, I think he said so in his story.'

'His *magnum opus*,' said Alison.

She looked faintly put out. Perhaps she had wanted her sons to be the only grown-up grandsons of their father.

'Your Thom is a year older than this Alexander,' said Juliet, to cheer her up.

'So I suppose you believe all this then?' said Alison angrily.

'Well, of course I do.'

'*I* find it all rather tasteless and novelettish,' said her sister. 'Hinting that Mother ought to have welcomed meeting her husband's by-blow!'

'But Ally, it was all over years before Mother and Father even met.'

'Well, how would you feel if Andrew suddenly introduced you to his long-lost bastard?'

'As a matter of fact, I'd be intrigued,' said Juliet. 'It might settle which attributes of Rose and Paul didn't come from me.'

Alison was a moment trying to work out what she meant.

'Well, we don't know what Rhoda's husband looked like,' she said finally.

Juliet was rereading to the end of the very last letter. Eventually she handed it over to her sister. 'You read this bit.'

Alison complied.

I expect you had already put two and two together. I didn't want it to be a shock for you. Archie *is* my son, there is no mistaking that. . . .

'He can't stop saying it can he?' said Alison.

When I saw him, for the first time, I was absolutely certain. Rhoda's husband never suspected and Rhoda herself sometimes

149

could not believe it. She might have lost my child, as women do early on, and Archie might have been a premature baby, she said. But she and her husband had no other children, and Archie was completely unlike his father. I think he looks a little like how I remember his Uncle Alec, after whom he was named. Rhoda had always really known the truth, Archie told me, and had told him when he went off to the war.

'In case he never came back, I suppose,' said Alison. Juliet took the page from her and read it aloud:

It took me a long time – a year to get used to the idea. I never wished to hurt your mother; that is why I have held off telling you before your mother's death, however far away in the future that may be. I asked my solicitor to communicate with Archie three months after Kitty died so I expect you will shortly be receiving a letter from him too. Alex is a most handsome lad. I am pleased that his second name is mine. He is only fifteen as I write but is a serious-minded boy.

I apologize if I have upset either of you. I reckoned that if you read my story first you'd be better prepared for the truth.

'I wonder if he'd have written his story in any case,' said Alison. 'You said he was obsessed by Rhoda.'

I won't go into the details of why Rhoda left me; she had been brought up to wealth and she was not in love with me. She liked me and was fond of me and it was only her unusual sexual generosity that led to her finding herself pregnant only three weeks after she said goodbye to me. . . .

'I expect she got the husband – he wasn't that then – Arthur, I mean, to go to bed with her as speedily as possible,' said Alison. 'Or perhaps she'd been with him earlier on, before she met Father in Wembley! Had you thought of that?'
Juliet was silent.

I long ago forgave Rhoda, though I never forgot her. It took me fifteen years to wonder whether perhaps it was all for the best. I am glad that Arthur Marriott never knew that Archie was not his. I'm afraid that Rhoda appears to have fallen out of love with her husband after only a few years. He was a ladies' man and a gambler, rich but unreliable, unlike myself.

It is Archie who has insisted, if you are willing, that he makes your acquaintance, however far away in the future that day will be.

If you have any objection to meeting him, he will of course not insist. He is an honourable man with a good mind and a kind nature.

I give you all my blessing.

You have a lot in common, all of you. I hope that you will one day introduce Archie's son, my grandson, Alexander Edward – they always call him Alex – to Thom and Mick, and Rose and Paul.

Forgive the melodrama, and remember I love you all, just as I came late in life to love Archie. What I discovered, and have now known for over twenty years, was the reason for my wanting to tell you about my youth.

Your loving father
Edward Bairstow.

There were tears making Juliet's throat tight as she finished reading this. Alison however was either unmoved or did not show her feelings so easily. 'This Archie Marriott shouldn't have written to Father right at the beginning in 1946 – the letter he *didn't* enclose,' said Alison. 'He should have left it to his mother to write!'

'He was only twenty-one. He'd just learned who his real father was. I think he probably did it against his mother's wishes,' said Juliet.

'Rhoda might have been angry, but I bet she was glad he'd written in the end. Why else should she tell him to write when Arthur Marriott died? Do you think Rhoda and Father went on writing to each other after that? It was some years before she died.'

'I don't imagine either would want to, really – and Father would always be loyal to Mother,' said Juliet.

'I suppose they might have written just once or twice.'

'Rhoda must have been in love with this antipodean cousin long before she met Dad,' said Juliet after a pause. 'From what you told me on the phone, it's obvious now why poor Father couldn't get anywhere with her.'

'But why couldn't she just have *told* him?'

'Perhaps she was hedging her bets.'

'I think,' said Juliet slowly, 'that after Eddie – Father – made love to her in London she might have intended to leave Arthur, but she was in love with him and she just couldn't. Seeing him again must have shown her she was in love with *him* and not with Father.'

'Father might have thought she left him because he'd "misused" her – you know how romantic he was. He'd be guilty about the sex – they all were, weren't they, in those days?'

'He'd think she was ashamed? Little did he know!'

'I'm sure he'd blame himself – full of guilt – he wouldn't want to stress that in his letter to us. I suppose before she found she was pregnant with Dad's baby she'd decided, if Arthur asked her, to marry him.'

'Yes, I imagine she'd decided even when she was being made love to by Father during those two days in London. She'd already know Arthur was to join the party in Europe for an extended tour. That's why she'd go, not to please the family. She'd already been his lover, I'm sure. Perhaps for ages.'

'Unusual for those unenlightened days.'

'I suppose some women did, they just didn't talk about it. All those trips to visit relatives – she'd arrange it all nicely. He was probably over here quite a lot on business,' said Juliet, thinking the young Rhoda had taken risks. Who was to say she hadn't been right to do so?

'Archie's existence is a surprise but not a shock,' stated Alison. 'As soon as she saw this Arthur again she'd find she still loved him. He was a wealthy man.'

'I don't think that would have counted with her,' said Juliet.

'Oh, you are such a romantic! I bet it did!'

'She'd know quite soon she was pregnant. Even before she met up with Arthur.'

'Long enough for her to give poor unsuspecting Marriott the impression it was his baby – she was a quick worker. Unless of course he thought her condition was the result of an earlier episode with him.'

'Don't you think that if Arthur had not asked her to marry him – when she told him she was expecting a baby, I mean – she would have come back to Father?'

'Yes, I expect she would. But her conscience – after allowing Eddie to make love to her – might have told her she ought to refuse to be tempted by her older lover. But as you said, she was in love with him so she couldn't give him up.'

'She said in that letter he quotes, *I am truly sorry.*'

'I expect she was. . . .'

'She must have revealed the pregnancy in Nice,' Juliet went on. 'It would have been two months after she'd been with Father – and she'd think this Arthur might be the sort of man who'd like the idea of an elopement, so she'd persuade him to "persuade" her to get wed at the British Consulate.'

'You don't know all that – you're just guessing. Maybe our brother Archie will enlighten us.'

'I can't believe her husband *never* knew that Archie was not his. I'm sure I'd have guessed,' said Alison. 'She told her son *before* his "father", Arthur died, so she must have sworn him to secrecy. Or maybe by then she'd been separated for quite a long time from her husband. Father hints he wasn't very satisfactory.'

'Oh, that might just be male jealousy!'

'But once Archie knew, he'd want to meet his real father. People do, even young men.'

'What if Father had refused to believe her, or refused to see Archie?'

'She'd know he wouldn't do that! Remember, she knew him very well when they were young. People don't change that much. I just think it's sad they couldn't all meet, along with Mother. I wonder if there were any other letters between him and Rhoda after the truth was revealed? He didn't send us any of those to read. She wouldn't want to come to England to see him because of Mother. I wish we had a photograph of her.'

'Oh well, there's a lot he's not saying, isn't there? It was Father who didn't want Mother to know anything at all about it – maybe Rhoda wished he would? Fancy waiting for us to be enlightened only after Mother died. I'd never have thought he could plan all that.'

'I think he was ashamed, you know, not only of having seduced Rhoda, but I believe he really loved Mother. Maybe not as passionately as Rhoda, but he wouldn't want to hurt her. He'd never tell her about those two nights he'd spent with Rhoda. If he mentioned her she'd just think it was an unrequited love—'

'Which it was—'

'Yes, but in those days, for a conventional person like Mother, his even having loved another woman might have put her off him.'

Alison said, in a rare burst of the old Alison, 'It's *men* who are romantic – more than women, I believe. Women are more practical in their affections.'

'Isn't it just that similarities of temperament are more important than the differences between men and women?'

'But what did Rhoda have in common with Father? Mother probably had more.'

They went on turning it all over in their minds as they made a pot of tea and reread the letters more closely. It was odd knowing all this about their own father years after he had died. What would they do about it all?

Juliet wanted to write to Archie straight away. Alison was more cautious.

'Well, you write to Archie if you must,' she said. 'I'd rather think about it a bit longer. It'll take me some time to get used to a half-sibling.'

Juliet thought, her sons have got some of those already. Alison's first husband Harry had married again and had a son and a daughter. Perhaps that was why her sister was rather sore about Father's bombshell? In some matters Alison was more conventional than she had been in the past, and yet she claimed she was now a feminist. Juliet had noticed she hadn't liked the idea of Rhoda's falling out of love with her husband. It was too like her Harry falling out of love with her.

Alison finally made preparations to return in the evening to Cambridge, her father's story in her briefcase. The letters were to be left with her sister.

'Do you think her brother Alec ever knew Rhoda's secret?' said Juliet on the doorstep, just as Alison turned to leave.

'I doubt it. He may still be alive. Perhaps this Archie sees him still.'

'Father nursed his own secret well. I'm so glad he saw Archie again a few years before he died.'

'You write to him,' Alison reiterated. 'That's what you're good at.'

She added that she would be prepared to see this half-brother if he came over, but drew the line at a long exchange of correspondence.

When Alison had gone and Juliet was getting supper ready, she decided she had got into a middle-aged rut. Reading the contents of those envelopes had put her in turmoil, yet might not these unexpected revelations revivify her? She had become used to feeling a little dull. She usually got on with her work, kept the house going, looked forward to an occasional holiday abroad, usually in Italy which, as Alison had said, had been their father's favourite country too. But now there was the possibility of acquiring a brother. . . .

She was missing talking to her children about it all, especially to Rose, whose absence she compensated for by talking to Booth, her old tabby-cat, to calm herself down.

'I've got a new brother. I expect you have dozens of brothers you've never seen.'

She thought, I'm quite presentable, and I have a good part time job, even if it's a rather boring job in a library. I still have a few ideas in my head, so there's no need for me to be nervous of meeting Archie Marriott. She supposed he still used that name? How would he take to new sisters not much younger than himself? Would he think she was a chip off the old block, or a suburban housewife with an interest in roses, cats, detective stories and the solving of crosswords. I'm no different from Grandpa Bairstow, she thought. His supreme delights in life, she well remembered, were his buying Grandma old jewellery, cultivating his roses, and doing the *Sunday Chronicle* crossword. Juliet mused over her grandparents as she prepared the supper. Grandma Bairstow had adored jewellery, wore heavy beads and brooches, the sort Juliet liked. What would Aunt Flossie have thought about it all – Flossie who had died seven years ago, who always smelt of her favourite scent, lily of the valley, and was a very kind spinster lady? Aunt Flossie would have been this Archie Marriott's aunt too, and Grandpa and Grandma his own grandparents! He had missed them all.

But Archie Marriott needn't be interested in herself as anything more than a relative he'd unaccountably missed knowing earlier.

Yet someone else's existence could alter the balance of a family.

A week or two later, Juliet sent Alison the draft of her letter to their half-brother, needing her to approve of it. She asked Alison to add her own message, or, if she did not like what she had written, to write the letter herself. Alison might not like her turn of phrase, and she thought that as the elder sister Alison ought to take the lead now and then.

'Don't let off all your guns at once,' wrote Alison on return. 'You can keep the gush till later.'

But she said it would do, if Juliet were to omit her thoughts about Eddie and Rhoda and confine herself to welcoming him to the family and expressing pleasure that at last they would know each other. Juliet had written that she thought it would have been better to have been able to sort everything out twelve years earlier. She'd calculated that Archie would now be fifty-seven.

Alison said she sounded too eager. Alison had changed, was more sceptical about everything, no longer the idealistic, optimistic extrovert she had once been. The experience of infidelity and divorce still festered, even if her new partner, Clive Sands, was utterly trustworthy and himself trusted her judgement. Alison did not approve of emotional statements. Juliet had tried to sound sensible and rational whilst in truth she was seething with excitement and anticipation, but she'd obviously failed.

Andrew, interested rather than intrigued by what had happened, also read the draft and pointed out a few improvements. He did not have that obsessive interest in family links which his wife had always had, and was sceptical himself about such things as genes and mysterious inheritances. Juliet supposed he was good for her, curbing her more romantic notions.

'We don't know what he'll be like,' said Andrew, 'He might be an enormous sixteen-stone ex-rugger player with an obsessive interest in beer.'

'Not likely,' said his wife.

Archie Marriott (he still kept his 'official' father's name) wrote back almost immediately. He had rather stylish handwriting and a good turn of phrase. First he said how sorry he was their mother had died. He still missed *his* mother, he said. He added that he had often been tempted to write to them but had promised their father he would not do so until he had heard from them. He told them a little about himself – he had a business in Wellington – and about his wife, a teacher of drama, and his son Alexander, who appeared to be involved in some ecological activity. He and Alexander proposed to come over to London in mid December if that would suit them.

'To enjoy a good old English winter', he wrote.

'He and his wife were in Oxford five years ago,' Juliet told her sister. 'And when they were in London they looked up our address on the map. Father must have briefed him about my married name. Anyway, Archie had wondered whether to walk past our house and possibly see one of his long-lost sisters!'

Alison snorted when she read this. 'He sounds as romantic as you,' she said.

'Actually, I think we must both have inherited it from Father,' Juliet replied rather frostily.

'What else does he say?' asked Alison, sounding as if she was making a big effort to be interested.

' "I shall just come over with Alex",' quoted Juliet. ' "Thelma thinks it would be better the first time we met for us three to absorb each other without an in-law problem, though we shall of course look forward to meeting your husband. Thelma is very independent and is anyway busy with college work. She says she'll wait to hear all about it from me. You are in any case invited to come over and spend a holiday with us in New Zealand whenever it suits you – your sister and her family too".'

'So it's not just our long-lost brother who's coming over to see us but a cousin for the children?'

'That's right,' said Juliet. 'Isn't it exciting! He's twenty-seven. Archie sent a photo – I'll send it on to you. He looks a nice young man.'

In a few months Archie Marriott and his son Alexander Edward Marriott would arrive. Rose and Paul Considine and Alison's two sons would meet a new uncle and a new cousin.

How would they all get on with each other, she wondered.

It was some time before she could find the time to write down some of her own memories, as she had promised herself. Her father's story had made her want to analyse her idea of him, to compare her memories with his. The writing could now be ostensibly for Archie. But writing was an indulgence; there was always the house to see to, and the garden, and the shopping, and the cooking, not to mention her part-time work in Bloomsbury. How did people ever have time on their hands? She forgot that she was always reading, and that this accounted for many hours. Soon there would be Christmas and then the half-dreaded, half-longed-for visit.

She would show only what she had written about her father to Archie, and then only if she got on well with him when he came to London. But to amuse herself she tried to analyse her parents' marriage, feeling a little disloyal even as she did so.

Their mother, Kitty Hall, had been an intelligent, capable young teacher, well known in the town when she married their father in 1929. He was thirty at his wedding, Kitty a year younger.

On her good days their mother was inclined to say that her marriage to Eddie Bairstow had been a love-match, and that she and he were ideally suited, each complementing the other, not at all alike.

She had been the sort of managing, competent person their father probably needed. Everyone knew her to be clever. Juliet herself had once remarked to her sister that she doubted their mother had been a truly self-sufficient character. 'But on the other hand I don't think Mother was a very feminine sort of person,' she had added.

'She wasn't as self-sufficient as a man,' her just-divorced sister had commented. They had often discussed how young men put everything into compartments, but it did not seem to Juliet after reading his account that their father had been like this. It was true though that his wife had appeared to feel she ought to defer to men, and in practice did defer, verbally and in public, to her husband, though she then usually did what she wanted. She'd been brought up to think men were superior creatures, but never believed a word of it.

How could I describe Father to a stranger? Juliet wondered – for he *is* a stranger though he's our flesh and blood. And Father is still inextricably entwined with Mother in my memories. I never knew him as an individual really.

Even before they grew up she and her sister had often wondered why their parents had married, and had discussed their characters. Their mother was the energetic one, the mover and shaker. Rhoda didn't sound a bit like her.

Juliet began her account one dark November day, and finished it just before Christmas.

CHAPTER TWO

Memories

Alison always said Father was a dark horse but I thought she was just being dramatic. She took after Mother in that. Father had been, or appeared to be, easy-going and happy. When I was a child I had liked him better than Mother because he was kind and easy-going.

My friends often said Father was most amusing, for he liked to entertain intelligent young women, so long as they would also listen to him. I think he occasionally needed a bit of an audience. Mother had once been his audience but she was too busy to put him first most of the time in my childhood and adolescence.

Mother had no sons – I don't know how they would have turned out if she had. . . .

Alison has two sons, thought Juliet, but, like Mother, she is competent, even rather bossy. Mother always appeared to approve of this, though not if it came into conflict with her own wishes.

Oh dear, she'd better not write *that* if she were going to show this to anyone but Andrew.

Alison had had a very different youth from her own. Enjoying America, married to a successful academic, and a first-time mother in her twenties she'd seemed ecstatically happy. But eventually her husband had fallen in love with someone else, which had led, inevitably it seemed, to their divorce and her eventual return home.

Mother and Father would never have been unfaithful to each

other, she decided. As for divorce, it would never have occurred to them. They thought they were happily married. Perhaps they were. Adolescents judged their parents sternly. As you grew older, and up, and looked back, you thought they could have chosen a worse partner for themselves. She remembered resolving, during the period when she did not get on very well with her mother, that she would let her arrows shower upon her, would try for a day or two to bear criticism nobly and in silence, but she always failed. Somehow, she felt that suppressing her bad thoughts even to herself would be being untrue to herself.

Her father was luckier than she was in this. As far as she knew he had not had any conflict with his own parents, or he had not alluded to any. They'd have been only too relieved that he had come back from those trenches. Maybe they had spoiled him. . . .

She returned to her typewriter:

I was seen as the dreamy one. I nurtured the idea in myself that I was highly strung, though my mother, capable of drama when necessary as far as her own interests were concerned, was down to earth towards her children's fancies. Father was more sympathetic towards my sensitivities, even if I never had the impression that he ever bothered his head too much about his children. It was Mother who agonized over us. I must confess that I see my own childhood a little differently from the way my father described it. I arrived late on the scene of course.

Mother was a fairly astute woman. Had her husband ever hinted to her about his disappointed love? She always seemed to me to accept what he felt for her as only her due, but I don't know if she ever knew the extent of his earlier passion for another woman, or whether she ever guessed he had been in love before, or had any idea about what she would certainly have called romantic infatuation.

Mother was very respectful of her husband's intellect and literary powers, knowing they were of a different kind from her own. When I was a student I thought that my father should have gone to university, should have had some training, but a little later I began to realize that he had read more than most people I knew, and he didn't need or wish to make a job of literature. It was his life-blood, his joy, his inner life, his *raison d'être*. He was lucky – I have always thought so – lucky to have such a passion, even if I now know he had not been lucky in love, never mind in business.

Mother always called Father 'Edward', never 'Eddie', the name his own family called him by. I think she wanted one part of him that did not belong to 'them'. She was a very possessive woman. Father always left domestic matters to her, matters that included the more tedious procedures involved with bringing up children. That was par for the course at the time, I suppose. It probably still is, in spite of all we hear of the New Man. But our father could never have been a strict *paterfamilias*, and his sins were those of omission rather than commission. For example, unlike Mother, Father would never answer one's persistent enquiries if he happened to be reading a book. Mother would always put down whatever she was doing if you needed help or a question answered.

I'd have been interested to know what Mother and Father were like together before their children came along; I suppose many people would like to know that about their parents. Naturally, we were always told that it was a love-match, and I'd have been surprised to have been told that there had been someone else in Father's life. Surprised, but also pleased, for I often thought Mother did not quite deserve her husband. He was always very grateful for her housekeeping, her hard work, her brains, and her contribution to expenses. With the wisdom of hindsight I now wonder if he had changed since he was a young man. Had Rhoda left him unable to love another woman as much? Suspicious of the sex? Or *better* able to love? Mother never discounted the feelings he had for her: he was a good husband if not a magnificent provider. She would have liked to be better off financially, but Father never complained on that score, nor of her sharp tongue. She'd often analyse his family mercilessly: dear old Grandpa Bairstow, who died when I was seven, and Grandma, who had once been a beauty and was easy-going and cheerful, if a little timid. Father's sister Auntie Flossie was a favourite with both Alison and myself and she adored our father, her only brother. But Mother often used to sniff and say she'd have done better to find herself a husband. Countless women of Flossie's generation however were left on the shelf when three-quarters of a million young men did not come back from The Great War. . . .

She'd better hurry up and write something about her father if Archie Marriott was ever to read it. . . .

From the outside, I don't think Father changed his way of life very much after Rhoda had abandoned him. He went on doing the same work in the same place, and his writing efforts must have given him some relief. Otherwise I suppose he just suffered in silence. It would have been no good going away to find different work after his marriage for there was none in the depression that started in 1929. He never gave farming in Thirksay another try: I suppose the idea occurred to him several times, especially after the disappoint-ment of his hopes with Rhoda, and he could never quite let it go. But he stayed put, turned his life inward, and went through the motions of joining small town life.

Had he really enjoyed it, she wondered. He'd appeared to. Had he seen himself as a failure? He never complained about his fortune in life, but in worldly terms he was not a success. He wasn't suited to business, as Mother was always telling him. He'd failed with Rhoda, and not made a success of business. Also (what he cared about far more than business success and money) he had failed to get his poems and plays and short stories published.

I read some of his plays when I was a child, and I was puzzled by them. I know now that he was trying to write brittle sophisticated Noel Coward-type productions, and short stories with plots and twists and turns. He must have thought these would be more publishable than poetry, his first love. He went on writing parodies, and joined the debating society, and continued to attend the Woolsford Literary Circle, devoting each winter to the study of a writer he liked, presenting his yearly paper there. In spite of lack of worldly success the father I knew always appeared busy and happy – happier than Mother. Perhaps his marriage was his one real success?

Both our parents had lived through difficult times. Father did not lack will-power, and he did have some literary talent, but perhaps he had used up most of his idealism and energy on Rhoda? In spite of his romantic proclivities, he was easy-going, I mean in the conduct of his married life and towards his work, but I suspect he was always a little 'out of sync' with the times. Whatever he thought about himself (and he must have thought about his life a good deal, especially once he knew he had a son far away!) he did spend his life doing work for which he was not really suited. Was he also living with a woman who could only be second-best?

The fact that he had to work had probably been good for him. At several times in his life work had not been easy to find, and he was still working for various members of the Bairstow family around the time Alison was born. Did he guess that eventually the Bairstow family mill would be sold up, and that would be the end of that? He was old when he found work in the office of another firm.

As I hope I have conveyed, he was a good husband to Mother and a kind father to his two daughters. But if it had not been for us, his family, might he eventually have fallen in love again, written out of that experience, and had a different sort of life?

He died relatively young – young anyway for modern times. Even by the time he died, more and more people were living into their late eighties and nineties, but Father was only seventy when cancer caught up with him. If he had been luckier, he would have been amongst those very old men whose lives spanned a century, whom my husband and I recently watched on television talking about their army service in The Great War in France.

The Great War is just about to pass out of living memory, said a writer who was gathering together the shards of memory left in the minds of that war's oldest survivors. We watched their last return journey to the Somme, and her words remained with us. I found them unbearably poignant. For however long these old men lived, the war would be alive. But no old men, even those luckier than my father, live for ever. Perhaps that war will still remain in some way in the borrowed memories of the children of these men's children, and be told to their children and grandchildren.

I know it remains in mine because of Father . . .

It had given her a jolt to read what her father said about his daughters as little children, and about their home. Like seeing something through the wrong end of a telescope. Time was such an odd thing; what she saw as a long-distant past was much fresher in Eddie's mind when he wrote his story. But now she saw it doubly as part of his life and part of hers and Alison. And yet it was all done, all over, long ago.

She had so often recalled that bright and breezy new house; even, she remembered, the morning Eddie's story had arrived. Her memory of her childhood made her feel not only a nostalgic regret, but also a sort of fury that the passage of time cheated people of their past memories.

Another odd thing was that when she had looked in the *Radio Times* to see what the music had been which had transported her to the past, she discovered it was called *Green Tulips*, the very piece of music that her father had written about, the music that took *him* back too. Her memories had already merged into her father's.

Was that because similar kinds of people remembered similar things?

Poetry did the same thing for her as music, just as it had done for Eddie. Not just a poem in itself but the time when she had first read or heard it.

Her father would often quote a line from that poem of Cowper's:

cups that cheer but not inebriate

and these words took her back to the side of the roaring coal-fire

166

he had made up, and the sight of the tea-trolley wheeled into the dining-room loaded with blue teapot, blue cups, and silver cake-stand bearing a half-eaten Christmas cake.

Yes, Cowper had stood for married domesticity, just as her parents' oft quoted Tennyson reminded her of a time when she was about fifteen:

> I falter where I firmly trod,
> And falling with my weight of cares
> Upon the great world's altar stairs
> That slope through darkness up to God.
>
> I stretch lame hands of faith, and grope,
> And gather dust and chaff, and call
> To what I feel is Lord of all,
> And faintly trust the larger hope.

Her mother's quoting this one day had suddenly alerted her to the truth that neither of her parents possessed a genuine Christian belief. They had sent Alison and her as children to church and Sunday school only to give them the opportunity of choice, perhaps to believe in a god they had not truly been able to believe in themselves. Juliet could remember seeing her father in church once, and that was to give thanks for victory at the end of the Second World War.

How could she convey all this? And would Archie even be interested?

She realized she was writing for herself, not really for her newly discovered brother. Her mother's death and then the shock of her father's revelations had opened a flood-gate.

When I was in my twenties and was judging my parents' lives. I'd thought Eddie's was a mouse-like existence. Recovering from the war; jogging along; not being too ambitious; being happy, I'd thought, though I'd often pondered his amateur water-colours that seemed so nostalgic, so melancholy. They had reminded me of a now-famous Leeds painter who was nostalgic for the past even as a young man. As far as I knew, that painter had suffered no disappointment in love, but now I realize that Eddie was trying to paint his memories of Knagg Wood and the ghost of Rhoda. After Rhoda left him, had he gone alone to Knagg Wood and wandered its lanes? After his marriage he had painted less, though in the next war he went back to it. When my sister and I were small he still used to attend the classes on Greek civilization. He had a thirst for knowledge. I remembered his once telling me he had used to talk about intellectual things with a man called Alec who was better-educated than he was.

If Rhoda's brother Alec had not gone away Father might have gone on pouring out his heart to him, asking him to tell him more . . . or we might have met him; but I suppose he wanted to preserve a distance between his old life and his married life.

I don't suppose Alison has the same memories as I do of our shared childhood, for no childhood is ever really shared. Differences of temperament between people, the accident of the order of their birth, the way they react with their parents and each other, their varying talents, will all affect their young attitudes. I always had the feeling that Mother preferred Alison. They had the same rather sardonic humour and refusal to show their feelings in public whereas Father and I were both sentimental. I still find it painful to remember that October of 1970 when Father died. I have tried many times since – I even tried at the crematorium – to contemplate the reality of his absence, and my grief is all tied up now with my children's childhood and myself as a young woman. It was my Aunt Flossie who appeared most grief-stricken at the funeral. She had never married, and she died four years later.

After Father died, both Mother and Aunt Flossie received many letters, many from people Mother hardly knew. All the writers stressed Father's gift for friendship and kindness as well as their impression of his wide reading, and his gentleness. One or two said he did not belong to this harsh modern world and I think Mother agreed. He had been a very quiet sort of man, except when he was being enthusiastic about his reading. He'd never spoken much

about his youth to us, or let drop more than a few remarks about
the war he had fought in, and he had usually held his tongue over
matters like sex and love, except to agree with Mother when she
was warning my sister and me about the duplicity of men. Yet once
or twice I'd caught him looking pensive, and on one occasion he
said, 'Many men are not like that, Kitty!'

I had imagined as a child and as a young person that my father
thought rarely of his past, for as I have said, he hardly ever spoke
of it. But later, even before I read his story, I knew that he had tried
to write about it, for I discovered some scribbled memories of
Thirksay in an old notebook of his. Like me he had preferred to
write things down.

My parents lived through both the wars we British have fought
this century, and my sister and myself lived through the second one
as children. But if ever Ally and I asked him about 'his' war, he'd
be reticent about his service, hardly ever vouchsafing any details of
his time in France, even when we'd pestered him and asked him if
he'd killed any Germans. I don't think it was because he didn't
want to upset us, or because he did not wish to remember it or had
forgotten it. But like many of the men who had been through that
conflict, it had been too momentous to try and explain to those
who had no idea of the actual circumstances, too painful for mere
conversation. All I knew was that he had been called up when he
was eighteen, to fight at a time in his life that seemed to me then to
be long ago, though the war had ended only twelve years before
Alison was born. We never had any idea of the unpleasant and
often gory details, except just once he told us that some conscripts
wounded themselves in order to get to hospital and escape the
front line.

The sudden dislocation between a happy, well brought-up
boyhood in a hard-working family, spending holidays in the country, reading, discovering poetry, and filthy brutal trenches full of
swearing men of his own age who thought of nothing but booze
and tarts, must have affected him. Yet I would never have guessed
that Father had been under fire or stuck in shell-holes or had
buried dead horses: he had never mentioned to us such events or

situations. Once, though, he had hinted that not all soldiers had been brave, or ready to die for their country, and at another time he did say that, far worse than the fighting, even worse than the fear of death, was his realization of what most men were like. Was that what he had been risking his life for?

When in his middle age Father became a member of what is now affectionately called 'Dad's Army', he rather enjoyed the experience. He was patriotic, if he no longer thought that fighting settled anything for good. The Great War must have made a difference in his inner life, even if a woman had perhaps made more. His experience of the worst things human beings can do to each other in war had not stopped him falling in love, one of the best things that can ever happen to a person. The horrors of the war in France may have matured him and made him ready to love, for he had never lost his romantic ideals, but the final effect of fighting in a war had not been as lasting as the force of his innate romanticism.

The decisive factor in Father's life, allied to his desire to write, had been his romantic nature. He had clearly been deeply in love with Rhoda, with a young man's love, essentially a pure kind of love. Had he ever come to believe that romantic love had duped him? If he had he would never have admitted it. He has nothing bitter to say about Rhoda in his account.

Father often used to quote lines from another of his favourite poets, John Donne:

> *Love, all alike, no season knows, nor clime,*
> *Nor hours, days, months, which are the rags of time.*

As an adolescent I often puzzled over these words. I came first to the conclusion that time's 'rags' were what was left at the end of life, memories, worn-out things. Then I thought that the 'rags' were just day-by-day events – bits of daily living. But this did not seem quite right, so finally I consulted my father.

He explained that love did not belong to time, did not belong to winter or England, or the hours as they pass; it existed out of time.

Love was immutable. Only much later did I realize that at the beginning of this poem Donne was asking the rising sun not to shine in at the window where he lay in bed with his love but to wake others and leave them alone!

My sister and I lived through the war, the one they now call WW2, as children. In our part of the country we did not suffer very much apart from rationing, and the black-out, and the occasional incendiary bomb in a nearby town, but I suppose I must be grateful that my own children have had no war in their lives, apart from reports, brought to them on their TV screens, from Ireland and from more distant places. Alison's two, Thom and Mick, had the Vietnam war going on whilst they were young, but all our children, hers and mine, were born a little too late to worry about the nuclear bomb, which our own generation agonized over. Alison was divorced from her American husband Harry Fairweather just after Father died. She returned to England for the funeral and then decided to make her home back here with her two sons, who are more than ten years older than Andrew's and my children. I'd married Andrew Considine in my thirtieth year, and our children were born in the early 1960s.

Father's story is of more than filial interest for me. In it I recognize, separated by a different sex and another time and place, much of myself, his mind being recognizably like my own. There seems to be an inherent durability in personality and temperament, more than one might expect from a changing world whose signposts alter radically. My own fear of the violent, the anarchic, chaotic side of life is similar to Father's. His experience was forced on him in the midst of horrific slaughter, whereas mine is at least a partial choice. Have I inherited an idealistic temperament which shrinks from too much reality? I believe my children are more cynical.

I guessed my father had suffered as much disappointment over his writing as over Rhoda Moore, and had never ceased to hope he might one day publish his poems and stories. I was surprised to discover that he had realized right from the beginning, and even more as time went on, that his literary style, which was always old-fashioned, would be considered even more so as the 1930s and 1940s drew on.

I sometimes used to rehearse what I might tell Father if he suddenly returned to life. He was never interested in technological progress: 'Remember, Juliet – ends rather than means,' he would often say to me.

As I write now, the year he died seems to have been at the same time long ago and yet quite recent, the former when I think of the time of Rose's and Paul's childhood and youth, the latter, paradoxically, when I remember him as he was when I was a child. When I hear his voice the years since his death are like yesterday. Alison's and my children may have grown up, and that fact dates his death, but it would have been their growing up in which he would have been interested most.

Father would not have liked the way the world has gone; Mother hated the way the world had gone to pot in the seventies. Father might have been pleased to have colour television, and might have appreciated the improved food and wine but he would have very much feared the growth of crimes of violence, of drugs, of pollution. The media infect us now with global fears, and our country has changed. I sometimes think myself that there is no more safety anywhere, whilst in my childhood I felt secure. Which is worse, the shadow of war or the fear of one's neighbour? In my imagination, I describe to my father, the hotter summers, the changed life of women, which has usually given them two jobs instead of one, the rise in divorce, the tyranny of the car. Father would have been 'green' all right. He was a much better gardener than I shall ever be!

I talk to him in my head about his grandchildren and tell him of their successes. He liked little children, and Rose remembers him quite well; she was eight when he died. Paul was younger, so his memories are a little garbled.

Father's account of love in his youth seventy years ago is still making me think about my own youth, which was chequered if not rackety. I too was much concerned with love. I supposed real love *was* some sort of platonic essence, existing in some special realm of ideas. But where was that? Was it like happiness, only a transient feeling, existing only in and through people? Once I reached adolescence and studenthood, I had suffered a larger number of infatuations than Father seems to have done. When I read about his love for Rhoda I feel sure he would have acknowledged the feelings that I never thought to burden him with when I was young. At twenty-one however I knew already, unlike my father, that love was not immutable.

Alison and I were so much freer in many ways than our parents had been; we had escaped into what we chose to regard as a wider world than Woolsford, but the number of choices before us was sometimes the problem. We were luckier than our father, for we went to university, and our 'abroad' was more than a snatched holiday in the Bernese Oberland. Neither had we suffered in wet cold trenches nor risked our lives at the age of eighteen or nineteen. But the face that looks out of Father's sepia portrait, taken in his uniform before he went to France, the face belonging to a man who has not yet fallen in love, is uncannily like my own young face, and I had been in love, or what I imagined was love, three times before I was twenty. Whenever I looked at this photograph, I used to think it was a pity he had no sons. Although I now believe myself to have been very like my father, I did not realize it then, and so we could not talk about our common experiences. Not that he ever wanted to pry into my love life, or into Alison's, but he would have had more advice to give to a young man, I feel. I think he was glad when Alison announced she was to marry her American academic. That was Alison sorted out. I know Mother was torn between relief at having one daughter settled and regret that the couple would not be living in England.

In those days women were a continual prey to public opinion. It would not have been so bad if our mother, had not been so extraordinarily sensitive to it. There was always a conflict between what we wanted to do and what Mother thought was the 'proper' thing to do, for she had been brought up in a very puritanical way. Alison escaped – or I thought she had – but Mother regarded me as 'on the shelf' until I married. Once, she opined I might not be the marrying sort. I was careful never to reveal to her my various romantic escapades.

I'd gone up to Oxford the year after Ally had begun her studies at London University. There, she was enjoying life. I remember spending a good deal of time agonizing over what I called 'moral conduct'. Now I see this was because of Mother. Father ought to have given me a little more advice. He was not a censorious kind of man, but I suppose men worry about their daughters in a way they do not appear to worry about their sons. Anxiety prevented my father being honest with me. If I did what I really yearned to do, which was to say 'Yes' to the next attractive man who wanted me to go to bed with him, I'd end up either pregnant or the cause of great sorrow for my mother. In those days – the same in Father's youth too, I suppose, even for a man, and unlike our children's generation, you knew you just could not do what you wanted. Did it make us better people, waiting till we were really sure, or did it ruin our sex lives?

Yet all those years ago Rhoda had allowed my father to make love to her! That had surprised me when I first read about it, for I had realized that even twenty-five years after Rhoda's youth I had been initially more wary, fearing consequences. The pill had still not arrived, and we were also confused between the meanings of 'lust' and 'love'. I wonder if my daughter Rose has that problem. You don't hear so much about love nowadays. When I was young I remember thinking of real love as quite different from desire. Real love was the green-bitter ecstasies of poets and artists who took flight in an existence unlike my own narrow constricted one, for I had an elevated idea of the artistic life, even if I were not creative. Perhaps Father had given me that. In truth I wanted neither marriage nor career, but love-affairs and experience and life. Isn't that what all young women confess to wanting now, for a time at least?

For most of us it was always a question of 'love', that mythical ideal aroused by one man after another. Like a god taking on the shape of a swan, a young man would take on the shape of a mysterious object of desire, before the magic wore off and he was eventually revealed for what he was: not a god, but an ordinary young man. There were a few men who were like gods to me, men who were worthy of my adoration. I felt that then and still feel it now.

Removing the fear of pregnancy and making a god of sex may not have made anyone any happier in the long run; there are just as many abandoned women or miserable young men as ever and probably more dispossessed children, but I wish things had been different when I was in love with Daniel, or Jaime. At least Father had four years of his Rhoda, however unsatisfactorily their relations turned out. His generation was brought up with a much firmer idea of marriage too.

The eight years between my leaving university and my marriage to Andrew were all marked by countless moves from one London bed-sitting-room to another, by lack of money, and by those repeated fallings in love, a pattern from which I escaped into – for that time the maybe aptly named – wedlock.

My mother was the reason for my dislike of living at home, which in those days many people did until they married. Father would not have objected to my life style – I doubt he would have noticed, but I would have drawn the line at bringing home some of my conquests, or rather those young men who had conquered me. If I had been a man none of this would have mattered. As it was, I lost out, for I should have liked to return home for a time and take things easy when I was training for my librarianship examinations. I'd have been better off financially living at home than scraping an existence in London during those years of my twenties. I chose freedom – and penury – in a way Father, a generation earlier, and belonging to the favoured sex, never seems to have considered in his own young days.

When I look again at what he has written about Rhoda, those many unrequited loves of my own youth come back to my mind. Not that I existed in a constant state of misery but I was often dissatisfied with myself, and especially dissatisfied with my love-life. Father had been single-minded; he might have lost the girl he loved but he had been faithful and concentrated his feelings on one person, on Rhoda. I had spun from person to person, from idea to idea, yet we had it in common that neither of us had found requited love until we took the plunge and married someone who apparently loved us.

Good things unconnected with love for other people happened to me in the years before I married Andrew. I remember solitary rides in Oxford. I loved cycling in the days when you did not take your life in your hands on a bicycle, and I would often ride around Port Meadow watching boats and horses, and scanning that queer flat misty landscape with its tufted willows and little allotments. There was a bridge marked DANGEROUS, and another low bridge over which trains would pass, the canal underneath. It was a sort of dream landscape I was walking in at the very same age as my father had been marching in the scarred landscape of the Marne. I loved the autumn, just as I remember now that he did, those days of my childhood when the autumn sun would haze benignly over his little garden.

After Jaime the Colombian and Daniel the Jew there was a beautiful young man called Lancelot who turned out to be gay, though we didn't call it that then. My 'Wembley' had been the spending of an Easter vacation in London hoping I might come across him. I had not, and it had been a complete waste of time. I bounced back eventually and after several rather more carnal affairs abroad fell in love with another dark, curly-haired man. They always say that girls look for men like their fathers but my father had straight brown hair, what was left of it.

I arrived in London in 1953, at the age of twenty-one and penniless, to start my adult life. London was to be the scene of later loves, of Henry who loved me but was married, of Nicholas whom I loved but whose muse I could never be, of John who was my friend as well as my lover, and of an unhappy Australian called Clarence. It was at a party I went to with Clarence that I met Andrew and fell in love with him. In London I knew many people struggling along like myself; we old friends saw each other constantly. I found new friends too, people who are still friends. My father appears to have had only his musical friend, and Rhoda's brother Alec. No other real friends? I know he belonged to a tennis club and an amateur operatic society in the town but I expect they were not full of the sort of like-minded people he needed to meet. Nor was Woolsford. Would it have been better for him to have left home and gone as I did to London?

I remember enjoying solitude once more as I walked round fifties London in hours snatched from the jaws of work and quasi-penury. Again, the autumn sun, and the river with the gulls by Chelsea Reach ... Chelsea Hospital and its grounds ... Chelsea Old Church – blessed Church of England, I thought – simple but worldly, casual but magnificent. Walking from Chelsea, from Whistler Reach and Old Church Street towards the great flat wastes of Pimlico behind the Tate Gallery.... The river was never very far away, nor the endless high terraces built in the 1840s and 50s ... I found it all invigorating and blessed and was grateful for such afternoons, grateful for the graceful people I imagined had created this London of lovely places.

Like my parents, I was a theatre-goer too in those days, and an art-gallery frequenter. How like Father I was! I remember Beatrice Lillie with her pixie voice, the sardonic little girl, funny little legs under the skirt and thin arm muscles, pathetic as well as funny; sharp, subtle, Edwardian, a Stevie Smith without the poetry.

> *I was standing in the street*
> *as quiet as quiet can be*
> *when a great big ugly man came up*
> *and tied his horse to me.*

London was full of such one-woman shows in those days but if you wanted Shakespeare there was always the Old Vic, and if you felt like the Continent, which began in those days on Victoria station by the Golden Arrow platform, as it did for Rhoda, you could go to a French film at the Academy Cinema, or to a theatre honoured by a visit from the Comédie Française, or to a show by Maurice Chevalier.

Father's 1920s were my 1950s, usually described as grey and dreary, dull and prim, which they were not. No, in the fifties people were busy defying convention, forming pressure groups to change many old laws, and marching to Aldermaston. The fifties were for young people an exciting time of change, not just the antechamber to the sacred sixties. When they came along I was in fact spending my time putting nappies on babies. . . .

Oh dear, Juliet thought, it is all far too personal and definitely for my eyes alone. I can't seem to stop writing about myself. Could she ever show any of it to Archie Marriott? Would he even be interested? She could edit the bits about her father for him – it would give her a purpose when her new brother had gone back home. . . .

One morning in early December, as dawn lightened the bedroom, she woke and wondered if her husband Andrew, still asleep by her side, had played the role in her life that her mother had played in her father's. But how could you compare Andrew's life with Eddie's? They were such different people.

Had her father ever seen Rhoda as something totally separate from himself? Had he asked himself why she should love him just because he loved her? Men in love could often be blind.

In this way, her father's story and his love-affair and her own attempts to come to terms with them and with her own childhood were often to keep her wakeful, making her reconsider her own life, her own existence, that was there only because *he* had once existed. Could she now clearly recall how she had thought of her father before the day the parcel arrived?

In the next century, a hundred years after his own childhood, Eddie's great grandchildren might take over the bâton of that relay-race we call human life.

She had always hoped her own children would have taken something from their maternal grandfather, but neither Rose nor Paul was really like him. His literary genes had not come down to her children, who were both in their different ways, more analytical than poetic, more like their own father.

Looking for similarities across the generations was a parental preoccupation, but, in spite of the different sex, she came to the conclusion that she was the one most like her father. Perhaps, in the lucky dip of genes, any children her own children might one day have would inherit his nice nature and his talents. But she didn't want Rose to marry too young. Marriage was such a lottery.

She thought, I truly loved my father, but he has made me see him as I never knew him, as a *young* man. My own childhood is now clearer to me than my children's early years. Strange tricks they are, that time plays on us as we grow older. . . .

I want some continuity in our lives, something to be handed on. I might give my story one day to Rose and Paul to read, after we have met Archie and his son, and then send some of it to Archie himself. I wonder what Rose will think of it all.

And what will I think of my new half-brother? I suppose I am determined not to be disappointed, yet I do trust Father's judgement of people.

Am I waiting now for the future to collide with the past?

CHAPTER THREE

Rose

The arrival of Uncle Archie made my mother, Juliet Considine, very happy. My father too was quite intrigued, though he always takes things very calmly. Ever since the New Zealanders arrived for the first time Mother has been busy writing her family history, an account of people through history and up to the present, which is to include her memories of her father Eddie Bairstow. Mother likes things to be nicely rounded off and once said it would be nice if Paul and I added our childhood memories and our feelings about life. I'm afraid she'll have to count out Paul; he's not the type to write about himself in spite of being a psychologist! Neither does my Aunt Allson want to have anything to do with this *magnum opus*.

Apparently Mother has recently finished writing about her own childhood and her impressions of her father but she's still writing of her reactions to his story, and those letters with their old secrets. I believe she sent some of the earlier part of this autobiography to her half-brother Archie.

I have never really wanted to write about myself – too busy anyway! But I have been thinking about the family and I have reread Grandpa Bairstow's account of his life. When I first read it it only mildly interested me and my brother Paul. We saw it the Christmas we came home after the autumn term at university. However, when you are twenty you are really more concerned with your own life and not so interested in the past. Paul was even

180

then interested in psychology but not really enthralled by his grandfather's early experiences, or interested in him as a person. Edward Bairstow seems to have been such a literary man, poetry being second nature to him. Most young women were probably bored by this aspect of Eddie's. Rhoda may have been but was too polite to say so. Mother always found him interesting, but then she's very like him, I think. She admired that side of him, as did Grandma, I believe.

I don't know how far I shall get with my own thoughts but here goes. In a way it's a continuation, I suppose, of my grandfather's life, all part of a family story. I shall describe how Mother and I met Archie and his son for the first time and my impressions of them.

I was born in 1962 and from the beginning I was a very different sort of person from Mother, much more like Dad in temperament. He was a research scientist and now works for a Civil Service department. How Mother ever got married to a scientist is a mystery to me and perhaps to her too. My father doesn't go in for mysteries. He says there is enough mystery in the natural world without making it up. I expect he just found her attractive. She is an emotional sort of person, rather sentimental and very bookish, like her father, Edward Bairstow.

I have never kept a diary, except when I was about eleven, for the same reason that I don't really like writing about myself. I have kept records of the weather though! Dad encouraged me to do that. My mother on the other hand has always kept what she calls a 'thoughts diary'. If you ask her what she was doing fifteen years ago, say, she won't remember things like the Falklands war, or further back when there were was a three-day week and we sat in the candlelight. I do remember that and she'll say, 'Fancy I'd forgotten that, but I think that was the year I read so and so,' or, 'I think that was the time I had that wonderful dream about the bluebell wood.' It isn't that she doesn't take an interest in the wide world, she does, but it's all important because of some link with her own life. I don't mean to say that she's egotistic because she has always looked after Father very well, and us when we were little, but she finds practical life a strain however hard she tries to do it well. Her real nature will peep out and surprise her.

When I was a child I think Mother thought I was more like her sister Alison than herself. Apparently I was active and quite bossy. My poor little brother Paul had to do as I said. But when I was about thirteen I changed and became more 'girlie'. Really, I think we are all different from our relatives and our ancestors, even if we have some shared genes.

Mother is a great one for tracing likenesses and often says I look a bit like her mother and Alison's, Grandma Kitty, who died when I was twenty. That was just before the famous story of my grandfather was sent posthumously to Mother and Aunt Ally, the story that was to point some of us in a certain direction, I suppose.

I studied ancient history at university so I must try to tell it how it really was, which is quite difficult. My brother Paul did not only achieve a first degree but a Master's in psychology and is apt to say things like, 'What do you mean by *"was"*?'

Just now a dirty-looking London pigeon has landed on our pocket-handkerchief of lawn. Perhaps he (or she) just needs a dust. The pigeons are so greedy; as bad as the magpies in their own way. Some of them fly over from the park and they are a sort of sepia colour and quite pretty; perhaps they are ring doves. I shall have to ask Dad who always knows which bird is which. Mother would not know for sure, though she might pretend she did, but she is better at finding pictures of things or spotting the right quotation for you in one of her books than actually being a fount of information about the real world. Except for children. I must confess she seems to know a bit about *them*. She just had to learn. She is keeping a second-hand bookshop now, having once been a librarian.

Where shall I begin? I suppose one theme could be: how does a person react when a long lost half-brother turns up?

Or I could write about men in general. They have a bad press at present. Not all men are testosterone-driven and aggressive. Women, when they are romantic, which is not so often as men (I've talked with Aunt Ally about this) also have to be practical, and it's hard for those like Mother who are not. But when the male hormones are deflected into 'romance', the resultant emotions can be powerful indeed. It seems that grandfather was very romantic. Was he obsessed with Rhoda Moore? Mother says not, and he seems to have recovered eventually, but I think that much romance is a cover for infatuation, or even obsession.

I could begin my side of this story in a different way, though I'd have to check my facts. The kind of history I studied did not start from earth's beginnings. I suppose historians have always considered that the history of human beings starts with the same thing as *In the beginning was the word*.

I could write:

Earth has lasted three and a half billion years so far.
There were 700 million years of evolution.
People have calculated that 100,000 years of human evolutionary history followed.

Well, so what? Where are we now? Have we stopped evolving? I believe it's a very, slow process.

I could go on:

Remember that it takes light, travelling at 180,000 miles per second, one thousand million years to reach us from some of the galaxies.
Is the universe still expanding?

Whether it is or not, or whether we know all the above facts, does the knowledge make one's puny life less or more important? Facts and figures slip and slide in my mind so I'm never quite sure I've got them right, in their billions and millions, or trillions. But they do cut one down to size.

My cousin Alex, who writes poetry, as well as being a naturalist, once sent me a poem about the sky at night. I wonder what the sky looks like at night in the Southern hemisphere?

I remember only two lines of his poem:

Space-spun, pin-prick reels of stars
Pocking Heaven's indigo ponds.

I rather liked that. It was from a collection, he said, called *Inner and Outer Space*, and I wanted to ask him if it had been published, but then I thought, if it has he will think I doubt his powers, and if it hasn't, he will be embarrassed, so I didn't. I learned later from my mother that he had published at least one 'slim volume'. I don't suppose there is much money in poetry.

To return to the Universe(!) My father says that the more you know, the better you understand and then you can see the whole of human life, and your own life, in perspective.

As I have explained, Dad is a sort of scientific civil servant, but I have not noticed that all his undoubted knowledge has made his dealing with petty irritations any easier!

The immense size of the universe is beyond *my* understanding but so are the billions of synapses in one human brain, even the brain of a dolt or thug. Here we are on earth with our magnificent brains, the brains that tell us all the above facts, and we cling to this tiny – or huge, depending on your vantage point – sphere of rocks and seas, this earthy particle that is spinning around the sun.

And this sun is only one sun among a *hundred thousand million other suns* in our galaxy alone. Our galaxy is only one among a billion galaxies. I don't think I'll go on. . . .

Mother, a glutton for punishment, says it all makes her dizzy but she forces herself to try and understand it. I told her I had read that the stars, and everything else in the universe, was made of the same stuff as ourselves.

'Well, that's a comfort,' she said. 'Nice to think that every new baby is a star baby.' That's the kind of remark she makes.

When you look into the future it's not so comforting. Dad says there'll be first of all a short-term global warming, then a hundred difficult years, and then, within ten thousand years, another ice age. I like to think that Europe and our little England were all connected in one piece less than ten thousand years ago at the time of the last ice age. Paul told me that when I was about ten. I was older than my brother but I'd thought it was *millions* of years ago, not thousands.

'This time though we shall have the technology to do something about it,' says our father.

Or will humans be just as much at the mercy of Nature? In many ways I'd like to believe that, that there is something much bigger than ourselves, call it Nature. Or God. You can see why I am not a scientist.

My brother Paul is more interested in the self that is conscious of itself; only one small atom but made up of millions of cells. Paul was always interested in theories about the differences between people. When all the other little boys were thrilled about moon landings he was indifferent. He's much exercised by the idea of cloning and genetic engineering, doesn't regard it with the horror I seem to.

I wonder what my grandfather would have made of all this. Mother says she thinks he lived in many ways at a better time for the human race.

'Well, there *was* the Great War,' I said.

Mother is a pessimist about the present. She cries easily, especially over pictures of war and anything about man's inhumanity to man. In this I am not like her. I don't show my feelings so easily, but I agree that it's when events are personalized, in letters or diaries, or people remembering horrible things that have happened to them, that you despair.

If you understood all the things I've mentioned about the universe and the galaxies and the human brain, *would* it make life easier or more exciting or less exciting? I don't suppose there is an answer to this question. Paul says everything is a 'process'.

I ought to describe the people in my story but I have always found it hard to convey the exact look of an individual. I think you learn more from someone's voice and gestures than from their facial contours, and those are even harder to communicate in print. But here goes: my father, Andrew Considine, is of medium height, fairish with blue eyes and an aquiline nose, and is a man of decisive gesture. He is no great talker, however. He says he has enough talk going on at his work-place, so he leaves women to do most of the social talking. He is always grumbling about the piling-up of bureaucratic jobs, especially the official passion for forms, and duplicates and triplicates of everything, even though computers and spreadsheets and databases are supposed to have made everything easier. I think he quite enjoys his work though, when he's allowed to get on with it.

He is more optimistic than Mother and can be quite sociable, but only on his own terms. He can be tetchy sometimes. Like all men he is a bit selfish and can abstract himself from mundane goings-on if he has a piece of work to do. He worked his way up from a working-class background; his father was a fitter in an engineering firm in the Midlands, and Dad got a scholarship to Cambridge.

Mother is of medium height and used to be thin but is now a bit overweight. Not that she seems to mind. She is mentally much quicker than you might think; she often looks as if she is thinking about something else. She used to catalogue books at an institute in Bloomsbury but she got fed up with that a few years ago and rented a local second-hand bookshop, saved up, got a mortgage and now both owns and manages it. She loves doing this; as far as I know she doesn't make much money, but she keeps her head above water. Quite a lot of her work is mail order.

My brother Paul is about the same height as Dad but has brown hair and eyes. Like Dad he is quiet but not as patient. He is also quite lazy. He too loves his work. I suppose that apart from me, the family is lucky to enjoy what they do for a living.

I have to confess that I never really wanted a prestigious career. Aunt Alison used to despair of me, for she is a feminist, and thinks women should carry on with their full-time jobs even when they have babies. Not that she carried on with *her* job when she was married; I suppose that is why she's changed her mind. She got married young to a 'wonderful' man who later unfortunately fell in love with someone else, so that in the end Aunt Ally divorced him. She has a partner now, not a husband.

186

As for me, I have worked at all sorts of things since I got my degree: bookselling – Mother got me that job; as a secretary – I did learn the useful skill of typing; as editor of the small magazine of a voluntary society; as a dogsbody to a scientist friend of Father's, and my present job which is to do with international copyrights but is mainly clerical.

When Uncle Archie arrived with his son Alexander from across the world to visit us, his long-lost relatives, it was at the end of December 1982 and they stayed for the whole of January 1983. It doesn't seem so long ago, though it's almost ten years now. I was in the middle of the Christmas vacation of my last year at college, and Paul had just started at a university in the North, and came home too for Christmas – he likes his home comforts does my brother. Our mother had been so excited on the telephone to us when she discovered she had a half-brother she'd never seen, that we felt impelled to try and show some enthusiasm when we arrived for the vacation.

I don't think either Paul or I had been difficult adolescents and of course by the time the Marriotts came over we were almost grown up, even in Mum's opinion. I think she relied on me to help her over any sticky bits there might be with the long-lost brother. As I've already said, and you might have expected, Paul wasn't really interested in families, in spite of studying psychology. I remember saying to him, 'Well, you'll soon have an interesting psychological situation to study on your own doorstep!' But he explained that the sort of psychology he was doing at that time had more to do with rats than people.

Mother was working at the same time as being busy at home preparing Christmas. Her new brother and nephew were to arrive in London a day or two after what Dad calls Saturnalia, and she said she had a lot to get through before then. She always panics over housework and cooking and shopping and getting done all she thinks ought to be done like buying flowers and polishing silver and dressing the tree and posting presents to her friends and writing letters and cards. There was a constant bustle.

We had a slight contretemps not long after I came home when I said it was not necessary to do all she did – we'd all enjoy Christmas anyway. I had a suspicion that she'd rather relished us both being away from home, once she'd got used to it.

'I thought I had plenty of time,' she moaned. 'But it's always such a rush when all the family is together. And you know you take for granted that your pillow-cases will be full of presents when you wake on Christmas morning, but who do you think is Santa Claus?'

'But you needn't go on with all that,' I said.

'I thought you liked it,' she said, and so I felt guilty. Of course we like it, but we could do without it and open our presents in some less time-honoured way. It was she who felt things ought to stay the same. The thing is that Mother doesn't really enjoy family life. She makes big efforts but you can see it doesn't come naturally. Once I asked her why she rushed around all the time. What was she rushing for?

'So I can sit down with a book!' she said.

That year she had father's mother to entertain as well, which was a bit of a burden because my only remaining grandparent was then a dour lady in her eighties who had devoted her life to looking after men, and Mother thinks that Grandma Considine thinks she – Mother – doesn't do enough for Dad and the house, and is not very good at what she does. I did offer to help and it was then that Mother said,

'I'm so nervous. There's Christmas to get through before I can meet Archie – he sounds so nice. I just wish I could meet him by myself away from you all.' And she burst into tears!

They didn't last long, they never do, and she blew her nose and said, 'I'm sorry.'

'Well, why not arrange to go to his hotel or something before he comes here? I'm sure he'd rather meet you first before meeting all of us,' I suggested.

'He'll want to see me with my family,' she said.

'How do you know that? Tell you what – shall just you and I go and meet him first and then you can relax when he comes here,' I said.

188

'Oh, Rosie would you? That would be so nice – then we shall have got all the preliminaries over.' So that's what we arranged to do.

They were staying in a hotel in Kensington, a really nice small one that Mother said had a reputation for being stylish.

Dad said, 'You mean *dear*?'

Mother replied, 'No, they could go to a much more expensive place but I happen to know that this place scores on simplicity. You must have heard of it, it usually caters for academics.'

Then Dad said he'd never had to stay in a central London hotel, thank God, and why didn't she invite her brother to stay with us? He had nothing against that.

I heard Mother mutter, 'Nothing against it, but who'll cook all the meals?' She wasn't going to put her reputation on the line for any long-lost brother. She said she wanted to enjoy him before she returned to her part-time job in January.

Then Dad said, oh well, he didn't mind waiting a day or two to meet Archie – he had a lot of work to get on with, and Paul had other things to do with his mates.

'I'll cook for you all next year,' promised my brother.

Mother sighed and shrugged her shoulders.

I won't go into Christmas, which is much the same everywhere for people like us, I think. Actually, it all went very well. Mother's slaving produced a nice plump tasty bird which Dad was called upon to carve, and there were no disasters. The tree looked all glittery and she bought lilies to go on the table and fantastically luxurious crackers and we all got the books we wanted. Dad received a first edition he was really thrilled about.

Grandma said how quiet it was without children. She lived at that time with her daughter, father's sister Julie, but usually went for Christmas to her other son who is a bank manager in Walsall, with young children. This year they were going abroad for the festival season, which was daring of them, I must say. Grandma hadn't wanted to go with them to whatever tropical island they had decided upon. On 27 December she went back quite happily to her daughter Julie. We were alone again and Mother breathed a long sigh of relief.

The next day she and I were to meet her brother Archie and his son Alexander.

'I shall invite them to come to spend a day with us next weekend,' she said. 'Alison says she can come over then.' We live in a genteel suburb that borders upon a less middle-class area. 'I suppose New Zealand is full of suburbs like ours,' she said.

Mother telephoned to make sure they knew who would be coming to see them, and the time and everything. When she put the phone down she said it was strange hearing a voice that should be familiar but that had a New Zealand accent. They had only spoken once over the phone before, between continents, thinking it better to write. Several letters had apparently passed between Mother and Archie. His son however was an unknown quantity.

Mother was nervous but exalted. When she is like this Dad keeps out of the way and retires to his study. I could well understand why she was excited. When the morning came for our trip to London she was rather pale and quiet.

'I'll take my camera,' I said. 'And then you'll have a record of the day.'

I find it hard to remember exactly all I felt when we entered the lobby of the hotel and turned into the lounge where there was a bright fire and a little bar. Two men who were sitting by the window rose when we entered the room. So much was talked about later that I can't recall exactly what we all said at first. After all, at that time they were still strangers to us. but I don't remember any feelings of constraint. I felt everything would be all right.

Once Mother saw Archie she just smiled and smiled, even though there were tears in her eyes. Alexander was smiling too and he seemed very friendly, though not a chatterbox. We all shook hands and Archie busied himself getting a bottle of champagne. They did not appear to be at all nervous either so I could see Mother calm down and lose any nerves she'd had.

My new uncle, Archie, was quite tall. What is it about what people used to call 'the Colonies' that makes tall people?

Alexander was not quite as tall as his father and had fairer hair and a snubber nose, and hazel eyes, but they both had terrifically bushy eyebrows, and it was these eyebrows that made me remember Grandpa.

Mother kept saying, 'Oh, Alexander does remind me of Father – it's incredible,' and Archie said, 'We call him Alex – I assured you there was a resemblance, Juliet!'

'They called me Alexander after my great-uncle Alec – Grandma's brother,' put in Alex, and smiled at me.

'His second name is Edward,' said Archie.

'What did happen to that brother of Rhoda's – Alec?' Mother asked as we all sat down.

'He died several years ago. He worked in Scotland all through the thirties till the war and then he retired to the Yorkshire Dales. He married quite late, then divorced. He came over to see Mother when I was about ten. I liked him.

'Who owns Knagg Wood now?' asked Mother.

'It was bought by a nursing home and then that folded a few years ago and the city council bought it for development, but nothing happened.'

'I've never been there,' said my mother. 'But I feel I know it from Father's descriptions. I'll lend you our father's story if you want to make a photocopy,' she said.

'That would be very generous, Juliet, and I shall take you up on it.'

'Have you often been to England?' I asked Alex who did not seem bored by all this harking back, or else was good at hiding his boredom.

'We came over to meet Grandpa when I was ten,' he said. 'I haven't visited London since. Mother and Father have. I've worked in French vineyards though! I do like Europe.'

'Do you regard England as Europe?' I asked him.

'Yes, of course – island Europe – I wasn't brought up on Empire, you know!'

'What do you do now?' asked my mother.

'I've just finished my doctorate in natural science and I'm

hoping to get a research job in some think-tank but at present I'm involved with ecology and conservation.'

Archie said, 'He's got connections with Greenpeace, if you know who *they* are.'

We didn't then, of course, though we were to find out more later, by which time Alex had told me that his first love was poetry. I thought it was odd for a scientist, though I don't know why.

At this time, on our first meeting, I could see that Uncle Archie was a clever man, the sort that Mother enjoys talking to, even if he isn't a long-lost brother. Apparently, Rhoda's husband Arthur had started a small textile factory in the 1920s, one of the first; they certainly had the wool for it! Later, Archie had gone into the export of newsprint pulp from the great pine forests. In 1943 he had just missed serving in Italy; he had gone into the army at eighteen, expecting to be shipped over to Europe, but the Italian campaign had just finished by the time he was trained and in '45 he was about to serve in the Pacific when the atom bomb was detonated.

'Thank goodness you didn't have to serve over there,' said my mother.

I was wondering what Archie Marriott's son Alex's priorities were. Was he mainly a political animal? We talked together a bit whilst Mother and Archie were engaged in discussing family. Alex's radical alignments arose from idealism. That he was a was a demonstrator and sympathizer for Greenpeace arose out of his first degree, which had been in zoology. He had worked for a time for an English marine biologist who had settled in New Zealand, and who had told him what man was doing to his Earth. This had fired Alex with reformist zeal.

He must have been in his mid or late twenties. Talking to him that first time I'd never have guessed about the poetry. I suppose I expected modern poets to be wild-eyed and difficult, even perhaps experimenting with drugs. Not with degrees in zoology anyway. Later, Alex was to tell me that he suffered from looking respectable, but he said it with a laugh.

Well, my mother and Archie talked and talked about Grandpa

and the past. I'd already read the famous autobiography when I got home before Christmas but had not felt it was really anything to do with me. Like most young women – and most young men – I suppose I was rather self-obsessed and not always interested in other people's reactions.

Alex told me he was glad his father had found his real family and that he hoped his mother would soon come over to London too.

By this time we had moved into a pleasant little dining-room and were eating a simply delicious lunch. Archie ordered everything with great aplomb.

'What was your Grandmother like?' I asked Alex.

'Granny Rhoda? She died when I was nine but I thought she was wonderful. She was very good looking – I thought so even when I was a little boy. She sometimes came out with rather sad remarks, though. I thought it was because of Grandpa Marriott – he hadn't lived with her in their house for ages.'

'What do you think the real reason was?'

'Oh, Father thinks she was often depressed because she had married the wrong man. But it was a smiling depression. I suppose she must have felt guilty till she told Father who he was.'

Alex spoke with no self-consciousness. He was an unusual young man. I found him physically attractive too, but at the time I was madly in love with a post-graduate in Oxford, so I was safe from Alex's charms.

'Do you really think she did – marry the wrong man?' I asked him.

'Well she ought not to have married either of them, perhaps. But I'm not sure – my mother thinks she was used to being well off, you know, and Eddie wasn't. Wasn't well off, I mean. Of course she was madly in love with Grandpa Marriott.'

'She didn't behave very well,' I said and then felt he must think I was a bit smug. Who was I to be censorious? It was all long ago, anyway.

'It was all so long ago,' I said.

'Yes – we have to live in the present. Father does, really, but it's bugged him all these years that your mother didn't know about his existence.'

I looked over at the two of them. They were still talking earnestly and animatedly – Mother was quite flushed and looked very happy.

'What relation are we to each other?' I asked Alex, feeling a little reckless myself, what with the food and wine and the unaccustomed company.

'We are, I calculate, half first cousins,' he replied solemnly, and then burst out laughing. I laughed too; it seemed such a silly relationship.

'You'd like my brother, another of your "half first cousins",' I said.

We arranged for them to come over at the weekend to meet Dad and Paul and Aunt Alison. Mick and Thom would come over too if they had nothing better to do.

It was already dark when we left, late that afternoon. I think we were put in a taxi and arrived home about seven o'clock.

'Flown with wine,' said Dad. It was one of his favourite quotations. Not that he had many. Mother wanted to tell him all about her day and I heard her talking for hours when I'd gone up to my room to study – or pretend to. I was quite pleased with the day too. I'd not met many young men I'd liked so much as my half first cousin. In my experience up to then, *liking* men was quite rare. They were easier to love.

The returning 'Colonial' brother found his two half-sisters waiting at our house on the following Saturday. Alex came along as well. Aunt Alison said immediately, 'Oh doesn't he look like Father!'

She'd brought Mick along and he was accompanied by his girl-friend, a lab assistant called Myrtle, whom he worked with. Thom was busy. Or, I suppose, uninterested.

Dad got on well with Archie. They were both intelligent, and they both smoked pipes, which gave them something to talk about as well as economics and the usual abysmal state of the world. Mother told me afterwards that she'd been frightened her sister wouldn't accept Uncle Archie as her brother but that she had reluctantly conceded, when she finally met him, that he was.

We saw our New Zealand relations several times before I had to go back to start the Hilary term at Oxford.

'You must all come and stay with us,' Uncle Archie kept saying. I know Mother had decided she would go if she could persuade Dad to accompany her. She always says she likes going places alone but I've noticed that she really prefers to have Dad there, at least to carry suitcases and sort her out at the airport. They talked about going in the summer, the Southern hemisphere winter.

Before they left to go back home Alex asked if I'd like him to write to me now and then. I was too surprised to say anything but, 'Oh yes – if you like – please do!'

I'd never met any male who liked writing letters or did not regard it as a chore invented by women. My brother Paul avoids it, and Dad usually gets Mother to write if he wants to keep in touch with people.

Looking back now I believe my mother found in her brother Archie a man she could idealize. I noticed he acted protectively towards her. Being seven years younger than he was, she rather looked up to him. I wonder how Paul and I would have got on if we'd never met till we were older? I suppose Dad isn't a protective sort of person; he takes her for granted, for I've noticed he thinks Mother is capable of everything from ordering the garden seeds to carving the joint, even if he's a better traveller than she is.

My mother once confessed to me that when she was about sixteen she'd imagined a kind of platonic relationship, a deep friendship, with an intelligent older brother. Archie lived far away, but he was quite an emotional sort of man, I think. I imagine that she fell in love with the *idea* of him, which was to keep her going when she was depressed or bored. I suppose she was going through the menopause at about this time. I noticed when I was at home that she would bring his name artfully into the conversation and a soft look would come on her face when she said it.

Paul noticed our mother's preoccupation too but I don't think our father had. Paul said that our female parent was a romantic and would prefer a one-sided relationship she could daydream over.

'Aren't you a bit harsh on her?' I protested. 'You think she's fallen in love with him.' I remember saying.

'Probably, but she will never admit it.'

'Has this a psychological explanation?' I asked him ironically.

'Well of course. He represents her father,' my brother replied solemnly.

'But she wasn't in love with her father!' I riposted.

'How do we know?' replied Paul.

He was going through a reaction to the rats, and reading Freud.

After the New Zealanders had gone home Mother wrote regularly to Archie, and to his wife as well, and they exchanged photographs and presents. I was to hear occasionally too from my 'half first cousin' Alex.

I know Mother and her 'new' brother wrote to each other about the books they were reading. She remembered who all my grandfather's favourite authors had been and told Archie about them. It often transpired, she told me, that her father's favourite reading had been the same as Archie's. This appeared to thrill her. Archie however was no poet. He was not what Mother called 'creative' – her highest accolade. But he would talk about reading Boswell's *Life of Johnson*, or Burton's *Anatomy of Melancholy*, both titles of books Mother remembered her father reading when she was a little girl.

'My father was quite reactionary when he was middle aged,' she told me. 'He believed in people reading in libraries rather than going to school, and that the art of letters was declining and becoming just another feather in an academic's cap. So Archie is just the sort of person he'd have approved of; quite old-fashioned in a way. Though I must say Archie is a much more successful businessman than my poor father.'

'He must have inherited that from his uncle and Yorkshire grandfather.'

Archie sent her a book he said their father would have loved:

The Influence of Montaigne upon English Writers and Thinkers.

'He guesses Father's taste so well,' she exclaimed happily.

'I expect they exchanged lots of letters after they'd met,' I said.

Archie did read novels, which apparently my grandfather never had, or not much, and this went down well with Mother, who was a great novel-reader. It was something to mention in one of my occasional letters to Alex, for I was an avid reader of novels too. Eventually he took me up and replied that he was more interested in the present moment and recording how things were in his own poems than in depending too much on the literature of the past.

I wondered if Alex was like Grandpa Eddie. Had Eddie always been 'literary', or had it only been love that had made him continue to write poetry after the first flush of youth? My mother said her father had certainly discovered the power of poetry by the time he was fifteen. I told Alex this. In his next letter he explained that he hadn't wanted to get muddied up with other people's words so had studied animals and plants instead of literature. I remembered that my great-aunt Flossie had collected country books and how I'd enjoyed reading them when I was a little girl. Next time I write, I thought, I'll tell Alex about that lovely book on hedgerows. I didn't know I was soon going to be caught up in love myself and that writing to Alex would have to take a back seat in my existence.

From the middle of the 1980s, after I came down from Oxford, the world – and our country – was changing too quickly for my mother to approve, just as it had once changed too quickly for her father. Many of my friends, women as well as men, went into the City and made their fortune there. Mother and Father were highly disapproving of these times we lived in.

They went for their holiday in Wellington during the following English winter, not as they had planned in the summer. Father had been very busy at work, and they decided it would be nicer to get out of England during the next winter.

I didn't go with them. I had begun on the long trail of suitable posts of employment that I have already mentioned. The post-

197

graduate student had been replaced by an accountant, a nice young man who happened to be musical. I found him a relief after the rather sceptical attitude to love found in my other friend.

It was a bit later, I think about three years after our first meeting, in the summer of 1985, at the time of my employment in a bookshop, that there was a piece of news about New Zealand that I only half heard on the news bulletin. Usually you never heard anything much about that place from one year to the next. It was in the paper the following day and I read it just before I had to leave for work:

July 10 1985

GREENPEACE SHIP IN MYSTERY BLAST

The *Rainbow Warrior*, the international protest ship belonging to environmental group, Greenpeace, was badly damaged today in Auckland Harbour. Two blasts, sixty seconds apart, tore the ship's hull apart below the waterline. Of the ten people on board, including one Briton, all escaped, except a Portuguese photographer who was killed. New Zealand police have not yet ascertained the cause of the explosions, but suspect it was sabotage. The *Rainbow Warrior* was to have led a flotilla of seven 'peace vessels' into the French nuclear test site at Muroroa Atoll in the Pacific for a Bastille Day protest action on 14 July.

Holding the newspaper I went in search of my mother. I hadn't heard from Alex for some months and was not sure whether he was still engaged in demonstrations or actually working on *Rainbow Warrior*. He still belonged to the group, but I had received the distinct impression from his last letter that he was more use as a sort of spy than as an active campaigner. It was, however, worrying.

My mother had a day off in the middle of the week and promised she would try to telephone her brother about it. She seemed to know exactly what time it would be over there, so far

198

away. I imagined it was a good excuse for her to hear Archie's voice. She rang me at work later that afternoon.

'It's all right. Alex is safe. I thought you'd like to know. Apparently he's had some sort of row with HQ and is no longer working for them.'

We discovered later that it had been two French secret agents who had been responsible, and they were jailed that November for ten years. It even led to the resignation of the French defence minister here in Europe.

I forgot about all this, but for the next few years I continued to communicate in a desultory way with my cousin Alex who was still doing research, but also, he told me, writing. He was unusual in that he appeared to like writing letters, and I rather looked forward to them.

I fell in love with Fabian Lee at a party on a rainy day in February 1987. By this time I was not living at home but sharing a flat with Lucy, a woman I had been at school with. I think my mother was really quite relieved when I went off. When I was an adolescent Mother had been obliged to adjust to 'letting go' and I know she found it painful. Once I heard her say to Dad, 'After twenty years of qualifying for being a good mother you're left with nobody wanting your qualifications!'

Dad had replied, 'If you had given birth to seven children you could have made use of them a bit longer!' He always joked about such things with her.

Mother would not have admitted it, and she had always urged me to be independent, but she was relieved she wouldn't have to worry any more if I were not back late at night. She would try not to listen for my key in the door but she found it hard to sleep if she knew I was still out.

Even at that time London's West End at night was pretty tacky, and now it's worse. Mother calls it 'The City of Dreadful Night' from some poem or other. Not that she finds herself there very often. After midnight, around Piccadilly and Soho, especially at the weekends, people a lot younger than my friends and I go clubbing and mill around in droves in what Mother also describes as Dante's Circles of Hell. Some of these young people have been known to strip; many are on drugs, most are a bit drunk, and some drive by in sports cars The scene has changed a lot since Paul and I were their age. I know this makes me sound like Methuselah but one thing Fabian did for me at first was to make me feel more carefree and young than I'd been with other boyfriends, who had been legion but not adventurous.

My new ecstatic feelings for Fabian didn't last long, I have to confess. I was for over four years his girlfriend, but madly in love with him for only about half that time. I can't even remember now what that sort of passion was like, though I can remember thinking at the time that it was like allowing oneself to scratch a patch of itchy skin, deep down to the root, an exquisitely excruciating joy. That sounds mad, but I think the sort of infatuation I had for Fabian *was* madness. I lived for the present whilst I was with him – we actually lived together only during our last year and I was never sure of him, so I suppose that kept me going and stopped me from releasing myself from him. I didn't know whether he was being intentionally cruel or difficult when he was unwilling to commit himself to our being together for good. I was surprised at myself, that I wanted what young women were not supposed to want any more. I'd thought I was less conventional. Love undid me, as the passion I had for him changed into a longing for a true partnership. It need not be marriage; I always told him that. Yet I thought that if people truly loved each other they would not want to be parted. He said I was bourgeois and that I wanted to have my cake and eat it.

'But that's just what *you* want! Where is *my* cake?' I asked him towards the end of our hopeless situation – hopeless for me, that is.

'Sex,' he said, and I thought, Well, he can have that with someone else.

I surprised myself thinking that love must be much harder to find than even 'good' sex, which we had certainly had. Inevitably, we parted. For a time I felt I was a failure but I was also angry, and

I suppose that cured me in the end. He soon found another woman and truth to tell, that relieved my guilty feelings. Had I asked too much of him? Not loved him enough? It was the old old story: young men want women and young women want babies. At least I didn't want babies immediately then, but what was my need to settle down and be sure of a man and for him to be committed to me, but an atavistic desire for security?

It took me about two years to allow myself to feel I was not a cold calculating woman but just a person whom another person had not loved enough. As for being 'in love', I had been 'in love' and what good had come out of it? Perhaps one day Fabian would fall in love with someone and then the tables would be turned on him? Or perhaps not, or only when he was middle aged.

I went out with several other young men, though there were long periods when I was quite glad to be by myself. I never wanted to live with any man again. Then I nearly made another mistake.

There was a man at work (by this time I was working in the office of the publisher of a political weekly) who obviously thought highly of me. Derek Ross had curiously large brown eyes and he would look at me with a dog-like devotion. Wasn't that what I wanted? I felt sorry for him, though I didn't encourage him, apart from consenting to go out with him to the cinema and for rather nice meals. He liked listening to me, he said. In spite of his Scots surname, Derek was from a Welsh mining community, had roots in chapels and choirs and, I was told, possessed a nice singing voice. His ordinary voice was rather hesitant with a slight lisp.

I know I am not making him sound very attractive but the truth was that there was no chemistry there, at least not on my side. He was a man who would certainly marry and make someone a good husband, and I hoped he would find a nicer person than me. I was not however prepared for the sudden proposal he made at the end of an especially nice meal in Fulham.

After telling me a good deal about the pension he had secured and detailing his insurance policies he took a breath and said, 'Will you marry me, Rose? I know you are an old-fashioned girl.'

I was taken aback though I suppose I should not have been. I decided the best thing was to be honest. I explained that I did not love him and that though I knew some people did not regard love as a necessary condition for marriage, I thought in my case it was.

'I'm sorry, Derek,' I said. 'Please don't be hurt. I've enjoyed being with you.' This was not strictly true; I'd just been weak-minded about him. I went on piling up all the wrong sentiments like, 'You are a nice person. You will make someone a good husband,' but his face had fallen and I felt a real louse. But then I thought, here we are in 1992 though he is stuck in about 1892. I am thirty years old, old enough to deal with disappointments, and so should Derek Ross be too.

He never took me out again but blushed when he saw me during the day at work. Soon after that I got another job.

Well, by last year – 1992 – my love life didn't appear to be going anywhere though I had not exactly decided to renounce the male sex. So many people my age don't believe in marriage any more – at least my friends *say* they don't, though one or two have taken the plunge since. I had begun to wonder if any relationship between people of our generation could be permanent. Even the church marriages contracted in their mid twenties by a few university friends were beginning to fail.

As I have intimated, I didn't want to live with anyone again – what Granny Bairstow had called 'living in sin'. This was not because of any notions derived from my 'old-fashioned' morality, but because I had noticed that in so doing women – young ones anyway – often got the worst of both worlds, the conventional one and the 'free' one. Anyway, Fabian as a partner had been quite enough. Even three years later I would wake up in a cold sweat thinking how I had very nearly sold my soul – and for what?

My thoughts often led in this direction, which was a frustrating one. Sometimes I decided to concentrate upon self-improvement; I'd join a gym, do some jogging, drink less, go for long walks, look for a job that was better paid and where fewer neurotics were to be found. I actually managed to accomplish some of all this!

But I shall have to leave this unfinished account of myself. Life has caught up with me – and it.

Perhaps I'll finish it one day when I am a little less preoccupied. . . .

CHAPTER FOUR

The Death of Archie

Thus the whirligig of time brings in his revenges
Twelfth Night Act 5 scene I

Juliet Considine had been keeping a diary ever since writing her memories of childhood and youth, but on that February morning in 1993 when she heard the news of her brother Archie's death, far away on the other side of the world, she could not write a word.

Archie was only sixty-seven, had that very summer taken semi-retirement from his business. There had been no warning; not long before he had been given a clean bill of health. For many months afterwards Juliet had no heart to write, or even to read a book that needed concentration.

Why had he come back to them, especially to her, only to be snatched away eleven years later? Life was cruel. Only her self-employment in the second-hand bookshop, which she could do almost automatically, saved her from depression.

Rose had found a job where the touch-typing her mother had once made her learn, very reluctantly, was to come in extremely useful. The small international company that chased authors' copyrights also valued someone who could spell as well as type. There were no young men in this new office of Rose's, which was a relief to Rose. Instead, there were several much older women graduates, competent and friendly people whose conversations were not limited to 'men I have known' or 'men I wish I knew'.

Rose at thirty-one still had her old sense of humour if a little less of the optimistic spirit of the young woman of eleven years before who had impressed her cousin Alex. Rose's circle of friends, both men and women, was wide, but her experiences had chastened her. It might be true that the kind of man who was both clever and kind, and whom one also found sufficiently attractive, just did not exist. Her old lover Fabian Lee had disappeared completely from her life and she thought of him seldom. Thinking of him for too long depressed her. She had failed with Fabian and was not sure whose fault it had been. She referred to him privately as Good Riddance, the name her friend Miriam Hardacre always called him by, remembering him with a shudder. That shudder though had not been expressed by Miriam as long as she or any other friend had thought he might become a permanency in Rose's life. Once they split up her friends all agreed he had been a disaster area.

Rose and her women friends often discussed what men appeared to want, or need, from women, and what women needed men for. Even this tightly knit group who had gone to university together and in two cases been to school together, could not agree on their conclusions. The young women were all now over thirty and all wanted a man who would be faithful unto death. Some confessed they were inclined to be possessive and were easily jealous. Most would prefer to be married but dared not always admit to this for fear of frightening off the man of their dreams, or appearing old-fashioned.

Miriam Hardacre said both men and women wanted somebody who would love them and whom they could love. Sarah Williams said she wanted to be 'valued' but had spent a good deal of her time in the past telling boyfriends how *she* valued *them*. Lucy Thompson wanted to be 'needed and desired'. Imogen Roberts liked children and family life, and dreamed of her own, but never met men who wanted the same.

Rose Considine said she'd like a man with a good brain who didn't mind an independent woman – a man who liked being alone as much as she did. She also needed someone to whom she could give something that nobody else could give. What Rose did not say because it sounded too earnest and high-minded was she wanted both sexual attraction and a man with a similar temperament and interests. She looked for requited love, and joy, but also for the fondness and shared habits that came from shared opinions and tastes. And, yes, she needed a man who liked children and family life, and a man who would be loyal.

Miriam then said she required a man who had achieved something in life, if not yet all he wanted.

'Do you think *you* have achieved anything?' Lucy asked. Miriam was in PR and quite successful.

'I'd rather have a successful husband than be successful myself,' said Imogen. The others groaned.

'Isn't it just that you want somebody who will add to rather than detract from your existence?' offered Sarah.

'Having babies does detract from your freedom – and probably your looks,' said Lucy.

'You can't have everything,' said Rose, irritated. She wanted to say that she did not want a man whose taste irritated her, but that sounded rather trivial.

'I need a man steady enough to hold me on an even keel,' said Imogen.

'More chance of success if you're reasonably self sufficient,' said Rose.

'You have to be able to live with yourself if you are to be happily married. My mother never could and that's why her marriage was a failure,' said Sarah.

Afterwards, Rose thought, I hope I don't give the impression of being too self-absorbed. Sometimes her friends did come over like that. It was this awful problem of self-consciousness. Everyone talked about sex and relationships all the time: the media, the theatre, your friends, and yet the only thing to do was get on with your life and try to ignore it all. She often thought she never wanted to open a newspaper or a book again.

Rose had a fair amount of self-esteem, and had never admired people who depended too much upon others for their self-validation. It was always pleasant to be admired, but it must be even pleasanter to feel one had added positively to someone else's life? She knew she had often been too aware of the imagined opinion of others – about which she had probably been quite mistaken.

Nobody had mentioned money, she thought, or men who drank or gambled, or difficult in-laws, the sort of problems that filled the women's magazines and airwaves. She'd be more anxious about disagreements over politics or religion, or personal habits, tidiness or lack of it. Her mother had always said there had to be compromises in marriage: over when to have a baby, how to bring up children, where to live, where to go on holiday, how to decorate the house, who'd do the housework, how much time they wanted to spend reading, or going out. It seemed there was an endless list of problems that had not substantially changed since her parents were young, even after all the years of feminism that had occurred since then. And, added to all this was the new compulsion – or desire – or often necessity for women, partners or wives, to continue working when their babies were still very young.

After all, did being in love matter? Did that love have to be mutual? One partner would usually at any given time love more, but this position could change as time went on. There had to be something else waiting for when the first flush faded. Was it friendship? Really, thought Rose, I'd like to forget all this and just rely on enthusiasm for each other's company! But what sometimes made a man sexually attractive to a woman was often that he found *her* attractive. This did not appear to work the other way round. Being made to feel desirable was what made a woman feel sexy, wasn't it? Women liked to hear words of love and desire, declarations of regard, expressions of feeling, and they wanted to believe them. But how rare was it to be able to trust such declarations?

Most people seemed to think that a partnership depended on sex. But Rose remembered Derek Ross. He had found her attractive but she had not reciprocated, had just not found him sexy! Maybe it just depended on 'chemistry'. Or was it that feelings, mental sympathies, were more important?

Such thoughts would drift in and out of her mind as they drifted in and out of the minds of most of her women friends. There were plenty of men pleased to take Rose out – or stay in with her – in the small West London flat she rented, and she had not yet renounced the male sex.

Her cousin Alex, the naturalist, with whom she had maintained a sporadic correspondence that had never actually come to a full stop, had not written for several months. She had not yet replied to his last letter, had been feeling guilty that she owed him a reply, and now she had to write to him about his father's death.

Alex Marriott grieved greatly for his father. He knew he could be a great support to his mother in practical matters, and wondered whether he should move back in with her for a time. But Thelma would have none of this. She had always been spiritually independent, having no wish to rely on her son more than was necessary for a time.

Alex was good at his work but it was not as important to him as his writing. His mother knew that if he wanted more money, and more power in the world of work, he would have to put more of his time and mental energy into his job. As it was, he did enough, and nobody had ever reproached him with laziness, but he lived for when that work was finished, when he could read, think, and write his poems. He was thirty-seven when Archie died, and still living by himself in a suburb of Wellington in a small wooden chalet-type house that was not far from his parents' solider residence. There had been rumours that he was gay, countered by his friends who insisted he was a confirmed bachelor and probably a bit of a loner. One friend hinted to him that he had been the object of other friends' defence of his life style and that amazed him. Was he becoming an eccentric, a licensed hermit? He still wrote, and considered himself a poet, if one a little out of touch with the present fashion.

His mental preoccupations were modern ones; there were plenty of professionals now all over the world who worried about the way science was going, especially as far as global warming or advances in knowledge of genetics, or the animal food-chain, were concerned. Alex was not a specialist; he had done some decent research in the past but had balked at political action at the last moment, and he still wondered why. His interests were wide; he often wished he could retrain as something other than a labora- tory researcher. The march of scientific progress in the world of the 1990s both excited and, more often, depressed him.

When the concept of 'downsizing' reached New Zealand, he seized upon it gratefully. He disliked the whole idea of 'living to work' that was in vogue, that was converting the most successful workers of the developed world into harried ant-like creatures. He was fully aware that the world did not owe him, or anybody, a living. When he was a little boy he had decided that if he had to work, what he would most like to be would be a warden in a nature reserve, someone who was willing to live in some out of the way place to keep an eye on butterfly haunts or bird colonies. He smiled at himself now. In his twenties he had felt himself linked to the conservative, romantic and pastoral English rather than the pragmatic materialism of antipodean Lowland Scots. On the other hand, hadn't he felt he needed more of a challenge? Perhaps dirty little old England would fill the bill.

His mother, a descendant of Scottish settlers, was unselfish enough to encourage him to make his dreams a reality. If he wanted to make his mark as a poet, there would be more scope in England. He had always intended to go there again one day, the chief reason being Rose Considine. He had never breathed a word to anyone, even his mother, about this. He had found himself attracted to her on his visit to London but she had been very young, with all her life before her. What had he to give her?

He began to distrust the philosophy of some of the new and influential political lobbies, whose leaders and followers came from Australia; he was chary of their philosophy. He understood why some people were so alienated from the powers that be; he himself had once believed – still believed – in better ways of husbanding the land and the oceans; he felt strongly still against nuclear weaponry. But some people, living in a vastly different setting, had taken over ideologies from the States in forms of political correctness which he distrusted. It was all talk, mostly talk about language, and intellectuals had nothing to lose by this appearance of care and concern. It was true there were plenty of social problems amongst the Maoris, once inhabitants of islands in the Pacific, whose situation appeared to correspond with those of Amerindians, but there had been enormous interbreeding and the problems were different from those of Australian aborigines.

There was a whole pool of idealistic young who espoused ideas about another minority: animals, along with other causes, and their 'rights' were at present being sentimentally taken up. He did care for animals, but he could not equate their position with that of the human race, or any half of it – and he did not believe that animals had the same 'rights' as human beings, men or women. Animals had no responsibilities towards each other – lucky them. It was human beings who had responsibilities towards them.

Alex believed in other causes; he had been since his youth what he discovered was called a feminist, which was hardly a minority cause either. Maybe he had been more sentimental ten years ago, but now he was sceptical, distrusting the fervour and dogma of any closed system of thought. He had always intended to return to the Old World, knowing himself for a moral conservative, and he was restless now in his grandmother's adopted country. It might have been better if the European had never gone there. If it were possible he would be happy to leave the place to the Maoris.

After his father's death, he decided that he did not fit into his beautiful country and would definitely risk going to England. He had always had the strange feeling that he lived on the wrong side of the world. Perhaps it was because at his rather old-fashioned school they had used a map with Europe in the middle at the top, but when he read stories of English children digging down to find Australia he had felt that if he dug down there would be nothing except the South Pole.

He was careful not to express these feelings where he lived, for he knew they would not be popular and that he was prejudiced. He had indeed always tried to fit in well with his compatriots, but as time went by he had realized he needed the challenge of Europe. Just recently, he had published one or two poems in London. No longer was Britain as a matter of course the Mecca for most Australians or New Zealanders; he truly loved the beauty of his native land but felt he had been adopted there, just as Rhoda his grandmother had been. He must see if he could belong in Europe. All he wanted to find there was an honest job with time to write. Then he might do a Candide: 'cultivate his garden'. He could look for work connected with the research he had been doing for the last few years in conservation, though the jobs he found advertised appeared to consist more in supervising minia-ture game reserves or working for ministries or companies concerned with the world fish-harvest. Qualifications in animal husbandry would appear to be more useful than his research work, but if he were willing to earn less, and have more time, there might be other possibilities, in Cornwall, on the Essex marshes or in the North Yorkshire National Park? He dreamed of some sort of nature wardenship in the north of England, but if he could find nothing suitable at first he could take a job with computers in London. He could manage spreadsheets and databases. Computers were only a means to an end, just as any work he undertook would only be a means to make a living. Then he would be free at last.

But all this ratiocination paled before his desire to see Rose again. How could he have left it so long? He knew from her occa-sional letters that she was not married; they still carried on a haphazard correspondence, that had sometimes almost lapsed on her side. His parents had been planning another trip to Europe for the following summer, and he had said he would go with them this time. Archie's death had cancelled all their plans. Juliet Considine had written to invite them all to stay with Andrew and herself, as Thelma and Archie had done three years earlier, and to use their home as a base to make a grand tour round the British Isles.

When Archie died Juliet wrote again, extending the invitation to Alex and his mother.

'Why not come along with me?' he asked Thelma.

But Thelma preferred to stay and continue with her teaching until retirement. Married at twenty, she had been a little younger than her husband and had two more years to go for her own pension. She would mourn Archie in the place they had lived in together for almost forty years. But she was keen for her son to find a life that suited him, even if it were far away.

'I'll come and see you when you're settled,' she said.

'You seem to be sure I shall find a job and stay.'

'Yes, I think you will; you'll go back to your grandmother's roots.'

Paul Considine, who was now working in Leicester, had promised to come home for a few days for the Christmas of 1993. Juliet was still depressed. She knew she had invested too much of herself in the existence if not the presence of Archie. Even though he had usually been thousands of miles away, the fact of his being alive had comforted her. They had written to each other regularly and she had cherished this correspondence, imagining he did too. It was as if her father had returned to watch over her, and it calmed and cheered her. His death was a double death, for Eddie Bairstow died again in Juliet when his son died.

She did not tell her husband such things but Andrew had some idea of how much Archie had meant to her. In his opinion Juliet had not been in love with her brother but had relied on him to make up for the deficiencies that no husband, however loving, no marriage, however long and successful, could completely fill.

She had not talked so much about him in the last two or three years, but had been increasingly happy, as she had been since the day of the discovery of her brother's existence. Andrew had never been a jealous or possessive husband; indeed he had always preferred to keep a little distance from his own emotions. This had stood him in good stead when Juliet and he were younger and he had been able to offer rational calm in the face of her occasional turbulences.

It stood him in good stead too, now that his wife was mourning her brother. He offered a shoulder to cry on whilst keeping silent and listening patiently to Juliet's outbursts of sorrow and grief. Archie and Thelma had enjoyed a happy marriage and he was sure that his wife had never entertained jealousy for her brother's wife. He did not enquire into any fantasies or daydreams she might have had.

Juliet had indeed at first nurtured some flights of infatuated fancy but had kept them strictly under lock and key. She could scarcely have admitted even to herself that their becoming real would have necessitated the deaths of two people. But when she and Andrew had spent that long holiday in Wellington, she had relaxed. No need to imagine Archie, since he was there in the flesh. She had got on very well with Thelma, and Thelma had told her that having two new sisters had given her husband a new lease of life. Juliet had been a little surprised: she had not seen it that way round. Not that her sister Alison took any part in all these emotions. Alison was glad that Archie existed, sent him Christmas cards, but entertained no fantasies and thought Juliet a little unhinged. Andrew observed the brother and sister together in New Zealand and got on very well with Thelma himself. On balance he was glad about the discovery of Archie, and trusted his wife to behave sensibly, whatever her feelings for him might be.

Once Juliet's feelings had indeed settled down, and the years had gone by, Archie's presence in the world had kept her going when the nest had emptied and Andrew was so absorbed in his work. Then she had suddenly found the energy to rent a second-hand bookshop which was now doing very well. She was sure that it was Archie who had given her this energy. She had of course revealed to him her early plans for it, and he had approved of them and been encouraging.

She was beginning to feel now that the part of Archie into which she had become spiritually absorbed had been only the mirage of a person. In her heart she had always known that he was not really his father all over again in either temperament or talents. Apart from Eddie's lack of worldly success, there was a certain aura around Archie which most women would find attractive. Archie was handsome and successful, more sophisticated than she remembered her father to have been, and she sometimes found it hard to believe that he *was* her brother, amazed at how easy their relationship was when they were together.

Gradually in the months that followed his death, Juliet began to see it as inevitable. It could have happened earlier; she might have missed ever knowing him at all. She wrote a long letter to Thelma who told her in reply all the details of the fatal heart attack and her calm belief that she would see him again one day in a Christian heaven. Juliet decided not to attend the funeral and the cremation. Superstitiously, with one part of her mind, Juliet wanted to be able to envisage Archie still there going about his business on the other side of the world. Try as she might, she could not believe in an after-life, only in a kind of parallel imaginative life. She spoke to Rose about her lack of faith and Rose was a great comfort whenever she came on one of her regular visits home.

'We must encourage Alex to come over,' decided Juliet. Rose urged reserve. Her mother had always said that Alex was just like Grandpa Eddie, but her mother knew that Rose distrusted all this family heredity stuff. It was true that on the many snapshots Archie had sent her mother, Alex still resembled Grandpa when young, as far as the nose was concerned and the hairline and the mouth, but that didn't mean he was like him in any other way.

'But he does *write!*' said Juliet triumphantly.

When she heard from Thelma that Alex was going to look for a job in the old country she was overjoyed.

Alex finally arrived in London in January 1994. He had applied for several temporary jobs: there was a National Trust property situated between Wensleydale and Swaledale that needed a sort of caretaker; an estate manager was required for a large farm and house on the Plain of York; and there was a position for a game-keeper and general caretaker on the moors of the South Pennines. But possibly nobody would want him, so he had brought quite a lot of money with him. He had lived abstemiously up till now, so there was for the moment no urgency. He was unsure which of these jobs he could be really keen about. Possibly none of them. If so he would take up that other sort of temporary work, computing for a business, whilst he made up his mind. He could earn enough to manage, even if London prices were fairly shocking.

He found London dirty and cold, as he had expected, but full of interest. He delayed telephoning the Considines until he had been a week or two in the capital and found his feet. It would be too easy to stay with them. Juliet had already invited him to take over Paul's old room if he was stuck for accommodation, but he did not intend to accept. He would visit them whilst waiting for an interview, and in the meantime go to theatres and cinemas and art exhibitions. He also loved long walks and planned visits to Hampstead and Kew and Greenwich and longer tramps in Kent and Hertfordshire.

He refused to rent a car. The traffic was terrible in any case and he wanted the feel of the place. He noticed a good deal of crime reported in the London evening paper, and in local papers but almost as much relatively speaking was now happening in most of the developed world. He saw many drugged or drunk men and women at night in the centre of London, refused the importuning of sellers of crack or of female bodies in Soho and round the main stations, and managed to enjoy himself in more sober ways.

He finally telephoned Juliet and Andrew and accepted an invitation to Sunday lunch in their suburb. Juliet had also persuaded Rose to invite him to a party she and some friends were giving in a fortnight.

'He'll want to meet some young women,' she said. Rose was sceptical. If she knew her cousin he would not need introductions to anyone.

CHAPTER FIVE

Alex and Rose

Rose felt shy when Alex finally arrived on her parents' doorstep at noon on the Sunday. She had been helping Juliet to make lunch. Not being sure if he was a vegetarian, and Juliet having forgotten to ask, they had played safe and were providing soup and stuffed aubergines and fresh fruit salad with crème fraîche.

Juliet met him at the door, and, tears in her eyes, held him tight. He was a part of Archie. He did not squirm in her embrace or try to release himself but comforted her with words.

Rose, watching from the kitchen, thought how kind he was, and went up as they drew apart, shook hands with him rather than giving a cousinly kiss, and said, 'I was so sorry that you lost your father.'

He kissed her on the cheek.

Andrew ushered him into the large high-ceilinged sitting-room where sherry was waiting. 'We're a bit old-fashioned,' he said. 'I hope you like dry sherry – if you don't there's whisky.'

The claret was already opened to breathe, and smells were wafting into the hall from the kitchen. Alex stood there and smiled, and offered to help them in the kitchen, an offer that was brushed away. At first they knew they had to talk about Archie, had better get it over. Rose hoped her mother was not going to break down. But Juliet had herself under control and looked merely sad.

'It's so good to see you,' she said.

Rose had heard her mother the evening before state once again her oft-reiterated opinion that of them all it was Alex who was the most like Eddie. She hoped she would not go on about families. Alex was a patient man, as she well remembered, and she hoped he was old enough not to mind the harking back. She went back into the kitchen to see to the meal – her mother tended to forget when she was excited – and covertly peeped at him from the door as he sat chatting with her parents. They were talking about London, and about Thelma, and about Alex's plans.

'Yes, I've got various interviews,' he was saying, 'but I'm not sure what I want to do.'

Juliet looked a bit worried. How old was he? Thirty-seven? Thirty-eight? She hoped he was not going to turn out to prefer the *dolce far niente* to honest labour.

She need not worry, thought Rose, who usually knew what her mother was thinking about. Alex was a hard worker who even so – she knew from her correspondence with him – did not believe that the meaning of life was to be found in work. She was more interested in his poetry than in his jobs and wanted to ask him about it when her parents had had their turn.

The lunch went very well. Alex had a good appetite but was neither a gourmet nor a strict vegetarian.

'I suppose you New Zealanders must have been weaned on Canterbury lamb? We used to eat a lot of that when I was a child. All "Empire" produce,' said Juliet.

'My grandmother used to make Yorkshire pudding,' offered Alex.

'Oh I haven't made that for years. Andrew likes it,' said Juliet. 'You really have to cook it in an oven along with a roast, so the meat juices can drip on it. We don't eat roast beef so much now – for only two of us it doesn't seem worth while.'

Alex offered an opinion about the dangers of feeding cattle on the wrong diet, as cattle were vegetarians. He seemed to know a lot about all that.

'So much has gone wrong in the developed world,' he said.

'We've got to try and redress the balance before it's too late – half of the world rich and the other half starving. . . .'

Rose said, 'Sometimes I think we'd all better go and live off smallholdings and grow our own vegetables, but I'm a hopeless gardener – ever since I dug up Dad's strawberries thinking they were weeds.'

'Yes. Rose is a prime example of correct theory and hopeless practice,' said her father, 'Though her heart's in the right place.'

After lunch, Juliet wanted to show her nephew the old family photograph album with the pictures of mutual ancestors, and of course of Eddie and his sister.

'Oh you do look so like him,' she couldn't help remarking again.

Alex bore all this in good part. He saw he could do no wrong in this house. He wanted to talk to Rose, and offered to do the washing-up with her.

'I'm afraid we've never had a dishwasher,' said Juliet apologetically. 'Most people do, but it's not worth it for two.'

If she were not careful she'd sound nostalgic for family life, for the days when her children were little. She'd better leave off talking about domestic affairs and turn the conversation to work. Alex gave her the opportunity by asking politely about her second-hand bookshop. Then they talked about Paul and his work as an industrial psychologist in Newcastle.

'Right,' said Rose. 'I'm going to make the coffee.' Alex followed her into the kitchen and quickly disposed of the plates and pans.

'Do you ever have time to go out in the evenings?' he asked her. 'Would you like to go to the theatre? There's *Cymbeline* on at the Barbican. Or do you prefer the cinema? I expect you're booked up for some time.'

'That would be nice,' she replied. 'I wanted to ask you about your poems – but perhaps you're one of those people who don't like to talk about their writing. I'm sorry not to have written to you for so long – time's begun to rush by. I'm getting as bad as Mother, she's always lamenting that.'

'Do you like always to be busy then?'

'No, not really. It's London that makes you rush everywhere and we spend so much time getting from one place to another. I don't think you'd really like to be a Londoner, Alex.'

'Perhaps not. Why don't you work at home, in the provinces, or in the country? In New Zealand they're all doing work from home on their word processors.'

'I'd love to, but it's not always easy to find work that pays well enough. Houses cost half the price away from the Home Counties – away from commuterland, but then there are so few jobs away from London, or any big city, I suppose, that pay well. I suppose you could write your poems anywhere.'

He laughed. 'But I might not be inspired to write anything,' he said. 'London – any capital city as big – is a shock, and that galvanizes you into recording impressions. But that's not the same as having the time to work at something – and also having worthwhile thoughts. Good thoughts – original thoughts – don't come easy.'

'No, I know that.' She felt sure he was the sort of person who would have many original thoughts.

Before he left she promised to go out for dinner with him. They had a lot to talk about and you didn't go to the theatre to talk to people but to listen to others.

'I'd like to read more of your poetry. You sent me some the year before last and I never told you the impression it made on me. I want to read some more before we meet again!'

He said he would do that, and they arranged to eat together in ten days or so in an Italian restaurant she knew well.

Andrew brought in some wood and put it on to the sitting-room fire. They drank tea in the gathering dusk and finished off the rest of the Christmas cake.

'It's how people imagine England,' said Alex. 'Tea by the fire!'

'Not many people have open fires now. I suppose you can just as well drink tea by the fire in New Zealand,' said Andrew.

'Oh, Grandma did in winter, though it was never very cold. But she used to toast her bread there! It reminded her of home.'

Juliet thought of Rhoda all those years ago sitting by the fire, thousands of miles separating her from home, and her son from his sisters who were doubtless also toasting bread by a Yorkshire fire fifty years ago. She had never really thought of Rhoda as homesick.

Then they talked of politics and how things had changed in the past few years in both countries. Juliet asked about how many people of his acquaintance went to church, and how she envied his mother her faith, and so on.

Rose looked at him surreptitiously and thought, he is too good to be true. I wonder if most women would have that impression. Or is it just that he is exceptionally pleasant, or exceptionally tuned in to us, or that I feel the two of us could get along together unusually well? Why had he never married? Was he too serious, too cautious? Would her friends like him? She felt a curious reluctance to introduce him to Miriam or Sarah Williams. But she invited him to the party in two weeks' time. By then she would have had time to get to know him better.

During the week following his visit to her parents Rose found herself thinking a good deal about her 'half first cousin'. His poems, sent along to her without delay, were often about the land, about animals and birds, about death, about the shrinking natural world, sometimes mentioning or using Maori myths as symbols. She felt profoundly ignorant about them. Who was it 'went walk-about' – Australian aborigines or Maoris? You had to know the background of so many peoples now, especially all the tribes that London was full of, along with the Anglo-Saxon tribe of course: refugees, survivors from African wars, dispossessed colonials, and East Europeans wandering from their ravaged lands.

She decided one gloomy afternoon at work when she should have been finishing typing a report, that what ought to matter was how you felt yourself to be, how you saw yourself when you were with another person. With her cousin Mick, for example, she felt herself shrivel. She saw how he regarded her – or how she thought she did – as rather spoilt and indulged.

With her friends she had a quite different picture of herself.

Now, with Alex Marriott she saw her inner self talking to him as though he already knew that self and so she need not present it; could indeed 'be herself'. She had realized immediately she had seen him at her parents' house that she could feel strongly about him, and this frightened her a little.

Since Fabian she had reined in her feelings. Alex got on well with everyone, had never made any special beeline for her, and she did not want to get involved again with a man who, however intelligent, did not wish to commit himself. If he had been the committed sort, surely he would have already married? So she would be careful, enjoy his company, not deny herself that, no, but be wary and never give herself away.

Alex invited her to an early supper in a restaurant near St James's the following Wednesday. Rose usually found social occasions quite nerve-racking, but this evening she tidied herself up after work, somehow without feeling the need for much prinking.

Often, when going out with a man, or to a party, she had taken so long perfecting her hair and her face and her dress that when the time came to present herself she always felt she'd looked better half an hour before. On these occasions she would try to remember that she was a feminist and that feminists saw no need for bandbox perfection. Of course you did not need to wear make-up nowadays, though many young women did. Juliet said it was a release from a tyranny, but Rose could not help noticing that her mother still used the lipstick and powder-puff.

Alex was already at the table. She had dreaded his late arrival, having waiters feel sorry for her and – she continued the story spun so easily by her imagination – leaving the restaurant alone after waiting fruitlessly for him. . . . I'm getting like my mother, she thought. Disaster never far away! But there he was, and he smiled when she arrived and eventually asked her to choose the wine. He had easy manners, was decisive as far as his own wants were concerned but not the sort of man to take charge in an assertive way.

She looked up from the menu and caught him looking at her with a long, serious look which he quickly changed into a remark

221

about the number of dishes available. They chose a simple but pungent pasta in basil and garlic, to be followed by profiteroles. Rose decided on some Verdicchio to go with it.

'Have you had a busy day? Tell me what you've been doing,' said Alex.

Rose found herself describing the female boss she worked for who, in her opinion, was always about to boil over, and the head of section who ruled them all with a rod of iron but who was frightfully shy away from the office. There was also a group of younger women graduates who scanned papers and wrote reports. Rose felt so much older than them; the gap between twenty-four and thirty-two was a wide one. They used designer drugs at weekends and had peculiar 'estuary' accents, talked about pop music she had never heard of, went clubbing and appeared as hard as nails.

'Did you ever smoke pot when you were a student?' he asked her at one point. 'Perhaps you still do. Lots of people still did in the early eighties, even at home. Quite respectable middle-aged people.'

'I tried it of course but it didn't do anything for me except make me feel a bit sleepy and bored. Paul smoked a few joints when he was a student but he's a very cautious person and decided he'd rather not bother. People younger than us take dangerous hard drugs for granted. Paul has to lecture to teachers about their effects; he says there's a big difference between the official line and the opinion of most of the young, who scoff at the danger.'

'I used to smoke cigarettes,' confessed Alex. 'I love nicotine but I managed to stop. I do so dislike those morally ascendant puritans; they give the impression that smoking's worse than mugging people.'

'Yes, that's what my father says. He smokes a pipe as you know, and Mother is always "stopping smoking". Your father didn't die of lung cancer though. He didn't smoke cigarettes, did he?'

'No, it was a heart attack.'

'I loved the poems about the mountains and the sea,' Rose said when there had been a lull in the conversation for a minute and they were still waiting for the next course to arrive. 'I didn't understand all the references but I could imagine the places, and I liked your poem about England too. But you haven't been here for over ten years!'

'I find a poem waits until you are ready for it,' said Alex. 'As a matter of fact I remembered your autumn garden, how it was when we came over in eighty-two, the afternoon we met your aunt. How is she, our Aunt Alison?'

'Oh, she leads a very active life. She goes all over the place with Clive – he's now her husband – they got married a few years ago. One of her sons, my cousin Thom, has become a businessman and I think she's rather proud of him. The other one, Mick, is a research geologist or something like that.'

'And now, Rose,' Alex said when they had finished the next course and were waiting for the dessert. 'You've told me all about the family and your work and my poems so now I want to know about you.'

'No, it's your turn,' she said.

'What can I say? I spent years doing my bit for Friends of the Earth and Greenpeace and others, but I think I led a very selfish life. What had I given up for the world? Do you think it's the old puritan conscience coming back? They must all have been dissenters, our ancient ancestors.'

'I don't think Eddie – our grandfather – was. He was just born at a difficult time. Have you read his verse?'

'Some of it. Father had pages of it in a suitcase. Your mother brought it over to us when your parents visited last time. Apparently he'd left it in the bank! Our grandfather wrote very classically, I mean, formally, but with poetic vocabulary that was very impassioned, except for the love poems to my grandmother. He kept copies!'

Rose wanted to say that Juliet thought Alex was a throw-back to her father but it might be a bit too near the bone to say so when he had been talking about love poems.

But he went on, 'I often wonder if it would have made any difference to me if I had not been Archie's son, if it turned out that *I* was someone else's child, that my mother had conducted an affair with someone else! Would I have written? Perhaps I'd have been a rugby player.'

Rose laughed. 'My mother never stops saying, as you will have noticed, that you're just like her father in all matters as well as in looks, and anyway you haven't got the build of a rugby player.'

'But if I were someone else's son I might have.'

'Why, is there any doubt? It wasn't like what happened with Eddie and your grandmother, was it?'

'No, no doubt at all, but I often think about what makes us what we are. It must be that I'll be forty in less than two years; you begin to see your life more objectively.'

She looked at him, at his hazel eyes and full mouth and snub nose and light-brown slightly wavy hair, and thin hands, and had a sudden vision of history repeating itself the other way round; Alex falling in love with her but then abandoning her, leaving her for some woman on the other side of the world. That would bring the wheel round full circle! How silly she was. He was not in love with her, but if she were not very careful she was going to fall for him.

Alex returned her scrutiny; he saw a fair-haired young woman with grey eyes and a small nose and cherry mouth; long, long fingers; trim little figure, nice little ears, sweet voice, shy look, but an unexpectedly witty dry humour. . . would she ever believe that he had never forgotten her? He had perhaps a disadvantage in her eyes; all this talk about history repeating itself; people's belief that he was a sort of reincarnation of his grandfather. That was not good. If he were forced to pretend he was not his father's son to gain Rose's interest he would have done so, but it was too late for that. He would just have to manage on his own with the ammunition nature had given him.

The party was a noisy affair and as Rose was one of the hostesses she could not find time to sit down and talk to her cousin. He seemed quite happy however, chatting to several of her girl-friends. The next time they met was at a concert in a church on Piccadilly. Afterwards they went for coffee nearby.

'The Bach was wonderful,' Rose was saying. 'Bach always cheers me up, even when he's not supposed to. It must be something to do with alpha rhythms and the brain, it makes me feel calm.'

'And therefore happy.'

'Yes.'

'I feel the same. I used to listen to a lot of romantic music and then I slowly realized I wanted form and fugue and pattern. I love Haydn too, last week I heard the Haydn Organ Concerto in D, and it was wonderful.'

'Oh, I love it!' What about Telemann? Do you think he's perhaps too much of a good thing?'

'Yes, but in a funny way quite soothing! What about Vivaldi?'

'Can music be too "listenable"? I do like romantic music too. Don't you like Field's nocturnes. And Purcell?'

'Of course. The Purcell tonight was heavenly.'

Discovering they had the same tastes in music pleased Rose no end. She was not sure if she had appreciated Alex's verse; it was rather compressed in thought, but she welcomed the flashes of description, of countryside, of birds, sea, and moods.

As they went to the bus-stop (Rose did not own a car either) Alex said, 'I want to go North sometime, you know, see where we all came from. Would you come with me? For a holiday. Do you know the place where my grandmother lived? My father talked about it a lot.'

'So did my grandfather, or rather, he wrote about it, if you remember. Knagg Wood wasn't it? Haven't you been North before?'

'No, I didn't have the time when I was here last. My father went later on. I have to look round. There might be a job for me up there, in North Yorkshire.' It was the first she had heard of this. 'Perhaps at Easter,' he went on. 'It would be less cold then.'

Rose could not think of anything she would like better, but felt she must not appear too keen. They left the idea hanging.

Alex telephoned her a few days later asking her if she would like to accompany him to an art exhibition at a small gallery open on a Saturday morning. He had heard there would be one or two Yorkshire paintings there.

I wonder if we shall like the same paintings too, she thought. That would be impossible! She had rather simple tastes in painting, preferring the figurative and the English to greater works of art, apart from Turner and Constable, who seemed to be everybody's favourite painters.

The exhibition was very small but there were two of her favourite paintings at the gallery that Saturday morning by Atkinson Grimshaw the Victorian Yorkshireman so beloved of the older generation. She had seen similar ones before on a visit to her mother's maternal aunt in Leeds some years earlier. She and her mother had escaped to the city gallery and then visited Harrogate, and in both places she had seen paintings by this Leeds Victorian artist.

'*Silver Moonlight*, 1886,' quoted Alex. 'Yes, that's the painter my father told me about. He said he painted places like Grandma's mansion.'

'Nearly all my favourites are in provincial galleries,' said Rose. 'Not always in the North; there's a lovely little Cotman watercolour in Norwich; *The Drawing Master – The Green Lamp*. I suppose I just like the period. But we've time now to go to the Tate to see some Turner before lunch – or have you already been?'

'Not yet. We could get some lunch there, I suppose.'

So off they went to Millbank to see the Petworth pictures from a little earlier in Rose's favourite century.

On the way she said, 'There's the V and A too. Another day? My favourite Samuel Palmer is there – and then the Courtauld for Cézanne, if you really like galleries. I love tramping round them myself, I don't go so much to the big exhibitions laid on – too many people.' Alex liked the sound of her enthusiasm.

They sat and admired the Turners, Alex saying he would get aesthetic indigestion but then willingly following Rose to see a decorative Matisse, then Dyce's *Pegwell Bay*, and finally the voluptuous Edwardian garden fairyland of Sergeant's: *Carnation, Lily, Lily, Rose.*

'Time for a drink,' said Alex. Rose liked a man to know his own mind and she was enjoying her day not only on account of the pictures.

'Do you understand the "conceptual" art we passed by on the ground floor?' Rose asked him as they drank some quite decent red wine and ate their lamb casserole.

'You don't need to understand it; we could make up similar things. The only difference between us and an artist of this kind is that we have no technical prowess, or at least I haven't. I couldn't actually make the idea concrete.'

'Yes, concrete's the word. It's more like heaving round stone or heavy metal-work than art. It's technological art, isn't it.'

'Well, invent some "concepts"! Even if you can't carry them into existence, so long as you give them a catchy title, they'll do. I suggest – let's see, a montage of discarded plaster casts of animals' limbs taken from veterinary surgeries and joined together to make a new plaster animal with the title *Modern Monster*.'

'Freeze dead goldfish in ice in the shape of a bowl and have them on display with the title *Food for Inuits*.'

'Paint a picture with a dried umbilical cord you later incorporate into the painting.'

'What title for that?'

He thought a moment and then said *Rebirth*!'

'Breath produced in February in cold, non-centrally-heated English house captured as vapour and frozen. Title: *Cosy England*.'

'Rooms whose walls are mirrors with trick distortions, as in funfairs – or, wait! Better still, arranged as kaleidoscopes in which the visitors to the gallery act as the coloured pieces, making perpetually new patterns. I can't think of a title for that. You know if we could *make* all these things we might win the Turner Prize.'

Rose was unstoppable. 'Frozen waterfalls in a winter garden. Or a piece of frozen crest of a wave – in a showcase with frozen tears running down the sides. Title: *Winter Sea Grief*.'

'That's very poetic. We're quite good at this, aren't we.'

'Your turn,' said Rose.

' A concrete snowman made from an original child mould. Title: *Kevin Made It.*'

'Oh, how gruesome! Let me think. I know: a giant doll's house with rooms full of not *quite* life-size dolls that interact with the visitors, get them talking to each other. . . .'

'I'll supply that title: *Getting on with People.*'

'They're all like the kind of "art" you find in funfairs, and freak-shows, aren't they?'

'People's Art, that's right – or Madame Tussaud's. I went there with my – and your – grandfather on my first visit to London.'

'Really? Are such things linked to popular forms of religion? Primitive art?' She thought, I don't know much about his Maoris, and they won't be primitive any more, if they ever were. That's just how we think of them.

'Totems,' said Alex. 'The statues of primitive religion link with the models you might make as a child.'

'But what about these things here? Do they all come from the sort of imagination they test in so-called creativity tests?'

'I always loved them,' said Alex. 'So much more fun than IQ tests. A pity we're all theory, isn't it?'

'I can't make things to save my life. I bet you can though,' said Rose.

'Not very well. I used to do wood-carving as a boy—'

'There you are then! I loved making things when I was little. Paul was better at it though; he used to send his ideas up to *Blue Peter* on TV. Perhaps we should send the Tate a list of ideas for their next exhibition.'

'They say,' said Alex, 'that conceptual art will give way to "installation art" – at least that's what I've read. It's all over the world you know, not just here in England.'

They had by this time demolished their lunch and Alex went for two cups of coffee. Time just sped by when he was with her. They had the same sort of imagination, he thought. Not unusual, he supposed, for 'almost-first-cousins'?

Alex and Rose had many more conversations in those dark

February days, and in March, when the days grew appreciably longer and daffodils came out in the parks. They talked in galleries, over meals, in cinema queues, in the intervals of plays, at her flat – where Alex made no pass – but not yet at her parents' house. They had many tastes in common, it seemed, not only for the same artists or composers, and a few shared characteristics. But it had been Rose's experience that being like someone did not always lead to a good relationship. She had thought she was 'like' Fabian Lee, and they had argued a good deal. She did not want to argue with Alex Marriott, and they were not identical in all their opinions. Where they were alike, apart from their tastes in painting and music, and even novels, was in certain physical characteristics. She noticed that they had similarly shaped hands, those of both of them were thin and brown with long fingers and large nails; clearly some genetic print had survived in them both.

Alex was much more politically aware than she was. Rose had told him a good deal about her mother's pessimism and Alex said his father had been the same. It was to do with growing older and they themselves would most likely change one day. For the time being, though, if people of their age did not try to do something about social problems they all might as well give up.

'Yes, but people just don't agree on what the problems are, never mind what to do about them,' said Rose.

They had been walking on the Heath and were now sitting in a Hampstead pub on a March day warmer than usual, talking of London and England and what living here meant in the 1990s, and what was good – and bad – about it.

'I like the English,' said Alex. 'They may be insular and eccentric and conservative, but I'm no revolutionary. Except when I think of the mess you – we – are making of the environment. Yet there are worse things wrong in other places, I suppose.'

'The English,' said Rose, 'are mad about the countryside, though there's not supposed to be much left of it. They always say our literary tradition is pastoral and romantic, and that's how I find some of your poems, but with a tough backbone as well.'

He was silent for a moment, as though he did not wish to

discuss his verse, and then he went on, 'And the English like their privacy – they're not good at living in cities unless they are very rich, but our Romantic poets were used to London.'

They did not do so much direct talking about themselves as time went on, which Rose found refreshing. Instead she would mention some of the things that agitated people in the media; muggings, burglaries, rapes, sink estates, vandalism, drug-taking, child-abuse, generalized violence and the growing menace of idle young men with neither education nor work. What could anyone do about it?

'I wish I knew,' said Alex. 'But it no longer stops me writing, or prevents me from being happy.'

'Is that because we are young? They don't stop me being happy either, but older people are really terrified and depressed. Mother says life used to be much nicer. Father says it may have been nicer for some, but not for most people. But Mother thinks everything is worse now – she's been thinking that for at least twenty years. She'd be happy to return to a world of typewriters and bicycles and what she calls the 'wireless'; no aircraft, television, electronics or split atoms. Father says that the world was always terrible and violent.'

'Yes and Man's life nasty, brutish and short. It always was – still is. That's not the whole story though, is it? And we just expect it to be better after all our ideas of "progress".' For some reason his words comforted her. 'My father was like your mother,' added Alex, 'always on about the poverty of spirit that exists in the whole of the developed world, and furious about technology and consumer goods and ever-expanding "choices". I suppose that's where I must get it from, though he never really did anything about it. And it was odd for a businessman-cum-farmer.'

'Was he – religious?'

'No. I suppose he was too rational. Why? Are you?"

She did not answer his query directly but said, 'Religious belief doesn't seem to solve anything, does it? Though it might make you feel better.'

'Evil has always existed,' said Alex lightly, 'and disorder – and anarchy – that's what my father couldn't stand but my mother never believes that people are evil, just that they haven't had the right chances in life.'

'Do you believe that? I don't. Some people are just horrible – but then you do get people who had few chances and who made something good out of their lives.'

She told him about her Granny Kitty's grandmother who came from a poverty-stricken Norfolk agricultural background and who had left school at eight in 1859.

'Mother put it into her "story of herself". Great-Grandma married a widower twelve years older than she was and they uprooted themselves to go two hundred miles for work. She was the stepmother to two little girls as well as having nine more children of her own. She was a widow forty-three years; she kept going sewing shirts. Can you imagine what her life must have been like? Yet on all the photographs she looks quite happy and sane!'

'Were her children like her?'

'Oh, they all did well. She had strong religious beliefs; she was a Methodist, and I suppose that saved her. And the need to work day and night to keep going. My mother remembers her tasty meals of tripe and onions.'

'Perhaps some characters will always find that religion helps.'

'Was it only religion or was it her character?'

'What was her husband like?'

'He didn't drink and he used to read a lot. I suppose he was a good man. You know, I hadn't really thought about it but the "good" people are more usually women, aren't they? I mean in life if not in fiction.'

'She would not have expected anything more from life.'

'Well, she just got on with the life that was offered her. We are all spoilt, aren't we?'

'But we get on with our lives too – we have to – and there are so many good things in the world!'

'The good things of life,' mused Rose, 'depend a lot on civilization, don't they? I don't mean on a lot of money but on custom and habit and law and order. I remember a Sunday in a part of

France I visited a summer or two ago and how on Mother's Day the little restaurant was all dressed in pink – pink tablecloths, pink linen napkins, pink roses. All this tranquil formal habit going on, whilst if you opened the newspaper, "Rome burned".'

'Why should you not enjoy all that? Did it make you feel guilty? Perhaps they were dressing the tables for you, Rose, with pink roses!'

'I never thought of that! Maybe that's why it impressed me so. Yes, I did feel a bit guilty, I suppose, because I do read the papers and watch the TV news. And we were brought up to have a social conscience. What kind of things make you angry, Alex?'

He replied straight away: 'That millions of children never eat a decent meal, or hear any decent music, or see a tree. . . . And pollution produced by ourselves, and the British having Trident – that makes me mad – and all the rubbish that comes out of America and the worship of the car. . . .'

'Are we just agonized liberals? That's what Fabian used to call me.'

She told him then about Fabian as they walked down Haverstock Hill. 'He was a Marxist but he said there was no longer any hope for real socialism, only for a modified sort of reform.'

'Did he care?'

'No, I don't think so. Oh, I don't know. He certainly wasn't any sort of feminist! I'm sure he now spends a lot of time surfing the net.'

'A terrible time-waster,' said Alex, 'when you know that all technology can do is in the realm of means, not ends.'

'I do find you so very comforting,' she said.

They went down into the dirty underground at Belsize Park. There were several beggars further along the line, and when they got out and went for a meal to Covent Garden, many homeless were lying on the streets.

Over dinner Rose said, 'How true are food scares? They're always going on about the effects of this or that. Do we really know what we're eating unless we grow it ourselves?'

'They are usually true – I mean the scares – but if you research the things that are supposed to be good or bad for you you won't come to any conclusions because they lack proper proof.'

'All the things that are wrong in the world . . . it's just endless! Where can you start?'

'They must stop letting land lie fallow and paying farmers to do so. You never know when you might need some land to feed your far too large UK population. Do you know we have a larger country and fewer than four million people, and you have fifty-eight million!'

'Wars might suddenly arise, if not now, soon in the next century. I mean apart from Africa or the Middle East – or, I suppose, Ireland. Terrorists setting off nuclear bombs, for example.'

In this and in many similar conversations Rose and Alex tried to set the world to rights, and tested each other's opinions. They went to listen to a high-powered debate at the House of Lords whose speakers were not tired old party hacks but cross-benchers, most of whom, Rose noticed, were men. Afterwards they discussed homosexuality. Alex said it was nature's attempt to prevent over-population.

'Is there any political party for whom you could honestly vote?' asked Alex. 'I'd vote green on many issues, if there were any candidates. The strange thing is that I'm not a political person; I'm more against things than for them.'

'You're just an old-fashioned individualist.'

'So are you!' He had gone into details about his work for the Greenpeace movement when he was younger. Rose could listen to him for hours though he also was a good listener. She asked him why he did not want to stay in a country which was to all intents and purposes so much healthier than her own. Alex said things were changing over there and that everything – transport, water, energy – was to be become deregulated, making it more like a Mrs Thatcher paradise, 'an unrestrained free market,' he explained. 'And that's anathema to me!'

Rose was surprised; she had somehow conceived of New Zealand as a place in a time warp.

'It's true you *can* have a simpler lifestyle away from the cities but, for example, even our kiwi bird is now an endangered species and a lot of the native trees are being logged.'

She was immensely attracted to Alex and realized that she was beginning to love him, though she continued to be terrified of repeating the pattern of their grandfather's courtship of Alex's grandmother. Not that she would desert him if he loved her, which she did not think he did, but still, there was always the thought that he might desert her?

It seemed he was determined to settle for good in England. She knew he had been for two interviews for jobs, in the south-west and in East Anglia. The northern prospective employers had not thought his experience justified an interview. One day in April he mentioned once more their going North together. 'Could you manage it at the end of next month?'

Rose had leave owing to her and would like nothing better than to go away for a little holiday from London, but she was uncertain whether he would think she might assume she would be going as something more than his 'cousin'.

Juliet and Richard continued to explode with annoyance when they read their newspapers. They took three, to get a balanced view, but Juliet found certain attitudes hard to take, and projected her own insecurities upon left-wing critics who, she felt, implicitly criticized the middle classes rather than trying to offer solutions to the problems of modern living that confronted the English, and the rest of the world, developed or not.

'We get on perfectly well with ordinary adults without a crash course in inner-city practical sociology,' she remarked one Sunday, incensed at loose talk of 'community'. 'Where is the so-called "community" in this suburb? It's split into hundreds of groups, but the only one most families know is the "community" of their own social circle. How many times do these journalists invite home the people they stand at the bus-stop with or shop at the supermarket with?'

'They don't stand at bus-stops,' said her husband. 'They all have cars, or if they're very young what we used to call motorbikes. Anyway, don't be taken in by their burbling – you've nothing to feel guilty about.'

'But if you don't agree with them, and claim you do understand "ordinary" people, they say you're Lady Bountiful arranging the lives of the poor.'

They worried about the lack of facilities for the homeless and the mentally ill, about children being bullied in the land of the free; they agitated to keep open the library in their village, the public library system being, said Juliet, the first thing to go or at least economize on for many local councils.

Andrew worried about air-traffic control, the near misses that had risen in number, and all the dangers that were the results of the onward march of technology.

'If you say things like that,' said Rose, 'politicians will reply, You wouldn't want to go back and have no air travel would you? What you are really angry about is all those "ordinary" people taking package tours to far-flung bits of the world. Yet for myself I wouldn't mind going back; I've no desire now to travel further than Europe.'

'What about when you went across the world to New Zealand!'

'Oh well, you win. But now Archie's gone I don't want to go there again.'

Another great bee buzzing in Andrew's bonnet at this time was the establishment of proper vocational qualifications before the British forgot how to build, plumb or do joinery, never mind losing their brightest inventors to other countries.

'The economy has effectively abandoned millions of unskilled males to the dole and the scrap-heap, to drink, drugs and burglary. Yet there are thousands of jobs they could learn to do,' he said. Alex was there for lunch, so he heard this conversation.

'But you can't force them,' said Juliet. 'Your father,' she went on, turning to Alex, 'used to say it was like that in Wellington too except that they had a very small population. And the French and the Italians have the same social problems that we have. . . .'

'Not quite so bad in Italy – their families are stronger,' said her husband.

'In Western Europe they don't dress like our young – shaved heads and earrings, and dirty trainers, and wrinkled T-shirts, and all-over tattoos. Italian men are quite smart,' said Juliet.

'Some Germans dress as those British do.'

'But they're neo-Nazis, aren't they?'

Andrew continued to talk about tangible things, like the possible privatization of the railways or the Royal Mail. He had less interest in his wife's indignation with the Church of England, to which she did not in fact belong, over their dereliction of the English language.

'We must return to the old Book of Common Prayer,' Juliet had been saying for years. 'Then perhaps through the old words a new faith will come from memories of the faith people once had. What about your mother, Alex, does she like the Alternative Version?'

'I don't think she minds so much about the language as about the meaning,' said Alex.

'And you, with your nostalgia for language, have no god up there to punish the wicked,' said Andrew to his wife. They were used to this argument. Andrew knew very well that what Juliet really wanted was justice for the virtuous and hell for the wicked, though she did not like to say so.

Rose and Alex, on a visit to her parents, would easily come to the conclusion that Rose's parents like most of the older generation, were preoccupied with change. Some of their worries were over the kind of problems that she and Alex talked about together, that she and Alex took for granted in the world they lived in. Yet, as time went on, Rose was finding that all these problems did not preoccupy her as much as they once had, and that when she was with her Cousin Alex she was very happy.

In the meantime, the Channel Tunnel would be finished the following year; the destruction of the ozone layer would go on causing concern (there had been attempts to address the problem at earth summit in Rio the previous year) but depletion and worldwide pollution would continue.

It seemed that change happened whether you wanted it or not. The world, or rather the post-Christian part of it, was hurtling towards the Millennium.

Alex was poring over maps of Yorkshire.

'Two National Parks,' he said, finger on the map, 'as well as the South Pennine moors. There must be *some* work up there, you know.'

'Will you definitely apply again if another job turns up?'

'Probably – though I expect they'd prefer a home-grown person. If there's nothing official, I could always lend a hand with a bit of hill farming; nobody wants to do that much now, it's extremely hard work for a poor return. But I'm still on the look-out for wardenships and estate-manager jobs, or conservation of flora and fauna, that sort of thing.'

'They're quite different, all those places,' said Rose, peering at the map. 'The Bairstow home county is so big. Broad Acres, they used to call it.'

'I know about the three Ridings. My father listened to *his* father about that. Apparently they altered the boundaries in 1974.'

'Yes, Mother was furious! Yorkshire lost bits of itself to the new Cumbria and they made "South Yorkshire" and chopped off part of the old East Riding too. Sacrilege! But I should imagine the best jobs would be in the two National Parks, on the North York moors or in the Dales, that's where all the tourists go.'

'They'll need people to keep an eye on things. I don't suppose there'll be much going around Woolsford, though.'

'Oh, they have a lot of tourists there now. Is that where you want to go for a holiday? You want to see all the family stuff?'

'I'd like to see Woolsford, and then we could drive over to the other parts.'

'There's the Vale of York, too, where I think some of Grandpa's family came from. Lovely agricultural land there. Mother said he'd wanted to be a farmer, and he said so, didn't he, in his story, so perhaps it's in your genes.'

'I think you'd need a good deal of capital to buy in there, unlike

237

the hill farms. Well, if I can't find anything within the next few months, if there's nothing doing, I can always apply for an office job in London, perhaps at the Min. of Ag. or the D. of E. They might need clerks there, and I've got my two degrees—'

'Not very well paid! You could try what you did in New Zealand – you *are* a naturalist.'

'The situation down under was very different. I don't think my actual experience will stand for anything. Maybe I'll just take a job with one of the conservation organizations – if they'll have me. Most likely unpaid!'

He did not seem very worried though, and Rose wondered if it was all moonshine, some romantic dream of his, a bubble that would soon burst.

Alex was a little amazed at himself, but still could not quite believe that Rose could be interested in him, and that his gamble might pay off. She probably regarded him as a safe man to talk to who would not make a pass at her. Some of her ex-boyfriends, so far as he could gather, had been dire. He would be thirty-nine later that year, and his father's death had jerked him into a considera-tion of what he had so far done with his life. He had with him an introduction to one of the small presses in London that still published poetry; he knew several writers through correspon-dence, and should be spending these few free weeks meeting them or getting on with some writing. Instead, he was thinking about Rose Considine.

He had enjoyed a few affairs back home but they had all petered out, either because he had lost interest, or the woman had known he was too much of a solitary for her taste. Now he knew that one young woman shared his tastes, or at least liked talking to him, but he had no way of knowing, without taking the plunge, whether she was as attracted to him as he was to her. And he was shy of taking that plunge, did not want to lose her.

What he needed was some magic potion that would reveal Rose's innermost feelings, but such potions did not exist, and the only way was to tell her what he felt himself. When he thought about her, his feelings grew wings,; he would have to make her believe he could love her. and that he could be more than a friend, more than a cousin. For the first time in his life he seriously entertained the idea of marriage. He had always known it would come one day into his head but he had not tried to encourage it before, even though he had never forgotten the charms of Rose.

Rose was more and more attracted to her cousin but believed it was unlikely he was attracted in the same way to her. But she could not help day-dreaming about him, which was very unlike her. He was so different from other men she had known, so very 'old-fashioned'. Perhaps it was because he *was* her cousin, so that even if they had only really got to know each other in the past three months, by now they knew each other too well.

Why should he feel about her as she was beginning to feel about him? She remembered his asking himself how different he'd be if he was not his father's son but some by-blow of his mother's, as Archie had been Rhoda's. Did he wonder if she'd like him better, or trust him more, if that were true? She consoled herself with the thought that history never quite repeated itself. She had no desire to be a victim like poor Grandpa. But of course she was not a victim, unless everyone capable of feeling was one.

She agreed they would go north for a week and explore the cities and towns of their grandparents and great-grandparents, and of her mother and Aunt Alison. Juliet was pleased they were to 'make a pilgrimage', as she kept saying, and Rose thought she might even offer to accompany them if she were not careful. Juliet however did no such thing. She too had her dreams and had immediately seen that this young man, this son of her dear Archie, was a good young man, good enough even to deserve her lovely daughter, though Rose had said nothing. She was careful not to enquire whether they would be sharing a room. Indeed Rose would have been furious if she had, for Alex had booked them first of all into a hotel in Woolsford with adjoining rooms.

One morning in the first week of May they took the train from King's Cross and hired a car when they arrived in Woolsford. The hotel did not appear to be full and the visitors staying there were chiefly business people. They would stay there for two nights, look round the city and then explore a little to the north-east of Woolsford before going on to Ilkley and Wharfedale.

'I've found the way to get to Knagg Wood,' said Alex as they sat decorously drinking tea on the afternoon of their arrival. He had brought down a map. They were to walk round Woolsford after tea, until the shops shut. He wanted to see the old Market where Eddie had bought his books.

'I thought Knagg Wood might just be a dream place, even if your grandmother was supposed to have lived there,' said Rose. 'Mother's never visited it, you know. I believe your father did when he came over the second time.'

'Yes, he wanted to go there alone. He said it had been used as a hospital and then left for a time and now it was too big to keep up, but the gardens were still there, all overgrown into the woods.'

'Who owns it all now?'

'I believe it's the city council but they can't find a use for it, it's too isolated for drop-outs or druggies to haunt. There was a rumour it might become a golf course.'

'How unromantic!'

'The other rumour was that the university would buy it for a place for weekend courses and things, but I don't know the latest. We can walk there from the village – there isn't a railway station any longer. We can leave the car down in the village.'

After tea they went to look for the covered market. Once the centre of the city was left behind, all the streets were hilly and steep. The place was no friend to pedestrians who were forced to walk through dark underpasses over which the constant traffic sped along. Sixties development was ugly and characterless even if one or two handsome Victorian buildings had been left. They were glad to go into the similarly Victorian market. There was even a bookstall there, though not the one Eddie had known.

Rose found a ninety-year-old volume, prettily printed between illustrated green boards with a half-page line-drawing of trees and a stile on its front. It was about the wrong county, Somerset, but was full of country lore and she bought it for Alex. Alex was looking for old guidebooks to the city and its environs but there was not very much. He bought some old postcards of the place. Rose enjoyed pottering and it was obvious that her companion did too. They had this in common as well as so much else, along with the usual and inevitable differences between male and female.

Before dinner they had a drink at the hotel bar and Alex looked at his present and his postcards whilst Rose read the local rag which seemed to tell of just as many burglaries and general unpleasantness as the London suburbs she had lived in.

'Do you realize that by the end of this century it'll be a hundred years since our grandfather was born,' she said.

'It only makes me think how quickly time passes. When I read his autobiography our Eddie seemed quite close. Well, we'll all be celebrating a thousand years soon, I expect. I always hear "a thousand ages in thy sight" when I think of that number—'

'Are like an evening gone,' she finished for him. 'Well, let's enjoy *this* evening!'

'I am, dear Rose, I am!'

Alex was reading aloud to Rose from the book she had given him. He read of an English hedgerow ninety years ago, a 'glory and a delight,' with its snowy blossoms of blackthorn upon a leafless hedge, and its 'wrinkled maple', its hawthorn and hazel, its straight saplings of grey ash and the frequent suckers from the long roots of elm trees. Briers hung down offering 'their sweet pink flowers' and white bryony, and the broad glossy heart-shaped leaves of black bryony met in a tangle with the little purple, yellow-eyed flowers of the woody nightshade.

'Listen to this,' he said to Rose. He read on to her of the hedger with his leather gloves and long leathern gaiters, who cleared away the useless stuff they called 'trumpery', who chose with care the likeliest growing wood for 'plashers'. 'With a deft blow of his hook he cuts the 'plasher' almost through, lays it and pegs it down; builds up the bank with sods and fills the new-made ditch with thorns, lest cattle should come and trample on his work. So the old hedge is turned to account. Nothing is wasted. There is wood to burn, and faggots for the baker's oven. The younger hazel goes for sticks for next year's peas; the straight ashen poles to fence sweet-smelling ricks. Even the 'trumpery' will serve as 'staddle' to make a dry foundation for some future mow. . . .'

'Lovely – show me.'

He handed over the book and she finished reading it to him. 'In the autumn the hazel-leaves are yellow and the maple-bush is turning to old gold. A wren is creeping like a mouse and hiding out of sight behind the old level plashing upon the bank; and a flock of linnets flies out of the hedge with a whirring of wings, alighting only a few paces in front, all on one bush. . . . Do you have some of our flowers and birds?' she asked him, looking up when she had finished reading. He was staring at her. Then he smiled.

'A few of them. Over here you're losing many of yours, and half your hedgerows have gone. . . . But it's a lovely book.'

After a pause Rose said, 'I still don't understand why you should want to live over here when from all you've told me New Zealand is such a lovely country, with far fewer of the sort of problems we have. Mother said she wouldn't mind settling there herself. She liked Christchurch when they went over there. She said it was so civilized!'

'Christchurch was built as a churchy place and used to be more England than England, a garden-city with a cathedral. But now, like everything else, it's got more like New York.'

'Cleaner and safer, though?' Alex still dared not say how much of his desire to make a fresh start in England, his compulsion to return to the old country which had grown in him since his father's death was because of her. It would seem presumptuous, ridiculous.

'All the things you care about,' said Rose, 'good farming methods and conservation and space and beauty are in New Zealand! What do you like about this crowded little island that's even smaller than yours? You told me there were fewer than four million people over there, not fifty-eight million or whatever it is here. . . .'

He thought, I can tell her it must be my grandmother's – or

grandfather's – blood coming out, but Rose is a rational human being and probably doesn't believe in such things. I think I *am* like Edward Bairstow though.

'I am a bit like our grandfather,' he said. 'I write, and it seemed natural at this stage to come to London.'

She thought, so he'll probably go back home eventually. She said, 'There are lots of novelists in New Zealand. I've even read quite a few of them.'

'Yes – some poets too – but I felt the greatest challenge would be here.'

'Why not New York? All the English writers say that the best writing comes from the States.'

'I'm not sure that's true any more, and England still probably has more poets to the square yard than anywhere else in the world. I suppose something tugged me back.'

'To live where there are so many things wrong?'

'It's true that we are much more egalitarian over there. And the climate – perfect! And lovely countryside; mountains and fjords!' He had told her about the trout-fishing and the beaches and the mountains, the swift rivers and the alpine lakes, the animals and plants and the good land-management, the good food and the home-produced wine.

'The *pakeha*, the European man, has changed the place,' he said.

Rose appeared determined to undermine his reasons for coming over to London. 'It's a pledged nuclear-free zone too,' she said.

She thought, would I like to live over there? Perhaps.

They finally found themselves a mile or two from Knagg Wood, left the car on a side-street where there were no yellow lines, and turned up a walled, country-looking lane that began with cobble-stones, continued with stone flags on each side and then nothing. It was steep, still overhung with horse-chestnuts and beeches, as Eddie had found it over seventy years before. All was green, the air fresh as if there was no city near. Fields spread out towards a valley a mile or so away and on one side there were the beginnings of a wood, with a few bluebells visible under the trees. The lane, following the wood, turned, and there was a gate and a path beyond.

Rose and Alex climbed on to the gate that had once been a stile and Alex said, 'Look!' and pointed across the fields to a clump of trees with a tall grey stone chimney piercing their tops.

'It's the house!' said Rose.

'I think it's the side of the house, but we don't really want the house. We want to walk in the woods first, don't we?'

'Look down there – there's another road.'

'It's the old carriage-drive that curves round to the main road. I expect in the past the gardens would have stretched as far as the woods down there.'

'You *have* been studying the map!'

'Well, it wasn't a very good one, but enough to see the woods and the lanes.'

They turned back into the woods and walked along under tall trees before coming out into a clearing where there was another gate, this time of rotting wood, set in the far hedge.

'All this is still the grounds of Knagg Wood?'

She shivered, not from a sudden chill so much as from a feeling of a ghostly past.

'Shall we go through the gate?' he asked her.

'No, let's walk on further into the wood.'

The sun was shining through a green canopy in little chinks of light like diamond chips. There was the distant sound of a brook. How peaceful it was. Alex was thinking, I love her, how can I make her believe that? They could go and gape at where his ancestors had lived, and it would be interesting, the neglected old house where his grandmother had spent her youth. But it was all in the past and he felt he held the present in his hand and was fearful of dropping it like some precious crystal goblet that would dash to fragments on the path.

Yet it was to be the past that would tilt the balance. They had walked on a little further and then sat down under the trees where there was a dry carpet of brushwood and leaves.

He turned towards her. 'You were only twenty the first time I saw you. Twelve years ago now. Do you remember? I think I fell in love with you a little then, though I didn't know it; it took me years to realize!'

He was thinking, before I met Rose, and with other people since, it was always: never the time, the place and the person. Now I have her here and I am frightened of ruining it.

Rose looked steadily at him.

'Are you not sure I love you?' he added. 'Must I kiss you to prove it?'

She laughed. But he did not make a move, just sat looking at her now.

'Don't be frightened about the fact we are related,' he said after a pause. 'All that business with our grandparents—'

'But it does worry me—'

'That history for once might repeat itself? That's just superstition! I'd have loved you eventually, Rose, whenever I met you, wherever it was, believe me!'

She was so very attracted to him and turned her head away so he should not see her face. She wanted things to be ordinary and pleasant, for there not to exist any constraint between them.

She only had to say: I love you too. But she got up instead and said, 'Let's just walk a bit further on.'

Somehow the little wood was enticing her, forcing her to walk on further. The sun still shone high in the sky, but the beech-tree trunks now were tall and mysterious, their tops were tangled together so that the path ahead was gloomy.

She stopped and leaned against a tree. The path began to drop at this point towards the boundary of the estate for there was a wall at the bottom and another gate.

'We've come right round,' she said. 'It feels ghostly. I wouldn't like to come here alone.'

'Look!' he said.

'What?'

He was taller than she was, so she had not seen it, but right

above her head, where she was leaning against the smooth dark-
ish greeny-grey trunk, there it was, an entwined E and R. It was
quite clearly delineated.

'Look!' he said again.

She stepped back and looked up and saw it too.

'You see? "E" that's our grandfather, and "R" that's my grandmother. It could be us too, couldn't it? Edward is one of my names
and you are Rose – like Rhoda it means a flower!'

She stared and stared at the letters. 'It might be someone else
who carved it.'

'Didn't he write about doing it? – I think he did,' said Alex, 'in
that story of his life we all read.'

'I can't believe it! Fancy your seeing it – with all these trees
around!'

In fact, when Alex entered the wood he *had* remembered about
his grandfather carving his initials on a tree, though he certainly
hadn't expected to find them. For once, Fate had led him to the
right place.

He took Rose's hand and kissed her palm, then he put his arms
round her. She leaned into his firm but comfortable body and he
buried his face in her dark hair.

'Seventy years,' he said. 'I can't believe it either, but for seventy
years it's been there.' Had it needed the magic of Knagg Wood to
seal their love?

'Waiting for us,' she whispered. Then, 'I love you too, Alex.'

'Don't let magic influence you, darling Rose,' he said, but she
laughed.

They both looked up, and looked a long time into each other's
eyes then, before their first – uncousinly – kiss.

He could not stop himself saying over and over again, 'I love
you, I love you,' all the way down the path and over the gate and
down towards the house which was now visible beyond long-
neglected gardens with several broken urns littering the paving
stones.

'Do you know, I don't think I want to go right into the house,'
she said, 'It's too sad, and I want to go on feeling happy. But I will

if you want to.'

They were holding hands and suddenly Alex knew that he no longer wanted to go into the house either. It had never belonged to anyone but his great-grandfather, and somehow it had rejected Eddie. They could look more closely over at the terraces but the place was a mess.

'I think when Grandpa left his mark he would have wanted us to find it, don't you?' said Rose.

They had photographed the ruin, and were walking back down the lane.

'Do you think the initials would photograph? Or are they like ghosts that wouldn't appear on the print?' said Alex.

'I don't want to photograph them,' said Rose. 'I thought of it up there. It's the sort of thing my mother would love to see, but no. . . .'

'We can tell her about it, and she can come and look for herself!'

That night Rose and Alex became lovers, Alex having crept into her single room where the bed was larger than his own.

Early in the morning they woke together, and Alex said, 'Do you remember that poem of Hardy's about the names carved on a grave?'

'No. Tell me.'

'It's called *During Wind and Rain*. My father told me Eddie used to quote poetry often in his letters and it was one of his favourites.'

'He was such a one for quoting poetry! Like you. Do you know this Hardy poem off by heart?'

'More or less, I think.'

'Say it for me. Explain.'

'Well, it's about time, and how people grow old, and things change, but he describes the people in their youth, and then right at the end, he says – he's speaking of the churchyard –

> *Ah, no; the years, the years;*
> *Down their carved names the rain-drop ploughs . . .*

247

There they are now, just names. Some people think it's a morbid thought. I suppose it's a strange thought to have when you're with the woman you love.'

'No, I think that's the sort of thought love makes you have. And anyway, Hardy's not morbid, just realistic. It's so sad,' she went on after a pause, 'but the rain must have run over *our* "E" "R" initials many times mustn't it.'

'Rose, will you marry me?' Alex said in a muffled voice.

'Yes, of course,' she replied.

Later, they woke again and made love and Rose said, 'Grandpa's love was unrequited; I mean, as far as I can see your grandmother was sorry for him, gave in at Wembley and then made a beeline for the man she really loved.'

'I bet she didn't tell our grandfather the truth about how soon she was to see Arthur Marriott either!' said Alex.

Later, he said, 'I think what came over to me most strongly in his story was disappointment over his writing. It makes me feel so sorry for him – apart from Granny not loving him the way he did her. But in the end he made himself be in control by leaving that account with the solicitor and then the letters revealing the truth. He could have told you all a lot earlier. I don't suppose it would have killed your granny to know he had another child.'

'She was very strait-laced. I think he didn't want to hurt her.'

'Without his unrequited love we'd never have met would we? You'd never even have been born, so I must be grateful.'

'All's well that ends well. Mother sees it differently; for her it was a sort of fate that gave her the brother she never had.'

And without Eddie falling in love with Rhoda in the first place we shouldn't be here, they both thought and did not need to say.

'That's all past now, dearest Rose.'

And you have published some of your poetry, unlike our grandfather, she thought. And you needn't hanker after love, because I do love you!

They decided that morning to leave Woolsford for Leeds and to go that afternoon to the art gallery where Rose said her mother and aunt used to go for a treat as children.

Everything seemed different now to Alex and to Rose in the heady incredible beginnings of love when everything has significance. Even the grey Victorian buildings seemed full of mysterious meanings.

They found the gallery, and came across there many treasures. They paused before Rose's favourite pictures, some of which Alex had never seen reproduced.

'Someone should paint Knagg Wood,' he said.

'Look,' said Rose, 'they almost did!' She stopped in front of one of the gallery's Victorian landscapes. It was a moonlit street scene of the 1880s.

'Our ancestors would have seen it like this, wouldn't they.'

Another painting from the same period was of a bridge over the grim River Aire, showing warehouses, barges busily unloading, seven people crossing the bridge or standing talking there, one a long-skirted woman in a black-and-white checked overdress over a black-and-white flounce, her companion dark-coated and holding a large umbrella; in the centre a head-scarfed girl was holding a large shopping basket . . . people once so lively and all long ago dead.

But the third picture was the one that Rose and Alex stared at longest. It had been painted before the other two and was called *Autumn Glory*. Great deciduous trees arched over the picture and through the trees you saw an old mill-house with mullioned windows.

'I do wish he'd painted Knagg Wood,' said Rose. 'It's a bit like this. You know, I remember Grandpa once telling me about the pictures he used to see here, and in Woolsford too. He loved them. It was when I was a little girl and was trying to paint a picture of the garden and he said how difficult it was to get it right.'

'We'll go there tomorrow!' said Alex.

After this they went to look at Girtin's Bolton Abbey.

Rose paused a moment before Lord Leighton's *Return of Persephone*, the girl yearning towards her mother Demeter's outstretched arms as she emerged from the underworld.

Alex suggested they looked at the Impressionists, and Sickert.

Neither of them felt at all tired; they were like butterflies flitting from picture to picture, sipping and tasting.

Everyone they saw that day appeared to smile upon them. Perhaps they really did, for they looked so happy. Happy as they walked round the art gallery, happy as they toasted each other in two glasses of cold white wine in the cafeteria, and happy as they planned the rest of their holiday.

Coda

Rose Elizabeth Considine married Alexander Edward Marriott the following summer in London. It was a lovely wedding. Juliet so wished Archie could have been there with his wife. Thelma Marriott had come over from Wellington and stayed quite a long time sampling England and Scotland.

Paul Considine was accompanied by his new girlfriend; Aunt Alison by her second husband Clive Sands and by Thom and Mick, both now married. All the older generation's many friends and relations attended, and all Rose's girl friends; Miriam Hardacre and Sarah Williams, now Sarah Johnson, and Lucy Thompson and Imogen Roberts, and even one or two old boyfriends, though not Fabian Lee.

Everybody said they had enjoyed themselves, even that it had been the most enjoyable wedding they had ever attended – with, naturally, the most beautiful bride.

After their marriage Alex and Rose went to the first place that offered a job for both of them that would also allow Alex to carry on writing. It involved keeping an eye for a year on a National Trust property in the Yorkshire Dales between Wensleydale and Swaledale. It was badly paid but they needed less to live on than would have been the case in London, and Rose said she appreciated the beauty of the place and the lack of urban hustle. There was a different sort of hustle of course, necessitating a knowledge of building and mending and planting and overseeing workmen and polishing furniture.

After the year was up they moved to an outpost of the North Yorkshire National Park where for six months they were to keep an official record of the plants and trees and animals. Rose wrote to her friends of their winter bird visitors: of the flocks of fieldfare and redwing that fed in the fields and the thrill of watching the shy roe-deer grazing close to their cottage. They would have been happy to stay there for longer, but it was badly paid, and they knew they would have to earn more if they were to have children. For three months, with an eye to setting up for himself, Alex worked on a farm in the Plain of York, not far from Thirksay. But there was nothing for Rose to do there unless she drove to Northallerton and stacked tins in the supermarket, so off they went to prospect in the south Pennines, not far from several ex-industrial towns. They loved the moors, but it would be a harsh life there and not one that Alex thought Rose would really enjoy. It was a disappointment, but at least they had tried.

Finally they both made the decision to return to London. Alex now had another book of poems ready; he was looking for a publisher for it, and needed to keep in touch with what was going on there. Rose went back for a time to work in the copyright office. They were quite glad to see her, but it was then that Juliet had the idea of offering them the shop. Juliet herself was quite capable of continuing to work there, but she was sixty-five, and it seemed to her and to Andrew to be a very good idea. The young couple could live over the shop; Alex could expand the business, advertise and purchase on the Internet for example, and Rose could keep up the correspondence.

Rose is determined that her husband should find time to continue his writing. On maternity leave, before leaving the office for good, she tries to finish her own account of her family history whilst they wait for the baby to arrive.

At the very end of the twentieth century, eighteen months after their return to London, a hundred years after Eddie Bairstow's birth, his great grandson is born.

They name him after three of his forebears: Edward Alexander Andrew.

At birth little Ned, as they call him, has fine features and a dusting of light hair, a slightly squashy little turned-up nose and dark-blue eyes that might one day change to hazel. He is an active, alert baby, in spite of not sleeping as much as the books say babies do. Very soon, before he is a month old, when either of his parents leans over his crib he gives them a broad smile. His mother feeds him herself and feels she has never worked so hard in her life. But things eventually settle down.

Rose and Alex will share looking after Edward, and the housework, if at first the shop is more Alex's responsibility. He is also a capable house husband. They are making just enough money now to scrape along.

The baby changes so quickly that Alex says they must take a photograph of him each week. By the time he is seven months old Rose is helping in the shop, the child in his pram by her side; she wants to do her share there. Ned – he is never Eddie – still sleeps in the afternoons. They don't have to commute to work, and they know they are lucky, with a child to bring up together in the next century. They hope one day to have another baby.

Alex has never stopped his writing, has suddenly found a new voice and finished a series of poems that he could not have written before his son was born. Some of them have already appeared in literary magazines.

Maybe one day they will sell up and try something else, even leave Europe, but for the present they are staying on in London. Thelma has been over to see her grandson and one day soon the new family will visit New Zealand. Baby Ned may grow up to be the kind of man who wants to live there permanently. He carries both Eddie, and Eddie's lost love Rhoda, in his blood, but his doting grandparents are what he will remember from his own childhood.

What will the year 2000, the new Millennium, hold for Alex and Rose and Ned and any other children they may have?

What, after all are children, dressed in the rags of time, but the measure of all things?

THE END
and
THE BEGINNING